Outstanding praise for Kim Wright

LAST RIDE TO GRACELAND

"Kim Wright takes us on a mother-daughter road trip with a twist, moving both through time and across the South as a young woman retraces her mother's route to find herself . . . Cory Ainsworth is the best kind of road trip partner—scrappy, smart, and wry."

—Joshilyn Jackson, *New York Times* bestselling author of *The Opposite of Everyone*

"The twists and turns kept me captivated from start to finish. If you love Elvis lore, you'll love this book!"

—Mary Alice Monroe, *New York Times* bestselling author of *A Lowcountry Wedding*

"Vividly imagined, *Last Ride to Graceland* is a gorgeous southern novel that captures those twists in a life where comic blends to tragic, and fate and luck collide. Wright is an exceptional writer, and her newest book is more than a simple road trip. It's a canny exploration of the dark, seductive legacy our mothers leave us."

—Dawn Tripp, author of *Georgia*

"Kim Wright has written a clever, charming, hilarious romp through the quintessential South. *Last Ride to Graceland* is the story of two women looking for redemption and finding it in the most unexpected, meaningful ways . . . [It is] a novel that makes us laugh one moment and weep the next. It is a study in contrasts and parallels and the way two lives can tell the same story. I didn't expect to fall apart while reading these pages, or to bump up against so many familiar longings. But I did, and I love this novel all the more because of it."

—Ariel Lawhon, author of *Flight of Dreams*

"Talk about the ultimate road trip: blues musician Corey Ainsworth hits the road in Elvis's car on a winding journey through the Deep South and her own family history. It's a little bit *Elizabethtown*, a little bit *Walk the Line*. I'm so glad I got to come along for the ride."

—Anne Bogel, "Modern Mrs. Darcy"

THE CANTERBURY SISTERS

"With originality galore, Wright has crafted a wonderfully entertaining tale with flair . . . readers looking for something different need look no further."

—*RT Book Reviews*

"Wright offers a modern-day tale imbued with Canterbury's enduring lore."

—*Booklist*

"[Wright] gives us another warm and engaging novel."
—*The Charlotte Observer*

"Che de Marin is a terrific traveling companion for more than 300 pages."

—*Star News Media*

"One woman's mid-life crisis turns into a hilarious and touching adventure in Kim Wright's latest heartwarming tale. A book for anyone who needs reminding that sometimes the journey to find answers is more important than the destination."

—Colleen Oakley, author of *Before I Go*

THE UNEXPECTED WALTZ

"A joyful novel about regaining your midlife groove."
—*People*

"Wright . . . expertly guides us through a moving, layered, and lyrical exploration of transformation."

—*Publishers Weekly* (starred review)

"Captures our fear of the unknown and the tender joys of coming into one's own."

—*Booklist*

"A moving tale of a middle-aged widow learning to spread her wings and live again. . . . It feels genuine, as new beginnings and second chances aren't always perfect and fairy-tale like, even if outward appearances suggest otherwise. With strong characterization and a cast of intriguing secondary characters, the story dances its way through all the right steps."

—*RT Book Reviews*

"Kim Wright's charming novel chronicles one woman's second chance at happiness and an opportunity to find her authentic self. The writing is pitch perfect—this is a winner!"

—Elin Hilderbrand, *New York Times* bestselling author of *Winter Stroll*

"An insightful novel about the unexpected places where we stumble upon second chances. Kim Wright writes with wisdom and grace."

—Sarah Pekkanen, internationally bestselling author of *Things You Won't Say*

LOVE IN MID AIR

"Wright hits it out of the park in her debut, an engaging account of a woman contemplating divorce. . . . Delivers fresh perspective and sympathetic characters few writers can match."

—*Publishers Weekly* (starred review)

"Astute and engrossing. . . . This debut is a treat!"

—*People*

"An intense, thoughtful novel about love and friendship, or the lack thereof, in a marriage."

—*Booklist*

"A breath of fresh air. It's a candid, often painfully funny look at modern love and friendship, with some surprising twists and turns along the way. A book to savor—and then share with your best friend."

—Susan Wiggs, #1 *New York Times* bestselling author of *Starlight on Willow Lake*

ALSO BY KIM WRIGHT

The Canterbury Sisters

The Unexpected Waltz

Love in Mid Air

LAST RIDE TO GRACELAND

Kim Wright

G

Gallery Books

New York   London   Toronto   Sydney   New Delhi

G

Gallery Books
An Imprint of Simon & Schuster, Inc.
1230 Avenue of the Americas
New York, NY 10020

First Gallery Books trade paperback edition May 2016

GALLERY BOOKS and colophon are registered trademarks of Simon & Schuster, Inc. For information about special discounts for bulk purchases, please contact Simon & Schuster Special Sales at 1-866-506-1949 or business@simonandschuster.com.

The Simon & Schuster Speakers Bureau can bring authors to your live event. For more information or to book an event, contact the Simon & Schuster Speakers Bureau at 1-866-248-3049 or visit our website at www.simonspeakers.com.

Manufactured in the United States of America

10 9 8 7 6 5 4 3 2 1

Library of Congress Cataloging-in-Publication Data

Wright, Kim
Last ride to Graceland / Kim Wright.
First Gallery Books trade paperback edition. | New York : Gallery Books, 2016.
Mothers and daughters—Fiction. | Voyages and travels—Fiction. | Family secrets—Fiction. | BISAC: FICTION / Contemporary Women. | Family Life. | Literary. | Road fiction.
LCC PS3623.R5545 L37 2016 | DDC 813/.6—dc23

ISBN 978-1-5011-0078-9
ISBN 978-1-5011-0081-9 (ebook)

*To my father, Harry Wright, who taught me
to believe in the territory ahead.*

It was like he came along and whispered some dream in everybody's ear, and somehow we all dreamed it.

—Bruce Springsteen

PART ONE
Beaufort, South Carolina

CORY

May 30, 2015

I was a premature baby who weighed nine pounds and nine ounces. Yeah, I know. Impossible. But you have to understand that this particular kind of medical miracle is common in the rural South. Jesus still looks down from billboards around here and people still care what their neighbors think. We pray and we salute . . . and most of all, we lie. It's why we have so many good writers per capita, and so many bad writers too, because all of us learned how to bend the truth before we could even half talk.

This may sound bad, until you consider that most people only lie to protect something they love, like their family or their dignity or their reputation. A sense of decorum can be a good thing. In fact, the world doesn't have enough of it. I remember my grandmother crying when she took me to a touring show of *Fiddler on the Roof* in Savannah, wiping her eyes when they sang "Tradition," and saying, "That's my life, Cory Beth, that's me up and down. Except for the part where they're Jewish."

So imagine yourself in a version of *Fiddler on the Roof*

where the traditions involve tying up rice in little pink net packets before you throw them at the bride, hiding the dark meat at the bottom of the chicken salad so the ladies in the prayer circle won't think you're trash, sending birthday gifts to people you can't stand because they sent you one back in 1997 and now neither one of you knows how to break the cycle. That's right. Imagine yourself in a very polite insane asylum. Then you'll have some sense of how I grew up.

· Beaufort, South Carolina, is the Old South. Not like Atlanta with its hip-hop or Charlotte with its banks or Florida with Walt Disney and all those serial killers. That's a whole different world. That's the part of the South that more or less won the war, and people forget that the rest of us exist. We're just a place they drive through on their way to somewhere else. When they're forced to stop for something—gas or firecrackers or barbecue or watermelons—they get back into their cars and shake their heads and say, "Can you believe that?" They think we're slow. But we're not really slow. We just take longer to get there. We meander and backtrack and beat around the bush, which I guess you think is what I'm doing now.

But I do have a point and here it comes: saying that I was born seven months and four days after my parents got married is just one way to figure the math. Another way is to say I was born seven months and nine days after my mama left Graceland, driving home in some madcap rush because she suddenly realized out of nowhere that she'd made a mistake. Maybe she shouldn't have gone on the road as a backup singer, shouldn't have dyed her hair and lined her eyes and chased the bright lights of rock and roll. Maybe she should've stayed home and married the local boy, the one who loved her so bad he asked her to marry him on the very night they both graduated from Leland Howey High. She couldn't see then that her true destiny was standing right in front of her. She was eighteen and had something to prove.

So Laura Berry left Beaufort, and when the door slammed behind her, it slammed right on Bradley Ainsworth's heart. She toured and he waited, tinkering his life away in the family concrete business until that day . . . that day in the late summer of 1977, when it was so hot that the air shimmered and he looked up, thinking at first it was the sweat in his eyes that deceived him. But no, there she truly was, Laura, the love of his life, walking toward him across the lawn. The makeup was wiped off her face. The boots were gone and the leather jacket too, and her hair was pulled back, plain as truth, and her arms were stretched out before her like some kind of sleepwalker. She was sorry, she told him. So very sorry. She'd seen the world and she'd seen enough. She'd left Memphis and driven straight through the night, crying and praying and drinking truck stop coffee just to keep her going. All she knew was she had to get home. Would he still have her? Was it too late?

In answer, he picked her up and swung her around. Swung her in a big circle, and when she tried to apologize again, he told her to hush, that their year apart had never happened. She was his girl, always had been, and there was no need to talk about it any other way. They'd get married the very next day, with her daddy in the pulpit and the whole town in the pews, and then the rest of their lives would come spooling out like silk, one sweet thing following another, just like they'd planned.

Seven months and four days later, there I was. So big and strong that everyone always claimed I lifted my head and looked right at Laura and Bradley in the delivery room as if to say, "Really? You're both sure? This is the story we've decided to go with?"

Bradley Ainsworth is a good man. He nursed my mother when breast cancer took her, way too young, and he did all the things a father is supposed to do. I can still see him pushing the chalk machine that lined the soccer field at the elementary school, eating the Girl Scout cookies I was too shy to sell, scowling at my dates and asking why they thought they were good enough to take his baby to the dance. He lives simple and true. He votes Republican and sits on the session of the First Presbyterian Church of Beaufort, and I'd never want to hurt him, but math is math and the facts are the facts and the truth can only stay hidden for so long, even in the South. I've known it all my life and it's time to do something about it. Most of the people I could hurt are dead, save for Bradley, and who knows, the truth might set him free too—just a little bit. Deep down he's got to know it, as good as I do, so we may as well both take a deep breath and say it out loud.

Elvis Presley is my real daddy.

I'm not just pulling all this out of my ass. It's not just the undeniable biological fact that my mama must have already been knocked up when she went tearing from Memphis to Beaufort, driving wild-assed through the night and plotting how to foist another man's baby onto her gullible high school sweetheart. And it's not just the fact I've always known, deep in my gut, that I was raised by the wrong family and in the wrong place. The fact that I always knew there was something in me that was meant for greater things, or the fact that I can sing.

And I can, you know, like an angel and like a devil too.

But I'm getting ahead of myself again. Telling the end before I tell the beginning. The real proof of my identity started revealing itself yesterday afternoon, when I went into the bar to get my check.

I work at a place named Bruiser's. I don't know why. I don't mean I don't know why I work there, because they pay me and the musical performance opportunities in a town the size of Beaufort are limited. What I mean is, I don't know why they call it Bruiser's. It makes it sound like a biker bar, like some sort of dive where fights break out, and it's actually a sweet little café located right on the inlet waterway. I play out on the deck and they serve peel-and-eat shrimp by the bucket. I cover Jimmy Buffett, Joni Mitchell, Chris Isaak, maybe even a little Van Morrison. Some of my own stuff now and then, although the owner doesn't like it when I do. People start going to the bathroom or calling for their checks.

Anybody who works at Bruiser's can eat free before their shift starts, and nearly all of us take advantage of the owner Gerry's uncharacteristic generosity on this particular point, even though we know good and well that we're just eating whatever didn't move the night before. The servers sit with the other servers, and cooks sit with cooks, and the talent for the night sits at a separate table, which I imagine would be fine if you were a band, but can be a little lonely for a solo act like me. I bring a book. I don't always read it but I keep it in the car, just for Thursday and Friday afternoons, so I can pretend to be busy as I sit there, peeling my shrimp, squeezing my lemons, watching the sun go down across the bay. It feels like high school, which pretty much everything does, in the end. So it's yesterday and I'm almost finished when I look up to see Gerry coming toward me carrying a beer, which is all foamy because the line starts to spit when it's near dead, and a message.

"Your daddy called for you," Gerry says.

"Does he want me to call him back?"

"Nah. He just said tell you to ship him his waders."

"His waders? I don't know how to ship him his waders. I don't even know what a sentence like that means."

Gerry's brow wrinkles. "Wait a minute. I wrote it down."

He goes back into the restaurant, sipping the foam as he walks. I play at Bruiser's every weekend during the season, which is probably why Bradley knew to leave a message for me here. I push my plate away and consider the table of servers clustered on the level below me. College kids, mostly, either up from the design school in Savannah or down from the College of Charleston. They have that old-money, new-clothes look and they like the idea of slumming it, a dozen of them sharing a rental on the waterway, sleeping on the beach all day and serving at night. Slumming's fun when it's temporary, when you know you can go home to your real life at some point. Kids like this come to the lowcountry every summer, drifting in and out with the tide, and I used to sleep with one or two of the boys every season. They were young and pretty and there for the taking, just like a pile of yesterday's shrimp, and I was younger and prettier then too.

Julie Mackey was my roommate through most of my twenties and she used to get a new tattoo every Memorial Day to mark the start of the season. She called the summer boys "the buffet." "Let's cruise the buffet," she'd say in the middle of May, when the bars and lifeguard stands started hiring and we'd walk through town, checking out what this particular season had in store. "Looks like I'm going to need an extra big plate this year," Julie would sometimes say. She sang for this down-and-dirty cover band and could growl out a song just like Janis Joplin. That same sort of grit in her voice, in her life. "Looks like I'm going to be going back for seconds," she'd say on summers when the buffet looked especially bountiful, and whenever Julie talked like that, you always got the feeling she was getting ready to toss aside a cigarette, even though I never knew the girl to smoke.

Julie's married now. Got a couple of kids, and I don't know what she did with the tattoos, with that stoned-looking sea turtle on her shoulder or the merman on her breast. Her growl has tamed down to a purr and I see her sometimes—this town's the size that you see everyone sometimes—but she never seems embarrassed to run into me. We probably both should be a little embarrassed—she by what she once was, me by what I still am. It's a fine thing to run wild in your twenties, even okay to hang on to that life as you round thirty, but now . . . to be thirty-seven and still working the buffet? Not so good. My eyes slide past the server boys and toward the bay where the sailboats bob and the light's gone all pink and purple.

So Bradley's trying to get in touch with me. He wants me to ship him his waders, whatever the hell that means.

I've had some financial embarrassment as of late. My iPhone

contract's been canceled. It's temporary, just until the first of the month, or maybe just until the first of the month after that, but I guess Bradley must have called me and gotten some message about how his daughter is a coming-up-on-forty loser who lives in a trailer and plays waterfront bars and sleeps with the wrong men. Frat kids, transients, bassists with a coke problem, salesmen with a wife problem, an associate pastor who's begun to doubt that God is listening. Those are my boys. I don't know if AT&T would say all that on a recording, but they're probably thinking it, and besides, Bradley knows well enough that his baby girl's teetering on the precipice of becoming white trash. I'm the reason he hasn't run for the school board, even though everybody keeps telling him he should.

It's mysterious. Bradley went down to Clearwater to fish over the Memorial Day weekend, and if he forgot his waders, as he evidently did, why wouldn't he go into some Dick's Sporting Goods or Bass Pro Shop down there and pick up a set? Mailing them to Florida, assuming I can even find the damn things, is going to cost a fortune. But then again, Bradley has big feet. Size fourteens, the feet of a basketball player. I plop my own on a chair and study them. Size fives, with high arches and short toes. Small as a child's.

"What're you singing tonight?" one of the servers calls over. He obviously started drinking at about noon and he's already sunburned. I don't know why he's talking to me. I guess he's just trying to be nice.

"Haven't decided yet," I call back. He's tilted so far in his chair that he's about to go clattering onto the deck.

"ABE," he says with a wink. "Anything but Elvis."

How the hell does this boy know I don't sing Elvis? I squint at his grinning face, trying to decide if he's one of the return kids and I'm supposed to remember him from last year. I don't think I ever slept with him, but I wouldn't bet my life on it. I don't have a good memory for faces, or names, or the capitals of South America, or the order of the presidents, or anything in particular except song lyrics. I can hear a song once and know all the words, which is a useful gift when you're a troubadour for hire. When you're a girl who works the waterway, moving from one club to the next and never quite sure what her clientele du jour will be. Motorcycle gangs one night. Golfers the next. Then a place that caters to snowbirds from New York and Pennsylvania, those states where it seems like nobody ever stays home. So I have to be prepared to cover any song they request and I can, up to a certain point.

But every place that hires me knows I won't play Elvis. I can't. I don't know exactly why. I start up and something always happens. My throat closes or I get a cough or I stumble around with the lyrics, have trouble calling them up even though I know every line, as good as I know my own name.

Here's the perfect example. There was a night almost exactly a year ago, again at the start of the summer, when I was sitting on this same deck, maybe even sitting at this same table and looking out at the waterway at just this same pretty angle, but on this particular night two rather odd things converged at once. The first was that my mother came in. Or I guess I should say she came out. She must have come into Bruiser's and walked through the indoor part, all the way through to the deck, which was crowded that night, and it took me a moment to spot her. Mama hardly ever dropped by Bruiser's, and never without Bradley, much less on a summer weekend when the place was packed. And—stranger yet to say—she climbed up on one of the high-top chairs that somebody had pulled over by the railing and she ordered herself a peach daiquiri. It was what she drank when she drank—a rare occasion in itself, just birthdays and cruises—but she liked those fruity, brunch-type cocktails that come with flowers and fruit bobbing in them.

It threw me to look up and see her sitting there by herself, raising her drink to me and smiling as I started my set. It wasn't like she hadn't heard me sing a thousand times, even though she'd heard the Church Cory a lot more than she'd heard the Bar Cory. But I still think I would've been okay with it if the second strange thing hadn't happened right on the heels of the first. I opened with Van Morrison's "Moondance"—one of those rare songs that's appropriate for any situation, including the sight of Laura Berry Ainsworth sitting on a high top drinking daiquiris all alone on a Saturday night—and then this drunk Yankee (is there any other kind?) yells out, "Play 'Blue Suede Shoes.'"

"Blue Suede Shoes"? Seriously? Nobody covers that, and besides, like I said, Bruiser's isn't the kind of bar where people get liquored up and start screaming out requests at six in the afternoon. I didn't know what to say. He was loud. It would've been impossible to pretend I didn't hear him, so I obligingly started up with the "one for the money, two of the show" part, but then I segued it into something else. Some sort of old rockabilly, Jerry Lee Lewis or some such, and I slid off the bar stool and worked the crowd, walking between the tables with my guitar, because people like that. If you sing hard enough, they forget what you're singing, and even the guy who wanted "Blue Suede Shoes" seemed okay with it. So I dodged that bullet. I'd avoided singing Elvis without having to directly say ABE into the microphone, which sounds weird and bitchy, considering that I sing everyone else. Only when I looked over, Mama had gone. Her chair was empty, except for the daiquiri glass perched on the wooden railing, just a little puddle of pink sludge left in the bottom.

I'd hardly ever known Mama to drink, but I'd never known her to drink fast. Later, much later, when she finally told me how sick she was, I put two and two together and figured out that the night she showed up alone and unannounced at Bruiser's to hear me play was also the day she had gotten the diagnosis. Not just breast cancer, but stage three with a certain very rare mutation that makes whatever's going to happen to you happen fast. The ragin' Cajun kind of cancer that takes you from daiquiris to the funeral home in five months flat.

Gerry is coming back, with the note in his hand. "Okay," he says. "I wrote down everything your daddy said to tell you. First off, he says the water's rougher than it was last year. They're surf fishing, not going out in the boat. That's why he needs his waders."

I nod.

Gerry nods. "He says you're probably thinking that, shit, it'll cost a blue fortune to ship 'em all the way down there, but you gotta remember how big his feet are. Big old stupid feet you can't fit into regular waders. He's the one who said that. Not me."

I nod.

Gerry squints down at the note. "So he says to go out to his fishing shack on Polawana, you know the place, and get them. He says they're in the shack, not the shed, and I'm supposed to stress that. The shack, and not the shed, got it?"

"Got it."

"Don't go in the shed."

"I won't go in the shed."

"Because the waders are in the shack."

"I think I can remember."

"And send them to him collect on delivery at the Clearwater PO."

"Yes, sir."

He crumples the note in his hand. "What're you playing tonight?"

"Beach Boys. Maybe even a little Chairman of the Board, some Drifters. You know, the summer stuff. Herald the start of the season. Give 'em what they want.

"Good girl." Gerry starts to walk away again but he turns back one more time. "And remember," he says. "Look in the shack, not the shed."

"Jesus," I say. "It's like you guys think I don't have any sense at all."

When I get to Bradley's three acres on Polawana the next day I head straight for the shed. I don't go out to Polawana very often. It's Bradley's equivalent of a man cave, where he goes to fish with his buddies, and it's where he would escape sometimes, when the pain of watching my mama fade away got too much for him.

And even those rare times I've gone out there, I don't think I've ever bothered to venture all the way to the shed. It's right on the water, just this dilapidated little hunk of rotted wood where he keeps parts for his boat. My shoes slide in the muck as I make my way down the hill, holding on to the reeds to steady myself as I go.

I've already gotten the waders. They were right inside the door of the two-room shack, leaning against a wall and looking kind of scary, like the legs of a man whose top half has gone missing. I carried them out and put them in the driver's seat of my Toyota and then, on second thought, I strapped them in. And I should have driven away then and there, task completed, but there was something in the way that Bradley and Gerry had both kept saying "The shack, not the shed" that filled me with some nameless, nonsensical desire to visit the shed. That's how my mind works. When Granny would leave the house, she'd say, "Don't stick beans up your nose," which she meant as a joke, obviously, since there's absolutely no reason why a sensible person would stick beans up her nose. But the words always hit my soul like an order from God, right up to that day when I was seven and wound up at the regional hospital and learned firsthand that getting a bean extracted from your sinus cavity is a profoundly unpleasant experience.

And another profoundly unpleasant experience might be waiting for me at the bottom of this hill—20/20 stuff. *Dateline*. *Southern Fried Homicide*. I've seen all the shows and every one of them starts the same way, with some asking-for-it girl out poking around by herself in the boondocks, just like I am now. But I walk over to the shed anyway and look through the grimy, cobwebbed window.

All I see is a car.

Actually, all I see is a piece of a car, a bumper. One of those low-slung muscle car bumpers, and it's surrounded with bubble wrap. Not just one layer of wrap, but more. I pull back from the window and knock a spider out of my hair.

It takes several yanks before I get the door unstuck and manage to roll it up. When I do, I see the whole vehicle, pointed straight at me. The tires on one side have gone flat, making it tilt off center, and the bubble wrap, crisscrossed at several points with duct tape, has turned what must have once been the clean, elegant lines of the chassis into a lumpy, gray mass. But there's no denying that this machine has power. A wounded tiger's still a tiger, after all.

There is no way on God's green earth that Bradley and Laura Ainsworth ever owned a car like this.

For a moment I can't decide what to do. I try to circle the car, but it's so big that it's claimed the whole shed, with the back bumper pulled up all the way to the wall. I edge sideways along the driver's side, running my hand over the bubble wrap, half of it popped, and all of it dusty. I look around for something to start cutting the duct tape, but it seems that all the shed holds is the car. There aren't any fishing tools out here, or any parts for a boat. There never were. It doesn't shock me in the least to learn that my mama spent years holding something back from me, but the fact that Bradley helped her hide it? For some reason, that shocks me to the core.

There'd been a knife up in the shack. A fishing knife laying on the counter beside the sink, with a long, curved blade, and likely sharp. I scramble up the bank and get it, holding it out as far away from me as possible while I slip-slide my way back down, because with my luck I'll probably lose my footing and impale myself and my body will roll right into the river and I'll never be found.

I get back to the shed and try and figure out where to start.

I don't want to puncture the wrap and scratch the car, but it takes way more effort than I would've guessed to saw through the duct tape, so I decide to tackle one corner at a time. First the tape, then the bubble wrap, then the beach towels beneath that. First there's one that says HOTEL CALIFORNIA and another one that says SUPER BOWL X CHAMPIONS PITTSBURGH STEELERS. Another one says ALOHA FROM HAWAII and has a big orchid.

But when I peel back that final layer of 1970s nostalgia, the left bumper on the driver's side is freed and for the first time I can see what I'm working with. The car is black. Shiny. Its cocoon has left the finish just as flawless as the day it rolled off the dealer's lot. And when I give the next segment of bubble wrap a yank, a whole clump falls off at once, revealing the flank. I put my hand on the driver's-side door and, with a prayer to nobody in particular, open it.

The interior is red. Leather everywhere. Everywhere except where there's gold. Not tarnished. Shiny as God, even now. A Styrofoam cup sits in one side of the cup holder, the rim smudged with cherry red lipstick. There are other cups in the floor of the passenger side, along with crumpled paper bags. A napkin, flecked with brown, as if someone tried to wipe chocolate off their mouth. And a map. A plain old filling station map like I remember from my childhood, the kind that was always impossible to fold back into eight perfect segments. The person who last drove this car didn't even bother trying. The map accordions its way across the red leather seat and onto the floor. Sunglasses, oversized, aviator style, dangle from the rearview mirror.

And there's a smell that wafts up too—not the mustiness you'd expect, or the raw, wet decay of the river, but something subtler and more refined. A woman's perfume, spicy and sweet, some scent they don't make anymore, mixed in with a darker, more masculine aroma. The horse-barn smell of tobacco.

I've opened a time capsule.

I leave the knife stuck in the riverbank and struggle up the hill to my own car. It's about as far from a muscle car as you can get, a gold Camry, and I hop in and drive to the Exxon station on St. Mary's Island. They call everything an island around here, but it's all really just fingers of land connected by bridges, and the only thing separating one so-called island from another is marsh. They have a pay phone at the Exxon just after you come onto St. Mary's, a whole booth sitting right off the road and probably one of the last pay phone booths left in Beaufort, if not the world. When you break up with AT&T, you start to notice these things.

I keep change in my own cup holder, and as my fingers flick through the quarters, I think back on that Styrofoam cup in the black car, that perfect little imprint of a woman's mouth. Did my mother ever wear lipstick like that? It doesn't seem likely. I was born in '78, in that trough somewhere between the hippie years and the disco years, and the bright raspberry pink crescent on that cup was such a scream of color that I can't see anyone in that era wearing it. Certainly not here, in Beaufort, where decent people's lips are just one shade darker than their skin.

It was stage makeup maybe. One of the last remnants of Mama's time on tour.

I dig out six quarters. Walk over to the phone booth and look for the yellow pages, but of course the whole book is gone. All they've got is a black plastic cover flapping at the end of a chain. I have to go inside to ask for help, and the kid working the register doesn't have a phone book either. He just looks the numbers up on his iPhone, eyeing me suspiciously when I tell him what I need. One of the requests is dead common in these parts, since anybody who has a car break down calls Leary, but the other?

I don't meet his eyes. I pick up the ballpoint pen on the counter and write one number on one arm and the other number on the other arm. And then I walk back out to the phone booth.

Leary answers on the first ring and says he'll meet me at the shack in twenty minutes. Then I twist my arm so that I can read the other set of numbers, which I wrote kinda screwy since I was trying to hurry. It pops me into a menu, of course, telling me how to buy tickets and book tours, and all the prices and hours, but I keep pushing zero, and after a few minutes of "Love Me Tender," an honest-to-God person comes on the line.

"I think I may have found a piece of Elvis memorabilia."

The Graceland operator is most notably unimpressed. To be fair, I bet they get these calls all the time. People who see the perfect image of Elvis's face on a piece of burned toast, people who hallucinate and think the King spoke to them in a dream. But when I tell the woman that my mother toured with Elvis as a backup singer from '76 to '77, her tone of voice becomes slightly more enthusiastic and she says she'll have one of the authenticators call me back.

Authenticators. That's quite a word.

"He can't call me back," I tell her, craning my neck to look at the road. This rigmarole is taking longer than I thought and Leary's going to be at the shack any minute. "I don't have a phone."

I realize that's a strange thing to say to somebody when you're talking to them at the time on a phone and I might have lost some credibility points. But she says, "Just a minute," kind of flat and disinterested, like maybe she's just going to go to the bathroom and then come back and tell me she's real sorry but she couldn't find an authenticator.

Now the wait song is "Jailhouse Rock." I listen through three whole choruses before a new voice comes on the line. A man. Older sounding.

"Whatcha got?" he says.

Whatcha got. Not the warmest of greetings. The lady might not have believed me, but she at least had that singsongy politeness that people who work in tourist destinations all seem to have.

"What I have is a 1973 Stutz Blackhawk," I tell him, and my voice starts shaking like I'm about to cry. "A black coupe. And I'm thinking that most likely it's the car Elvis Presley drove on the day that he died."

That jerks him around. There's dead silence on the line for a minute, which I kind of enjoy, and then he says, "Now who did you tell me you were?"

"I didn't," I say. "But my mother was Laura Berry and she toured with—"

"Good God," said the man. "Good God. Are you trying to tell me that you're Honey's daughter?"

Honey? I don't know what this old duffer's talking about, but at least I have his attention. "I found the car in a shed—"

"And how is our sweet Honey Bear?" he says. "Is she there?"

Your sweet Honey Bear's dead, I think, but somehow I can't bring myself to say the words out loud. "Who is this?" I ask. "Who am I talking to?"

He says his name's Fred and starts rapid-firing all sorts of information. How he ran the road tours back in the day, how he knew my mother. What a pretty little thing she was, just as sweet as her name, and then he gets going on how if this car I'm talking about is the real McDeal—that's just how he says it, the real McDeal—then it's far too precious to be driven. If it's the real McDeal, it'll need to be hauled back to Memphis.

"You know," Fred says, "if what you have there truly is the last of the Blackhawks, then the only person who ever sat behind the wheel of that particular car was Mr. Elvis Presley himself. Which is why we can't let anybody else drive it now."

I hate to pop the guy's bubble, but obviously that's not true. Elvis died in Tennessee and the car's in South Carolina, so unless this old coot is saying a ghost drove the Blackhawk from Memphis to Beaufort—which I wouldn't put it past a Graceland authenticator to suggest—somebody else must have sat behind the wheel. Most likely my mother, Laura Berry Ainsworth, aka Honey Bear.

"Didn't Elvis give a lot of cars away?" I say weakly, although I know for a fact that he did. I've read all the biographies. I've made a study of the man. "Isn't there a chance he might have given the car to one of his backup singers?"

"Not the Blackhawk," Fred says with a sort of flat-out unarguable uncertainty. "It was his favorite." And then he starts up on how I need to give him my address and send him pictures and if it turns out to be the real McDeal they'll put somebody on a plane to come out and look at it. But under no circumstances am I to crank that car. He seems to still be under the impression that the Blackhawk teleported itself across four states, but at least he's finally stopped asking about Honey. I think he's figured out the answer isn't going to be anything he'd like.

I'm just getting ready to give him my address when I see Leary go by in the tow truck. So I tell Fred I'll have to call him back and he immediately gets huffy and calls me "young lady" in that tone old men get, and then all of a sudden, out of nowhere, I find myself in the mood to stick beans up my nose. What I mean is, I get stubborn. Maybe it's impossible that Elvis would have given his Blackhawk away, but it's even more impossible to imagine that my mother would have stolen it. She rarely talked about Elvis. Never talked about that year on the road. As far as I know, she only kept one memento, a picture of her standing in a dark paneled room wearing a blue satin jumpsuit with her arm around another girl. A black woman, similarly bedazzled, evidently another of the backup singers. When I asked her why she kept that one snapshot when she'd thrown away all the others, she pointed to the background. A man's face, reflected in a mirror, turned in profile. Looking down, looking a little sad, apparently unaware he'd been caught by the photographer too.

"It's the very best picture I have of Elvis," Mama said.

"Young lady, that car belongs at Graceland, at least if it's the one you claim it is," the voice on the phone is saying, but Leary's tow truck is rolling out of sight now and I hang up, glad it's a pay phone, glad that when Fred calls back it's going to just ring and ring into infinity, with nobody to hear.

Screw the authenticators. If that car belongs in Graceland, I'm the one who's going to take it there.

"**Well, shit,**" says Leary.

"Precisely. I couldn't have said it better myself."

"Look at the size of that hood."

"I know. A girl could lie down and die on that hood."

Leary sticks his head in the door I'd left open and looks around. "But it's kinda cramped inside, isn't it? That little jump seat in the back wouldn't hardly hold a dog."

"Look at the radio," I say. "AM/FM with an eight-track. I think the trim is real twenty-four-karat gold. That's why it isn't tarnished. And listen to this." I hit the horn and it blares out the chorus of "Never on a Sunday," so loud that the grimy windows in the shed start to tremble.

Leary leans back on his haunches. "Well, shit."

I love Leary. He and I went to school together and every girl needs to have gone to high school with a mechanic. He's come and picked me up when I got in a few scrapes throughout the years, and he's kept the Toyota going for a decade on little more than Everclear motor oil and a prayer. We never dated. Maybe he wanted to. Maybe not.

"Don't crank it."

"Why does everybody keep telling me not to crank it?"

He stands up and slowly walks the length of the car, shaking his head as he goes. "I don't know who else is telling you not to crank it, but I'm telling you because if it's sat here as long as it looks like it has, any gas left in it has turned to varnish. And if you flood the carburetor with varnish, you'll ruin it, and then we're really screwed."

He sounds so sure of himself. It's a side of Leary I've never seen.

"So what do we need to do?"

He raises an eyebrow. "We?"

"What do you need to do? To get it to run, I mean."

"Drain the gas, pull the plugs, lube the rings. Who knows, maybe the other fluid levels are okay; they don't decompose like gas. The tires are flat as a pancake, anybody can see that. Where the hell did this come from?"

"You know as much as I do. I just found it today."

"And you never knew it was here? Was this your daddy's car?"

"Can you see Bradley driving a car like this down Bay Street?"

"Not really."

"So it must have been my mama's."

Leary looks up from under the hood. "And I believe I'm going to have to call bullshit on that, Cory Beth Ainsworth. Your mama was a preacher's daughter."

"Maybe so, but that's not all she was."

"She spent twenty years as a choir director," Leary adds, as if that settles the matter. "And she directed me in the Christmas pageant three years in a row. Shepherd the first year, then a wise man, then you finish up as Joseph. That's how it goes."

There's no point in arguing. I doubt there's even a handful of people in town who know exactly where my mama went during her lost year. There was some talk about a Bible college in Georgia or that she sang backup on a gospel record in Nashville, but it was all so long ago that I don't think there's anyone left to ask. Leary is looking at me like I'm crazy and I need him too much to risk pissing him off.

"So you have all that stuff in the truck?" I ask. "Or at least enough so we can at least get it to where I can crank it?"

Leary sighs. "Those tires most likely have weather rot and, if so, you can't drive on them without risking a blowout on the open road. I can't let you even try, so don't bother jerking your chin at me. And I sure as hell don't have four tires in the truck. I don't even know where you'd have to go to get tires that'd fit a car like this."

"You said they might have weather rot? Might?"

He pushes back his ball cap and studies me like he can see right inside my head, and see all the wheels and gears going around. "Or they might have just lost their air over time. It seeps out. The longer things sit still without going anywhere, the more they get flabby and soft. Ya know?"

I know. "Inflate them back up," I say. "I'll risk it."

Still grumbling and predicting the worst, Leary climbs the hill to his truck to get his tools. I pull the butcher knife out of the bank and follow him, thinking. Well, not thinking, exactly.

I'm in a bit of a daze. The woman in the picture I found all those years ago . . . she was standing half turned to the side with her hand on her hip and her knees kind of swiveled together. A sexy-girl pose, and the other woman was positioned just the same way, only she was swiveling to the left, not the right, so that they looked like a reflection of each other, except that one of them was black and the other was white. The woman in that picture sure didn't look pregnant. She didn't look like she was destined to be anybody's mother or a choir director either. She looked young and pretty and even a little bit slutty under that layer of makeup, her eyes all big and startled, painted on in that comic book way of the seventies. She looked precisely like the kind of girl men might call Honey.

Leary's still digging out tools and muttering under his breath.

"You want a beer?" I ask him.

"You got one?"

"I can get us some."

"I guess that means you ain't planning to pay me."

"I'll pay you, at least for the parts." Leary picks up his toolbox and walks past me. The yard's big, as open as a prairie, but he cuts it close, his shoulder bumping up against mine, like he's trying to knock something into me. Sense, most likely.

"Better make it a six-pack," he says.

I've got four stops. First I go to the bank and cash the check I got from Gerry last night. Four hundred and twelve dollars, and if I had a shred of human decency in me, I'd turn the whole thing over to Leary the minute I get back. But I'm going to need some road money, so I divide the cash into two envelopes, and write Leary's name on one and my name on the other. Then I roll past the neat little split-level where I was raised and I get the picture of Mama with the bedazzled black lady and Elvis. I know just where she kept it: in the cabinet beside the TV where she put all the family photo albums, even though this picture wasn't filed and categorized and taped in like the others. It's always been just floating out there on its own, and I turn it over and see that my mother has written only a single word on the back. "Us."

Us?

Well, that's damn unhelpful. And not like my mother either. If you pulled out any of the other pictures from their albums, you'd find a whole encyclopedia of facts written on the back. Who's in the picture, the date it was taken, where we were headed to or coming back from, and sometimes even a little comment like, "Fun day!" or "My big girl." A hundred pictures of me and Bradley and Mama, and I would have sworn, until this morning, that we were the only *us* who had ever meant anything to her. But now I see I was wrong about that and probably a host of other things too. I take the picture and a box of protein bars from the pantry and a nearly full bottle of Excedrin Migraine too. Bradley won't miss it. Mama and I were the only ones who ever got headaches around here.

Then I run by the trailer, where I grab some clothes and my guitar, and my last stop is the Exxon, where I pick up Leary's six-pack. I decide to spring for Stella, because he's being a champ about this whole thing, and the kid behind the counter gives me the fish eye, like he's not the least bit surprised that the same woman who was prank calling Graceland an hour ago is now drinking in the middle of the day. He gives me the change all in ones, even though I've got eleven dollars coming back. I think it's an insult but I'm not sure why.

Screw him. He doesn't get me. Nobody in this town ever did.

"Well, I'm going to have to eat my words," Leary says when I get back to the shed. "'Cause all four tires inflated right up. I think you can drive on them good enough, as long as you don't push it on the speed. Weather rot doesn't always show up right at once and you don't want to have a blowout on I-95."

I look into the car. "You didn't try and clean it out, did you?"

"I bagged some stuff. Hell, girl, one of those napkins had a spray of blood on it."

"Blood? I'm going to need that. In fact, I'm going to need it all."

He shoots me another one of those Leary looks, but doesn't ask why. "The rest of the fluid levels in the car were pretty good. Even the wiper blades checked out. They had this thing wrapped up tighter than a tick, didn't they? Sometimes when a car sits idle this long you find dirt dauber nests up in the engine, shit like that. But I have to say it looked . . . pretty good. Better than it had any right to."

"So can I crank it?"

He nods. "It's gonna roar. Seriously, these old muscle cars are loud as shit. This baby's got a big 425 engine and they have no emission systems what-so-fucking-ever."

That gives me pause. "Is it even legal to drive it?"

"There's no way it'd pass inspection." He considers me through narrow eyes, although the truth is, Leary's one of those people who squints even when there's no good reason for squinting. Like he probably squints indoors, or in the dark. It might be sexy if a girl was into that kind of thing. "Tell me the truth," he says. "Exactly where are you planning to take this car?"

"Why don't we have a beer?"

"All right," he says, and we both sit down on the bank. He kills his first one in two or three gulps, then starts on the second. It seems to settle him. It's nice out here on the water and I can't think why I hardly ever come. I'm taking it slow and steady with my own beer, because it's occurred to me that I need to start tonight, before I lose my nerve.

"You know, Cory Beth," Leary says, and then he flops all the way back on the ground of the riverbank and looks up at the sky. "While you were gone, I took my phone and Googled the car, and everything came up the same. Turns out there never was more than a handful of these Blackhawks in the States, and one man collected more of them than anyone else, a man by the name of—"

I lie down too. "Leary, you've got to promise me—"

"Now, I'm not asking you anything and I'm not telling you anything," he says, and then he rolls over and drains the second beer before reaching for the third. "I'm just saying it would scare me out of my skin to think you were going to try and drive this car to Tennessee. So promise me you're not going to, right?"

"I'm not going to drive this car to Tennessee," I say. "Jesus. Give me some credit. Gerry's expecting me to start singing in an hour."

"'Cause that would be a foolish thing to try and do, Cory Beth," Leary says. "That road out there can't tell you a single thing that you don't already know."

The engine does indeed have a satisfying roar, and as I pull onto the dirt road, it feels like the whole world is vibrating. I aim my long, black hood toward the setting sun. Leary looked it up for me. It's 672 miles from Beaufort to Memphis, and Google estimated it would take a person ten hours and fourteen minutes to cross this particular distance. But if that person is driving a car with bad tires and an out-of-date inspection and trying to keep off the main roads, then I figure it will take twice that long. Thanks to the beer run, I have $199, a pack of protein bars, and a single Stella Artois, which Leary insisted I take, and within the hour Gerry will be expecting me at Bruiser's. But somebody else is going to have to sing his Jimmy Buffett and his Beach Boys tonight. They must have a squadron of their own illegitimate daughters out there somewhere. Girls with tiny feet and daddy dreams and pretty voices, all of us rattling up and down the waterfront, looking for work.

The sun is intense. I adjust the visor, which hardly helps, so there's nothing to do but let it shine, bouncing back at me from every mirror and burning away everywhere I grew up. My mama must have driven this same road thirty-seven years ago. She was heading east, with the sun behind her, while I'm heading west, with it ahead of me, but she must have nonetheless passed this same old twisted cypress tree, this bend in the road where the waterway curves and you suddenly see it all at once stretched out below you, the whole bay waiting like a shimmering flat blue carpet, so beautiful that it hurts.

Honey was eighteen when she left Beaufort. Nineteen when she came back. Young. Crazy young. Young and pretty and pregnant and wiping off makeup layer by layer, excavating herself right back down to the girl she once was, the spell of Graceland wearing off just a little more with each mile that rolled by. It takes a long time to get from Memphis to Beaufort, especially if you're alone. But what she was thinking as she drove, nobody knows.

HONEY

August 19, 1977

I'm a failure. I've failed completely and utterly at everything I set out to do.

But at least I have the Blackhawk. I have it by accident, but I still have it, and this car makes a statement. It says that Laura Berry might have snuck out of Beaufort on a Greyhound bus, but she's coming back riding 425 horses right down the middle of Bay Street, roaring to the sky like some kind of avenging angel. The townspeople stop in their tracks and stare at the sight of the Blackhawk rolling by, even though they can't see me through the tinted windows. They probably wouldn't recognize me if they did.

They don't have to know that I'm driving barefoot with no possessions in the world except for an eight-track tape, a tube of somebody else's lipstick, half a hamburger, and a jar of tupelo honey. They don't have to know I'm coming home in shame. Just let them see the car. That's enough. Just let them see the car and wonder.

I pass the ice cream stand where I had my first summer job. The sporting goods store where we were all fitted for our cheerleader uniforms, the library, and the fire station, and the beauty parlor where my mama gets her hair done, and the Chinese buffet. This town was the whole world to me at one time, not so very long ago. Before Graceland. Before Elvis. But now it feels small and flat, a little foreign, like nothing more than a town I once saw on a television show.

According to the clock on the courthouse tower, it's just past noon, which means Bradley will be eating his lunch. He's probably unpacking an egg salad sandwich he brought from home right now and sitting down at the picnic table behind the rusted yellow tin building that holds his family's business. It doesn't look like much, but Ainsworth Paving and Concrete is enough to make his family royalty in this small realm, or at least raise them high enough that when Bradley asked me to marry him, my mother said, "You'll never do any better."

You'll never do any better. Quite a thing to say to a girl not even a full day out of high school. And when I told Bradley no, thank you so very much, but no, Mama went to bed with a sick headache and didn't get up for a week.

I think being a preacher's wife must have been a mixed blessing for my mama. She liked the title, but she didn't like being poor. She found it humiliating when an Avon Lady from the congregation gave her samples, little tiny white plastic tubes that looked more like cigarette butts than lipsticks, or when a plumber brought somebody's cast-off toilet over to the manse and installed it, saying he knew for a fact that it was better than the one we had, since he'd donated that one too. And then we had to all come into the bathroom and watch him flush and say a prayer of gratitude right then and there, gathered in a semi-circle and looking down into the swirling bowl. So I guess it's not surprising that Mama pushed me toward the kind of security she'd never had. She wanted nothing more than to get me into a house that was cool in the summer and warm in the winter and where all the appliances worked. Once a woman is married and stuck—and nobody's more stuck than a South Carolina preacher's wife—then all that's really left for her to do is to pray that her daughter makes a totally different kind of mistake.

"But I can't marry Bradley Ainsworth, Mama," I said. It was the morning after graduation. She was adjusting the blinds, trying to shut out all the light, which I knew was a sign that one of her sick headaches was coming on. "He's a good person, but I just don't love him."

She hesitated for such a long time that I knew she was thinking I had completely missed the point. Then she said, "Laura, honey, just tell me this. Have you really tried to love him?"

"I've tried real hard," I said, which was more or less true. "I know Bradley's the answer to everything I need, but I can't make myself feel what I don't."

She sighed. It was the sigh of a woman who'd spent a lifetime praying over secondhand toilets. "Well," she said, dropping the last blind so that the room sank into total darkness. "There's always the chance that someday you'll change your mind. The human heart is a mysterious thing."

I nodded and said, "Yes, ma'am," but what she didn't know is that I already had a bus ticket in my pocketbook, along with an ad ripped from the back pages of *Billboard* magazine. So let Mama talk all she wanted about compromise, and sensible choices, and what a bird in the hand was worth. I figured that in three days' time, I'd be in Graceland.

The bus trip to Memphis was hell. Felt like it lasted forever. Like North Carolina alone was long and flat enough to kill a girl, like every worthless man in America was waiting for me in every station where I'd get out to stretch my legs, all of them asking me what my name was and where I was going. I arrived in Memphis sweaty and tired, smelling like cigarettes. So I spent half the money in my pocketbook at the YWCA just so I could take a shower, and then I put on my only clean dress and walked eighteen blocks to the audition. A man named Fred listened to a bunch of us sing, one after the other, in the back room of a diner, the sort of place where a Rotary or Kiwanis Club meets.

I sang the best I could, hit every note on my run, but Fred gave nothing away with his face. In fact, he kept the same sour expression the whole time, whether a girl was good or she was bad. But at the end of the day he picked five of us to, as he said, "await Elvis's final approval." He called my name first. Then he said that Elvis was gone somewhere. I got the impression Elvis was almost always gone somewhere. But all that mattered was that Fred furthermore said they were going to move the five of us into Graceland until he got back.

We squealed and hollered. Put our arms around one another and jumped in a circle. This must have broken the hearts of the girls who weren't chosen, I guess, like that little room in a Memphis diner was cheerleading and homecoming court all over again. But in the moment I couldn't stop to think about the others. I could only think that I was right on the cusp of getting everything I wanted. I may have started the day in a Greyhound bus station, but I was going to end it at Graceland.

It was early summer, that season of endless days, and for the whole next week we had the run of the place. We could swim and race the golf carts and try on the tour costumes with their fringe and beading, modeling them for one another, walking up and down the diving board of the pool like it was a Paris runway. The cook would fix us whatever we wanted, day or night, and what we wanted was mostly cakes and doughnuts. In some ways it was like the best sleepover a girl could imagine.

But in another way, Graceland was a trap.

We'd cheered when they'd driven us through the front gate. It had been glamorous, with musical notes woven between the gold-plated bars, and you almost expected to see Saint Peter himself standing guard. But when that gate clanged shut, I'd shuddered. I knew the sound from those times I'd done prison ministry with my daddy. He was always dragging me to some god-awful place to sing—trying to give hope to the hopeless as he said it—and so maybe I understood this particular sad vibration better than the other girls. Maybe I understood that Graceland was one of those places that was harder to get out of than into.

About a week in, when we were already bored out of our minds, everything changed. All of us girls were running through the mansion, drinking wine coolers out of coffee mugs and shooting water at one another with empty shampoo bottles. At some point I slid down the banister and plopped butt-first on the black-and-white tile floor of the foyer. And then and there, I looked up to behold the King himself, wearing a white spangled jumpsuit and gazing down at my crotch.

The other girls had frozen in their tracks. The whole foyer had gone dead silent, except for Elvis. He was laughing.

"What's your name, honey?" he asked me.

I said "Laura Berry," and he shook his head.

"Well, I'm going to call you Honey Bear," he said, and that was that. He stepped over me, still chuckling, and went up the long curved staircase that led to the second level and the private hall. The part of Graceland that hardly anyone ever saw, certainly not silly girls like me. A heavy turquoise curtain waited at the top of the stairs. Elvis parted it, stepped behind the cloth, and was gone.

We never sang for him at all, but the next morning the other girls were packing and crying and heading for home. I was the only one of that audition batch who'd be staying at Graceland, while for everybody else, their big adventure was over before it had begun. On her way out of the room, one of them turned, looked me right in the eye, and said, "Bitch." It was the first and last time anyone's ever used that word in connection to me. She must have thought I planned the whole thing. Planned to go sprawling at Elvis's feet with my legs spread to Jesus and my white cotton panties showing, and even though I didn't, she's right in a way. Nothing that ever happened at

Graceland was sensible or fair, but for some reason, I was the one who was chosen. For some reason, I was the one he pulled into the fold.

But that was the then and there, and this is the here and now. No use crying about it. No use wondering what might have been. I shake my head to erase the memory of Graceland and try to focus on being back in Beaufort. Pretty, sweet, unchangeable little Beaufort. The bridge that stretches over the waterway is the only thing I've seen since I hit town that seems at all different from the day I left. It looks like the water's gone gray instead of blue in my absence, but then I realize that's nothing but the tint of the window. I roll it down and, yeah, the bright, cool cut of the bay is still there. The wind hits my face and I catch a whiff of the salt and hear the gulls screaming out as they circle. And despite everything that's happened in the last four days, I smile. Being home isn't all bad.

After that, all that's left for me to do is to turn under the twisted branches of the old cypress, the prettiest tree on all of St. Mary's Island. The Blackhawk lurches and squeals in protest as it pulls onto the long, oyster-shell driveway that leads to Ainsworth Paving and Concrete. And as I roll up, I see Bradley sitting there, exactly like I'd imagined he'd be, at one of the picnic tables, all alone, sitting with his blue work shirt open down to his belt buckle. He's cut his hair. He looks good.

My heart softens, opens up a little in my chest. It's like right up until this moment I've been so preoccupied with how I'm going to fool Bradley that it never occurred to me that maybe I wouldn't have to fool Bradley. I keep forgetting his kindness, the sweet open planes of his face. If there's anyone who can hear this awful story I'm fixing to tell and still love me, it's him. And yet my hand is limp on the door. This car has been my bubble. I see that now. It's protected me as I floated between one world and the next, but the minute I step out, that bubble will break. I pick up the little jar of tupelo honey from the passenger seat, leaking but still mostly full, and I put it into my pocket, thinking I will give it to him. A gift from the road. It's not much, but it's all I've got.

Bradley is tilting his chin and frowning as he stares at the car. Everyone does. You've got to study a car like this from a sideways angle, because it's like looking at the sun. Behold it directly and it shall smite thee blind. But even though Bradley can't possibly recognize the Blackhawk or see me through the windows, he seems to sense that something big is happening, because he stands up. Starts walking toward me, slowly at first, then picking up his pace, so that by the time I'm finally out of the car and he knows it's really me, Bradley is running. He catches me up and swings me around, and the movement is so abrupt that for a moment it knocks the air out of my chest. "I want to tell you . . ." I start, but then I can't speak, so I grab the collar of his work shirt. The cotton feels strong and warm beneath my hands, and he stops twirling me. Just holds me, dangling, in midair, our noses almost touching.

"I brought you something," I say. "A souvenir. Because I have to tell you—"

"No," he says. "You don't have to tell me anything because there's nothing to tell. You never went away and this whole year never happened and you're my girl, always have been, always will be," and then he begins spinning us again, harder than ever. My jacket flies open and the jar of tupelo honey slings out of the pocket, sailing through the air in one final high, free arc before hitting the hard red clay of home and shattering for good. I don't know if this is the end of my life or the beginning—or both. Because some moments are like that, they kill you and birth you in the same breath. I throw my head back and watch the trees circle above me and I exhale, maybe for the first time since I left Memphis. I'm safe in the arms of a boy who is going to give me a second chance. And a third and fourth one too probably, before it's all over. Because I'm safe in this world of infinite mercy, infinite forgiveness, infinite grace.

And when you think of it like that, the truth doesn't seem to matter all that much.

PART TWO

Macon, Georgia

CORY

May 30, 2015

At first I thought this car was a time capsule, but now I'm thinking it's more of a treasure chest and that this bag of trash Leary threw together is the closest thing I have to a map. I'm like a pirate in reverse, somebody who's found the gold and who's now looking for the person who must have lost it. It's a funny thing to find yourself telling a story backward, to have the end but not the beginning, to know the what of a situation, but not the how or why.

I stop at a rest area about an hour outside of Beaufort and lay it all out across the passenger seat, trying to figure the route the Blackhawk must have taken thirty-seven years ago. The closest clue that I find, at least in terms of raw geography, is the Styrofoam cup with the lipstick smear. The side says JUICY LUCY in big, fat, graffiti-looking print, and below that are the much smaller words MACON, GEORGIA. And there's a crumpled white bag, gone dark with time and grease that evidently came from the same establishment.

What the trash suggests so far is that Mama took a serpentine route from Memphis to Beaufort, not cutting east to west along the more-or-less straight lines of the interstates, but rather scooping and weaving her way across the South, stopping in places as far-flung and illogical as Fairhope, Alabama. There's a napkin from a barbecue joint there, the logo featuring one of those fat, grinning cartoon pigs that seems happy as hell to have ended life as somebody's sandwich.

I don't need the crumpled map to tell me that Fairhope's as far south as you can get without falling into the Gulf of Mexico. I remember one time Mama was singing that Cher song "Gypsies, Tramps & Thieves" in the kitchen, and when she got to the part about "Picked up a boy just south of Mobile," I said that didn't make any sense, because Mobile's right on the bay, with nothing lying past it but water. They must have pulled up that boy with a fishing line. But Mama was quite insistent. She got out the atlas and showed me there was a narrow lip of land stretching around the bay, like a backward C, with Mobile perched at the top and some little place called Fairhope down at the bottom. She paused as we looked at the map, her fingertip grazing the ragged outline of the coast, then she flicked at the page, the way you flick away an ant.

"So the boy who knocked Cher up must have come from Fairhope," I said, partly because I could be a bit of a pissant when I was a kid and partly because Mama was always teaching me old song lyrics without bothering to explain what any of them meant. Mama liked Cher. She sang her all the time in the kitchen, especially the music from after she left Sonny.

I study the map. Beaufort to Macon is pretty much a

straight shot west. I can make it there before dark. Once I leave Macon, it'll take that long, slow dip through the fattest parts of Georgia and Alabama to get me to Fairhope. From there the trail runs pretty much due north, going west just enough to scoop by Tupelo, Mississippi, where a receipt from the trash bag tells me Mama bought something from a roadside stand. Something marked just "8 oz. jar" scrawled in red ink, something that cost her $2.15. Then a little more west and a little more north and I'm in Memphis. Back to the place where she began.

That road out there can't tell you a single thing that you don't already know. That's what Leary said to me on the banks of Polawana, and he undoubtedly spoke the truth. But right now I don't know anything, so it seems like this road stretched in front of me, long and flat and ugly as a runway, is gonna have to tell me something. I'm already in trouble with the money. Leary poured in a little gas from a can he had in his truck, just enough to get me going, and I stopped for more as soon as I was far enough out of Beaufort that I didn't figure anybody would know me. It cost $24.50 to fill the Blackhawk tank, which was bad enough, but then the needle started dropping almost the second I was back on the road and if I'm figuring it right I'm only getting about ten miles a gallon. Maybe not even that much. Which means it'll cost me twenty-five dollars to drive a hundred miles, and if I'm going as far south as Fairhope and then back up . . . The math is so depressing I have to stop.

Why the hell did Mama take such an indirect route? Was she trying to hold to the back roads too? Was she afraid, even in 1977, that a car like this made her too obvious? But that only makes a certain kind of sense, since I'd imagine that cops in small towns are even more curious about unusual people passing through in unusual vehicles than troopers cruising the interstate. Would she have been so frightened that she would have deliberately chosen to go miles out of her way just to avoid detection, even when it was clear she was trying to hurry? I conclude she was trying to hurry because of all the trash in the car—she may have stopped to order, but apparently she always took the food with her, eating as she drove, and the passenger's-side seat was reclined when I found it, lying damn near horizontal, suggesting she spent at least one night sleeping in the car.

But when I consider the evidence in another light, it isn't quite so surprising that all the napkins and wrappers in the trash bag Leary handed me are from local places, like this Juicy Lucy cup and bag from Macon. Mama hated fast-food chains. Hated Walmarts and Holiday Inns and big supermarkets too, anything that she thought stripped the individual flavor out of a place. She considered what she called "the homogenization of America" the great evil of our time. All right, then. She must have picked something up at a place called Juicy Lucy—likely a hamburger, if the perfectly round grease stain on the bag can be trusted—and that was evidently the last stop on her sojourn before coming home. I look deeper into the bag for a receipt, but there is none. Nor do I find any signs of gas receipts, so I guess she either didn't have a credit card or didn't choose to pay with one, which raises another interesting question. What had she used for money, in her flight from there to here?

It's a muddle. I sigh and lean back in the seat to ponder the limited charms of an I-95 rest area. The sun has almost fully disappeared and I watch a dog, long-legged and clumsy, like a puppy just west of the cute stage, sniffing around a trash can. Somebody's put him out. Turned tail and left him here, maybe a day ago or maybe a week, and he doesn't understand they're not coming back. My chest grows tighter as I watch him rise on his back legs, bringing his nose up to the top of the trash can. He's not quite tall enough to reach it, even with a stretch, but whatever's underneath that lid smells promising enough that he begins to wag his stubby tail, and there's something in that gesture, that undying little nub of hope that still exists in the most hopeless of situations, that makes me feel suddenly weepy and weak. He's not a pretty dog. It's hard to tell what type he is. Too small to be a hunting dog, too big to be lap dog, and so awkward with those skinny legs and big feet that nobody's ever going to want him.

I could toss him one of the protein bars. Call animal control, maybe, for whatever county I'm in, only he's not the kind to get adopted; he's too big and nondescript. But I sure as hell can't leave him here, not with all those cars going ninety miles per hour at the top of the ramp, because dogs make me feel guilty in a way people never do. I think it's how they ask for nothing and seem so damn grateful when they get it.

There's an eight-track sticking out of the tape player and I eject it. It's not a normal one, with a sticker showing the artist and the album cover, but a plain white shell of an eight-track, with only the word DEMO written across it, slanted, in black Magic Marker. I push it back in, still watching the dog, and for a second I think it's broken. There's a gentle roar, the sort of empty sound you get when you bring your ear to a conch shell, and then not music at all, but a woman's voice.

"Want me to set it here?" she says. "Is this close enough to pick up?"

The answer is indistinct, the low rumble of a man talking, but then a guitar begins. Acoustic, like mine, which is flung in the backseat along with the protein bars and three changes of underwear. Whoever's playing the guitar is pretty good. But they stop after a minute or two and I can hear the voices in the background again.

"Come on," says a woman. Different voice from the first one. Higher, breathier. "Just ease your way into it. You know you can."

It's my mother's long-ago voice. I always wondered how someone who spoke that soft could sing that loud.

And then the guitar comes in again, the same lead, played with a little more vigor this time. The lyrics start up too, a line about looking into the water, standing at the end of the pier, and it's clear with the very first word that I'm listening to Elvis.

He sings a couple of bars, then stops. Both women's voices are back at once, cajoling and comforting, like a pair of mothers trying to force medicine down the throat of a sickly child. The man on the tape may be king, but he's an uncertain king. He's singing a song I've never heard—somehow I think he's singing a song nobody has ever heard. Judging by the static and the background noises, I don't think this tape was made in a recording studio. I think I'm listening to something raw and personal. Elvis and Mama and this other woman—her voice lower and silkier than Mama's, and I get the impression maybe she's black, maybe the same black woman in the picture—were working on a song in private. A song about a pier and water, a man standing at the end of it and looking down. A man who's come to the end of his earthly powers and who now must, for maybe the first time in a long time, rely on something beyond his own strength.

The dog has given up on the trash can and is wandering along the sidewalk, barely out of range of the cars pulling in and pulling out. People not paying attention to some stray Georgia dog, people who just want to text or pee or text while they're peeing. Elvis mumbles something that sounds like, "Too much Otis," but even so he's still strumming, for I think the singer and the guitarist are the same person. It has the feel of that, of a man fitting the notes around the lyrics, making it up as he goes. "Too much Otis," must mean "Too much like Otis Redding," and the lyrics truly are a little reminiscent of "Sitting on the Dock of the Bay," but the tone is different. When Otis Redding sang that song you knew he had given up, and this new lyric . . . .

Waiting on the water, waiting on the water. Waiting on the water to carry me home.

Elvis is singing again, and I know enough of his history to know this melody is like his old stuff, the stripped-down music from the early years, even before he started recording at Sun Records. The sort of song he knew when he was just a boy, singing in church and playing the county fairs. I recognize the gospel tremor in his voice because I have it too, and so did my mama. It's the voice of anybody who started out in the church or maybe even just in the South, the voice of someone who can't even say the goddam word *home* without lifting the note just a little bit right at the very end, as hopeful as a dog at a rest stop, sure as shooting that waiting out there somewhere, somehow, is an angel just for them.

I roll down my window. I roll down Elvis's window, I guess is a better way to say it, and I holler at the dog. "Get out of the road," I tell him, and Elvis has stopped singing. He's still doubting himself. He slaps his hand against the strings of the guitar and he's mumbling again, something about a rip-off and I know how that feels, as if everything you write just sounds like a half-ass imitation of everything that's been written before. You're spent and you're tired and you know you've grown out of the cute stage and the world expects something new from you now, only you've got nothing to give them. Your hands come up full of air.

It's not a rip-off, I think, trying to will Elvis to pick up that guitar, to start playing again. *Otis Redding knew damn well nothing was going to come his way. But your song is different. You still have hope. And you can't get rid of it, country boy, no matter how hard you try.*

"Come on, baby, just sing," says my mother, like she always said to me. "Don't worry about Otis. He's waiting for death and you're waiting for Jesus."

That thought is so much like my own that I look toward the eight-track, half expecting to see my mother sitting there on the dash somehow, come back to me intact through time and space. But instead the car is filled with a louder roar, a horrible chewing sound, and when I try to eject the tape, I see it's come unspooled, and all the silky brown strands of music have gotten tangled and trapped. I hold the eight-track half in and half out with one hand and ease my other hand around the sides, trying to reach into the slot and unhook the tape, but it's hopeless. It's all coming loose in my hands. Elvis's last song—hell, maybe his only real song, since I don't recall any others he might have written, and I guess that's why my mother was trying to encourage him all those years ago. Because her "baby" was said in the same coaxing voice she used with me when I was sure I was going to fail algebra or was too scared to do the Christmas solo. Elvis was forty-two when he died, and Mama was nineteen, the true baby in the room, so why would she be talking to him with that kind of authority when he was old enough to be her father?

But the answer is gone now, falling to shreds no matter what I do to stop it, along with the voices of Elvis and my mother and the woman who was wondering if she should set something—the tape recorder probably—closer to the microphone. No, they weren't in a studio. It didn't sound like there was anyone else in the room. No producer or musicians, and I have the sense this song was something Elvis was afraid of, or embarrassed by, some part of himself he never planned to show the world. I gently set the busted eight-track, with pieces of greenish-brown tape stringing out like seaweed, onto the passenger seat.

I crank the car. It roars up so proud and mighty that I figure the sound must be costing me at least a dollar and a half. I back out of my parking place and start up the ramp. The dog's still there. I dig around for a protein bar to toss him but then I think he probably needs water more and I've got a bottle in here from the service station and surely I can find some sort of cup to pour it into. The ashtray pops out into my hand the minute I tug, and it's ironic, sure, ironic as hell to be giving a stray dog water out of a solid gold ashtray, but the day abounds with irony already, so why not?

Nobody's behind me and I ease the car over. Say something to the dog out the window and his ears go right up. He trots over to me without question as I open the door and lean out to give him the water and then, boom, he's up and over my lap in a second, knocking aside Bradley's waders and wedging himself down into the passenger seat with his tail wagging like crazy and his tongue hanging out.

"Oh no, you don't," I say, but it's hard to get a grip on him when he doesn't have a collar, so I give him the water and the protein bar, which fill him with so much unspeakable delight that he tries to kiss me, his long nails pushing into my thigh, and by then the fight had gone out of me. No point in trying to open the door and push him out the other side. He's taken up residence. He's sitting there staring straight ahead as if to say, "Let's get on with it."

What now? Events seem to be beyond my control and they have been ever since I looked in Bradley's fishing shed window and beheld this Stutz Blackhawk waiting for me, waiting in its bubble wrap cocoon. This car's driving me, and there's no point in pretending otherwise, although it is damn distressing to contemplate that I've been on the road for less than an hour and I've already managed to spend $24.50, destroy the final recorded words of Elvis Presley, and adopt a dog.

The cup Honey drank from thirty-seven years ago says Juicy Lucy but offers no address, and without a phone I can't do a search. When I swing off at a Walmart to buy the dog a collar, leash, chew toy, bag of kibble, and water dish ($21.72), the cashier claims she's never heard of the place. So I drive downtown and park in front of some dying strip center. It's mostly dark now, so maybe the Blackhawk won't attract too much attention here, and besides, attempting to parallel park this monstrosity on a city street is entirely out of the question. It's not really the kind of car you park. You have to dock it. I get the dog out. He's clearly never been walked on a leash and the skill doesn't exactly come to him quick. He strains diagonally to the right and then to the left, but we finally make it up the hill and into what appears to be the restaurant district of Macon.

At first I walk back and forth fairly aimlessly, with the dog lunging and jumping and peeing on every corner. There's no Juicy Lucy in sight, of course there isn't, and it's beginning to strike me that I've been very stupid, tearing off half-assed like this, with no plan and no money and no phone to look up things, like addresses and directions. This crazy interstate dog is getting ready to bite somebody and he probably hasn't even had his shots. I pass a cool little place with outside dining and a singer is setting up in the corner and I picture Gerry in my mind, no doubt pissed as hell that I didn't show up and didn't call, and I begin to wonder if I could go back to Beaufort now, even if I wanted to. Because I've been toying with the idea the last hour, even though I know Bradley's going to be, not pissed, but, in his words, "extremely disappointed" that I looked in the shed when he told me not to. Gerry might fire me for blowing off a Friday night and so there's a very real chance I could be returning to even less of a life than the one I left. But Leary would probably take the dog, which would be great, because this is absolutely the sort of dog that was born to ride in a tow truck, and this wouldn't be the first time I've disappointed Bradley and Gerry and they always seem to get over it. And at the rate the Blackhawk is guzzling gas, I've probably got just enough money to . . .

Just as I'm thinking all this, and half envying this guy who's setting up for a gig he probably hates, my eye falls on a chalkboard sign advertising Elvis Presley milkshakes. It's got to be some sort of sign. A sign that's on a sign. That's the best kind. Apparently, the milkshakes are made from banana ice cream and peanut butter with a straw made out of candied bacon. I haven't eaten since breakfast, unless you count the beer, and the thought of an Elvis Presley milkshake sounds so good my stomach rumbles.

Seven dollars.

What the hell. I'm starving and there's no point in going either backward or forward tonight and besides, several people at the sidewalk tables have dogs with them. Of course, they have little well-groomed, well-trained city dogs, not some wild-eyed stray coonhound kind of creature who is straining so hard he's about to break his cheap Walmart leash.

"You're going to have to be good," I say to the dog, who has no response, and I sit down at the table nearest the singer. He glances over at me.

"How long have you worked here?" I ask him.

He has to stop and think, poor bastard. "Six years."

"You ever hear of a place called the Juicy Lucy? I think it's probably some kind of diner. And it's been around a real long time. Maybe forty years."

He shakes his head. "I'm not a local. Dave here is a local."

Dave, who must be my server, is approaching with water and menu in hand. I wave him back before he can get close enough for the dog to bite him and we go through the whole Juicy Lucy's bit again even though it's beginning to dawn on me that what I need to find is not just a local, but an old local, or at least someone older than me and these guys. Someone who'd remember the seventies.

Dave's never heard of the Juicy Lucy either, but he says one of the cooks has been around forever and he might know. Then he asks, all sticky sweet like a good server, "But why are you looking for some greasy diner? We have the best food in town."

The trouble is, I don't know exactly why I'm looking for the place, aside from the fact my mother once ate food from there. I don't know what I'm looking for at all, or what questions I'll ask when I find it. It seems that I must not merely return the car to Graceland, but retrace the steps of Mama's whole trip, that the explanation for why she ran away is somehow buried beneath the question of how she ran and I'm going to have to dig through the trash of one to get to the truth of the other. The server and the musician are still looking at me, so I stall.

"Is that Elvis Presley milkshake really worth seven dollars?" I ask.

The musician answers. "It'd be worth $107," he says. "It's scary good."

"Then bring me one," I say, and as the dog jumps up against the table in a doomed attempt to eat the salt shaker, inspiration strikes. "My mother used to work at the Juicy Lucy back in the day," I say. "And she talked about the place all the time. I even named my dog Lucy, so I just thought it'd be funny to take a picture of the dog standing in front of the restaurant."

The server and the musician seem to more or less accept this explanation, even though all this leaping has provided evidence beyond dispute that the dog in question is male. But I guess no matter how much stuff he's got flopping around in the breeze, he's Lucy for life now, and someday this will be a funny story, if I ever find the right person to tell it to. The singer goes back to setting up his equipment. The server goes to get the milkshake and the cook.

I'm due for some luck and now, all of a sudden out of nowhere, I get a triple dose. The musician starts and he's good, with enough sense to open with a little Bonnie Raitt, who hardly anybody remembers and practically everybody likes. The music soothes me and, more important, it soothes the Lucy dog, who curls up under the table and goes to sleep as if to confirm that it's been a hell of a day and he for one would be happy to see the end of it. The milkshake shows up, complete with its bacon straw, and it's the best damn thing I've ever put in my mouth. I don't know if I'd pay $107 for it, but I'll gladly pay $7 and I'm starting to relax a little bit, lulled into a sort of bluesy sugar trance, when the cook emerges and says that sure, yeah, of course he remembers the Juicy Lucy.

"I don't know what your mama told you," he says, folding his arms across his big stomach, "and I hope I'm not speaking out of turn. But the Juicy wasn't some family diner, it was a pothead place. Like a bar where people got high instead of drunk and the cops closed it down for good more than thirty years ago."

Well, that's something to digest. Lucy's woken up and I throw him half the bacon, which gets his tail wagging so hard that the whole table starts pulsating. "But it had food?" I ask, remembering the bag with that great circle of grease.

"Well, sure it had food. Stoners gotta eat." He laughs, but doesn't unfold his arms. "Burgers and shit, but the food was just the cover. It was out by the airport. Not the airport airport, but one of those back roads that take you down to the shorter runways where the private planes land." He looks at the server. "What's the name of that road? The one where they found that poor little girl's body last year?"

"What poor little girl?" I ask. The musician is leafing through his music.

"Some dead teenager," says the cook. "All I'm saying is that there's not a big call for urban development out that way. But that might work in your favor, since the odds are high the building's still standing just like it was. It had this big pink and purple mermaid lady sprayed on the side like graffiti. You know, like that Beatles cartoon."

"*Yellow Submarine?*"

"That's the one. Damned hippie place." He moved toward the table, clicking an ink pen. "Here. Give me that napkin. I can't remember the road name but I'll draw you a map."

Perhaps at one time the phrase "private airport" conjured up images of status and exclusivity, but now the road that runs behind the main airport—which, as it ends up, has the completely unimaginative name Freight Road—holds nothing more than long-term parking lots, mechanics, a FedEx drop-off, and a couple of down-on-their-luck strip clubs, which claim to have BEER and GIRLS, but without showing any particular enthusiasm for either. I drive all the way to the very end and shine the Blackhawk's lights into an overgrown field and there it is, just where the cook promised. A concrete building so engulfed in kudzu that you can barely make out the name. But the JUI is clear enough, as are pieces of the lady herself, one shoulder and both feet, so the cook did have that part wrong. She's not a mermaid, she's some sort of goddess.

Either way, it's hard to imagine my mother—or even the dark-eyed, smirking Honey of that old photograph—ever hanging out at a place like this. I can only assume that she originally entered the pink-painted door of the Juicy Lucy halfway through her tour with Elvis, when the *Lisa Marie* landed on one of these short runways and taxied into one of these small hangars. I get Lucy out and let him pee. The headlights of the Blackhawk pump an arc of yellow-green light into the dark Georgia night, enough so that the whole front of the restaurant is eerily illuminated. I venture up and try the door. It's locked, but the windows, low and already half broken, would be easy enough to push out in case I decide to enter in the morning. Thanks to the combined costs of the gas and the milkshake and the dog, I'm going to have to spend the night in the car—that's a given. Mama obviously slept in this car once, and maybe she even slept right here, in front of the Juicy Lucy, in this same passenger seat that's still half cranked down. I consider driving farther up the road and parking under one of the streetlights near the strip clubs, which may or may not be safer, and which definitely ups the chance some cop will notice the car. There's no explanation for why I'm driving a vehicle that is more than three decades overdue for inspection and has no registration card in the glove compartment. I know because I checked. Just seeing the car in the name Elvis Presley would have answered a lot of questions—and raised as many more, I guess—but having a fancy old car with no registration at all would surely cause the cops to haul me in. And, awful as Freight Road is, I bet it's a lot better than the Macon jail.

The other option is to stay right here, parked in front of the Juicy Lucy. A place where I'm less likely to be found by a cop and more likely to be found by some sort of slasher-movie boogeyman. I don't want to be murdered any more than I want to be arrested.

"Are you going to protect me?" I say to Lucy, who is crunching kibble right out of the bag. I've got to break him of this snacking—that sack of dog food has got to last us to Memphis and back, but for now all I can seem to do is crank down the seat a few degrees and finish the last of the Stellas, warm as it is. A milkshake and a protein bar and two beers hardly constitute a proper day's sustenance, and I know I'll wake up hungry and have to spend more money on breakfast. I look over at Bradley's waders, which are still strapped in the passenger seat, even though they've been knocked all askew by the dog. I unstrap them and put the soles against the passenger side glass, facing down, in hopes that any murderer who comes knocking might logically deduce that there's a big man doing his private business in this car. A man so big that nobody in their right mind would want to mess with him.

And then we settle down, me in the driver's seat and the dog in the back and Bradley's boots up against the glass. The seats go almost totally flat and are deep and cushioned. This is a car that was meant to sleep in, I think. Or have sex in, or escape in. And despite everything, despite all the events of this bewildering day, I feel myself drifting off almost at once. My last thought before I go under is that I think I can smell honey on the seats. Not the person, but the actual stuff, rich and sweet, the kind of honest honey that comes straight from the bees, with ragged walls of comb half floating in the jar. The kind of honey you dribble over warm biscuits on Sunday morning, before your grandmother takes you to church.

And then, with the next breath, I'm asleep.

When I awaken, there's a man staring down at me from outside the car. He's tall, or maybe he just looks tall because he's standing and I'm lying flat. I struggle up, waking Lucy as I thrash, and roll down the window.

"Who are you?" he says. "And what the hell are you doing here?"

"Who are you?" I say back. "And what are you doing here?" For once in my life I'm not trying to sass anybody. They're two honest questions. I'm still half asleep.

"I own the land you're parked on," he says, the sort of information that partly explains things, but not really. The clock on the dashboard isn't working, but I glance at it anyway. No telling what time it is, but the sun is fully up and I have the feeling I've slept a long time.

Since he gave me a half-assed answer, I figure he deserves the same. I dig out the Styrofoam cup and hand it to him out the window. "I was looking for the Juicy Lucy based on this cup."

He rolls the cup over in his hand. Small hands for a man, I think irrelevantly. "This cup is from the Rookery."

"Oh shit. That's my milkshake cup from last night. Here . . ." I dig around. I'm going to have to get another bag. Start keeping my trash separate from Honey's. I hand him the Juicy Lucy cup and he falls silent, studying it deeply, like I've handed him something surprising, and of great value.

"This was my mother's old car," I say. "She died recently, and I found it. Everything in it was something she touched and used when she was young and I feel like—" Here I break off, for there is no logical thing to say next. My mother may have died recently, if you call seven months ago recently, but the car is old, so why wouldn't I have known about it for years? And it is so obviously not an average person's car. Even if you know nothing about Elvis, even if you don't stop to Google the words *Stutz Blackhawk*, anybody can see this is an extraordinary vehicle with a story to match. So I stop babbling and just sit helplessly, staring up at the man's aviator shades, which reflect me back, doubled, to myself. They're cop sunglasses, even though I don't get the feeling he's a cop.

"I named my dog Lucy," I finally say, even though I know that doesn't shed any light on anything.

He bends down and leans in the window. Takes it all in, from the map to the guitar and the waders and the dog and the empty Stella bottle.

"Looks like you're on the run from something," he says.

"No," I say. "I'm on the run to something. This is a . . . it's a voyage of discovery."

To my great surprise, he laughs. "Who was your mother?"

"She was a backup singer for Elvis," I say. "Traveled with him the last year he toured, right before he died, and that's how I think she first came here. Her name was Laura Berry, but the people on the tour called her Honey."

At this he reacts. Gets upset, or at least I think he's upset. It's hard to tell with those big, ridiculous aviator shades on, but he jerks his head back so fast that he hits it on the top of the window frame. "You're Honey's daughter?" He's the second man to ask me this in as many days and I'd never thought that being my mother's daughter was quite such a celebrity-making event, but evidently there was more to Laura Berry Ainsworth than her husband and child ever knew, because this man is gaping at me in sheer disbelief. He pulls off his glasses and he's older than I would have first guessed. Late fifties, maybe even early sixties, and something in him looks familiar.

"I've seen your face," I say.

"Doubt it. Doubt it very seriously, as a matter of fact. You from around here?"

"Can I get out and stretch? Let the dog pee?"

"Suit yourself."

I scramble out of the car, Lucy right behind me. He doesn't have his leash hooked to his collar and for a moment I panic, even though I'm still not sure I want a dog, much less this particular dog. But for some reason, Lucy decides he likes this man, standing up on his hind legs and doing a little dance of joy in front of him, and I snap the leash on.

"This dog's a boy," the man says, and then he spits. "Why'd you name him Lucy?"

"He sort of named himself."

The man studies me with solemn eyes, and in that precise moment I know where I've seen him. On a billboard, looking down at me last night as I was driving into Macon. He's running for something. School board. State legislature. Governor. Sheriff maybe, and wouldn't that be a pretty pickle.

"The dog named himself." The man snorts, but he scratches Lucy's ears nonetheless. "And you're here on a voyage of discovery. Yeah, I'd say you're Honey's daughter, all right."

"How well did you know her?"

"Not that well. They'd always park the Lisa Marie right over there, in that hangar, whenever Elvis had a gig in town, and he liked our hamburgers . . ."

The word *our* is a slip, small but telling. He doesn't just own the land, he used to own the Juicy Lucy. Or at the very least worked there. I could call him on it, but something about this guy makes me feel like I'll get further with him by playing dumb.

"So they'd send some of the band members or singers over to pick up a bag of burgers," I venture, even though it's hard to believe such a simple mission would have imprinted my mother on his memory for thirty-seven years. Of course she was traveling with Elvis, and that might have given her some special status, turning a simple burger run into the kind of story that would put the Juicy Lucy on the local map.

"You know what the secret to a good burger is?" the man asks me suddenly as we begin to make, by silent agreement, our slow way from the car to the restaurant. It looks less menacing in the light of day. The goddess is smiling down at us, and I'm just southern enough to find the curled vines of kudzu pretty. It's relentless the way it covers everything, turning cabins into fairy cottages and abandoned railroad tracks into leafy green rivers. Kudzu's forgiving, like memory. It hides what was, allowing just small bits of the past to peek out here and there.

"Grease?" I guess, and the man laughs.

"Well, good for you," he says. "Not many girls your age understand that."

For the first time I notice a FOR SALE sign on the door. "You're getting rid of the place?"

"Trying to sell it. Sell it or bulldoze it, all the same to me. That's why I was out here, to see it there was anything worth taking when I go."

When I tried the door the night before, I thought it was locked, but this man rattles the knob with confidence, and when it doesn't immediately obey, he puts his hip into it. The door gives way with a creak, and as it swings open I stoop to look inside. There's a lot to see. A counter, some stools, a pool table. A big, open area with what looks like the remnants of a beanbag chair and some sort of arcade game, cracked and broken in the corner. Indian bedspread curtains, a woven rug that has been half eaten by mice, and the same sort of pastel bubble graffiti that was on the outside is all over the walls. Flowers mostly, a frog on a lily pad, none of them particularly well drawn. The whole room is festooned in dust, the indoor equivalent of kudzu, with great ribbons of it hanging down from the rafters and windows.

"Why'd you close down?" I ask the man, pulling Lucy back before he gallops in and does something crazy like pee on what's left of the pool table.

"Times change," the man says with a shrug. He's made a gesture for me to step in and I do, but he doesn't enter himself. He just stands there in the doorway, blinking, sunlight streaming past him on both sides and making the dust sparkle.

"Did the cops do it? You got raided?"

It's the most obvious two questions in the world, but he bristles, takes offense. "What'd you say your name was?"

"I didn't. Cory Beth Ainsworth."

"Cory?"

"That's right."

"And where'd you come from?"

"Beaufort."

"And you say Honey's dead."

"A few months ago. Breast cancer."

"I'm sorry to hear that. And how old would you be?"

"Thirty-seven."

"Thirty-seven?"

"Yes, sir. I was born in 1978. Seven months and four days after my parents got married. Seven months and nine days after my mama left Memphis. So I think you see my situation. I would think it's rather obvious why I'm driving this route, and just what truth I'm trying to get at. May I ask you some questions? Starting with your name?"

He's staring at me. At least I think he's staring, because he's put his aviator sunglasses back on. But his feet are planted wide apart and he's got a hand on each side of the doorframe. Look-

ing back at him with the sun streaming in on both sides, I'm reminded of those old cowboy movies where the bad guy comes
bursting into the saloon and it hits me that maybe I've been stupid, getting out of my car and coming in here with a stranger. I
could scream at the top of my lungs and there'd be no one to
hear me, not here at the end of a rarely traveled road with nothing but the sound of airplane engines in the distance. Normally
a dog might be some help, but Lucy's just curled up on the
grimy concrete floor, licking himself.

"Name's Philip," the man says. "You can ask me your questions and I'll answer them as best I can, even though all I know
about your mama is that she'd come in with the other girls who
sang backup and he'd be with them too. I don't know what
Honey told you growing up, but Elvis was never too good to mix
with the common man. He wasn't the sort who'd sit on his
plane and send somebody to get him a sack of burgers. No, he'd
get off and come in himself, and whether you believe it or not,
little girl, he sat right on that corner bar stool the last time he
was in and he played up a storm. The blues and rockabilly, the
kind of music that gave him his start, and he remembered every
line of every song. Even though by that point he'd been singing
his Vegas crap for better than ten years."

"I believe you," I say. "He was playing the old stuff at the
end. Like he was circling back. Like he knew he didn't have
long."

The man shrugs. "Whatever you say. Your mother was just
one of the girls who came in with him. I don't know what there
is to tell you beyond that."

"But she came through town again," I said. "A year later. In the Blackhawk, the car I'm driving now. You'd have to remember that, wouldn't you? It would have been probably no more than two, maybe three days after Elvis died, and this time she was alone. Maybe scared. I'm thinking probably scared. It seems like all that would have made an impression."

He pulls off the glasses again. It seems to be his nervous gesture, this putting on and pulling off of his glasses. Everybody has one. His small eyes are red rimmed and I wonder if he's one of those people who has to wear sunglasses all the time because he's light sensitive. "And I'm sure it would have made an impression if I'd have seen her," he said. "But I didn't."

"You're sure?"

"I said I didn't see her and I didn't."

"But here's the thing . . . There's that cup and a bag out there in the car, both saying the name of this restaurant, plain as day. The Juicy Lucy in big pink letters, and that's how I knew to come here. I'm not suggesting anything, sir, because I've seen your face on a billboard and I'm sure you're a respectable man here in Macon, a pillar of the community. I'm just trying to get at the truth. Or at least my own little piece of it."

He leans back abruptly, pulling his hands away from the doorway. "Now look here," he says. "I could have run you in for trespassing and I didn't. You wanted inside the restaurant and I brought you in. And I've stood here and held my temper while you implied I'm a liar, not once but twice. Your mother had a sweet nature and I'm sorry to hear she's passed, but all that aside, I hardly knew her. So I'd say our interview is coming to an end."

"I'd love it if we could sit somewhere and talk. Maybe I can buy you a Starbucks."

"I don't drink Starbucks. The coffee's too fucking strong and it's a sign of everything that's wrong in America today."

Exactly like something Mama would have said. I try again. "I still have questions."

"Don't we all."

I look around the room, trying to imagine it years ago. The colors bright and unfaded, the music loud. The smell of grease and pot mingling in the air and Elvis on a bar stool holding court. The absence of chairs. His listeners must have clustered around him on the floor, sitting at his feet like the apostles with Jesus, and maybe it felt good after the big stages and venues to sneak away to a little nothing place like this and take the glitter off. I have a million questions to ask this man, but I hear myself blurt out, "Did my mother smoke weed?"

He laughs again. But it's a genuine laugh, not a bitter one, and Lucy looks up from his balls.

"You want the truth?"

"You know I do."

He spits on the floor. Put his sunglasses back on. "Then I'll give you what you say you've come for," he says. "Your mother was a wild child. She did it all and she did it all the time."

With that, the air seems to go out of the room. I stumble, even though I'm not moving, and throw out an arm to brace myself against the dusty wall. I'm filled with a sudden desire to get out of the Juicy Lucy, off of Freight Road, and far away from this town. I head toward the door and Philip steps aside to let me pass, as if he's aware that despite my big claims, he's said too little and too much, all in the same sentence. Lucy trots along behind me and we're almost back to the car when he calls out.

"Wait a minute," he says. "Don't I get a chance to ask my own question?"

I get the dog into the car and climb in myself. Fasten the seat belt, crank up that engine, which would suit a crop duster better than a car, and then he walks over and stoops down. He has to practically crawl through the window in order to be heard over the roar, so it looks like we'll be ending our relationship in exactly the same position we began it. As I put my hands on the steering wheel, I notice I still have the phone numbers from yesterday inked on my arms, the one for Graceland and the one for Leary. They're blurry but still legible. Meaning, I guess, that maybe I could still either go forward or back.

"All right," I say to Philip. "I'll answer you one question. Shoot."

I would have thought he'd want to know where the hell I got the Stutz Blackhawk, or where I was planning to go next. Why I have a bunch of numbers written on my arm like a Holocaust survivor or how I'd ended up here, behind the airport, in the parking lot of this broken-down dive. Any of them would have been good questions. The kind I'd like the answer to myself.

But instead he leans in and says the last thing on earth I'd expect him to say. "Just tell me this one thing, Cory Ainsworth. Do you need any money?"

As I drive back down the bumpy road, past the strip joints and freight warehouses, I keep trying to wrap my head around the fact Philip had called my mother a wild child. It's hard to see your own mother that way. I guess it's hard to see your mother at all. For thirty-six years Mama was the most important person in my life—the one phone number my fingers could always remember, even when they were drunk or lost or scared. Hers is the name I still cry out in those bad dreams, the kind where I think I'm falling. But in other ways, she was always unknowable—the first and last mystery of my life.

It's not like I think she was a prude or anything. Leary and the other kids in Beaufort might have seen her as nothing more than a church lady, but I always knew better. My mama was a survivor. She had that wary look of people who've seen things they never wanted to see, but now that they've seen them, they can't forget.

Here's an example. It was the summer between tenth and eleventh grade, so I wasn't even sixteen. I couldn't drive. But there was something in me that came up fast that summer, shooting out of the ground like kudzu, and I liked older boys. Mama made them come into the house and tell her and Bradley all sorts of stuff about their parents and their future plans. It's like she had a checklist in her head and she was adding up the pluses and minuses as they talked. But somehow she still didn't like Joel McGee, the boy I was seeing that summer, even though his father was an optometrist from Charleston and his future plans included med school and joining the family practice.

Nothing trumps med school. Nothing. Bradley rolled right over for him. Mama, not so much.

She said, "If you want to date a younger girl, then you'll have to play by younger girl rules," a line I'd heard a hundred times. Joel had nodded and assured her that he'd have no trouble getting me back by eleven and that yes, he would love to join us for lunch next Sunday after church. And somehow he even managed to work in the fact he played the guitar. I'd told him she was a fine musician, he'd said, that she'd taught me everything I knew. Maybe the three of us could strum a bit on the porch after Sunday lunch. He had a particular admiration for James Taylor.

Ordinarily, this would have charmed her, but Mama had an instinct for trouble. It's like she could smell it coming down the road a mile away, and when Joel and I left, she came out and leaned on the front porch banister, watching us get into his car.

When we got back that night, she was still standing there in pretty much the same position.

It was eleven thirty-five. I said, "Shit," and slid out of the car. Joel wanted to walk me to the door, but I wouldn't let him. No amount of James Taylor was going to save him now.

Mama followed me through the front door and across the den, down the hall, and into my bedroom, listening to my cockamamie excuses about movies letting out late and traffic on the bridge.

"You've been to Smuggler's Cove, haven't you?" she said.

That's exactly where we'd gone, and I don't know how a woman the age my mother was then—which, come to think of it, was pretty much the age I am now—knew where the local teenagers went to make out.

"He writes his own lyrics, Mama," I said, and went into the bathroom. It was all I could think of to say. Mama came right in after me, still nagging about how Joel was entirely too old for me, and I said he'd been a perfect gentleman and we'd only talked about music, and then I sat down on the toilet and pulled down my panties and a big clump of sand fell out of them and went splat on the bathroom floor.

It's hard to recover from a moment like that. Mama just looked at the sand there between my feet and said, "So maybe I'll leave you alone to take your shower."

She spoke with that cold, icy calm voice she saved for the times when I was in deep trouble. Her expression was an equal mix of disapproval and the absolute absence of surprise. 'Cause the apple never falls very far from the tree, does it? That's what people always say, and everybody likes the edgy girl, unless you're the edgy girl's mother, and everybody roots for the rebel, except maybe the woman who'd taken her own shot at freedom sixteen years earlier and was still paying the price.

"I'll give you some privacy," said Mama, in that tone that could make an angel's wings shrivel and fall off her back. I got into the tub and turned on the water as hot as it would go, stood under the steaming, punishing blast, letting it wash away any trace of Joel McGee and the sandy dunes of Smuggler's Cove. But I've never forgotten the look on Mama's face that night. Was this the same woman who had taught me to sing along with Cher when I was seven? Who had turned the pepper mill into a microphone and who'd braided my hair while it was still wet, just so it could come out wild and free? It seemed like she'd always been pushing me forward and pulling me back in the same breath, that she wanted more for me out of life, but then feared that if I found it, I'd leave her.

I guess it's no surprise that the next Sunday, Joel did not

come to dinner. Instead, Mama and I went out alone, to the Chinese buffet, while Bradley stayed behind at church to help count the collection money.

We hadn't talked about that Friday night. I had stayed home Saturday to play Scrabble with Bradley. We'd made popcorn and watched *Who's the Boss?* And I'd worn a pink linen jacket and pantyhose to church, even though it was hot. I had sung loud and hard on all the hymns. Nobody could say I wasn't trying. But when we finally found ourselves alone in the booth of the Chinese restaurant, staring each other down across our spring rolls, Mama just looked at me wearily and said, "Do you at least know how to take care of yourself?"

Here's the thing. I knew at once what she meant. It was one of those rare times where there were no veils or pretending between us.

"I'm a careful girl," I said. "You raised me that way."

We ate the rest of the meal in silence. I sat in my space while she sat in hers. And at some point after the plates were cleared but before we got our ticket, I blurted out, "You know, nothing happened Friday night."

She just looked at me.

"We didn't do it," I said. "I wanted to. I was ready. I got Connie Baker to drive me to Savannah when we were out for spring break and I went to Planned Parenthood and I got the pills and I took a whole pack and was halfway into the second one. So I know it was safe. But when I showed them to Joel, he said it was unromantic that I had preplanned it. He said I'd stripped all the spontaneity out of the night. He said I killed the mood."

Mama put her elbows on the Formica tabletop and laid her chin against her fists. "He claims he's going to med school," she said, "and you're telling me he doesn't understand the world any better than that?"

"I know. But you gotta remember, he's also a musician. A songwriter. And they don't even try to make sense."

She sat back against the orange vinyl cushion. Maybe a minute ticked by, maybe less. I was so nervous my heart was pounding. The waitress brought the check and the fortune cookies, but neither one of us said thank you, even though that sort of thing is ordinarily automatic for my family. I know what you're thinking. You're thinking this is an improbable conversation between a mother and a daughter, and you're right. But through the years when I was growing up, there were times when, out of nowhere, I'd catch a glimpse of the woman behind the mother. This odd little part of her that slipped out in certain moments, like when she was singing Cher into the pepper mill or skinny-dipping in the Polawana River. I guess the person I was seeing was Honey, although I didn't know it at the time.

Mama was frowning, looking down at the bill like something wasn't adding up. "So you're telling me that you were going to Savannah and getting yourself on birth control pills, counting it out for a month and a half . . . and that put him straight off the idea."

I nodded. "I think he wanted to be the one who, you know, the one who decided when it was time."

"And on that golden day, just pray tell what was Mr. Joel planning to do?"

"I don't know," I said miserably. "Pull out, I guess."

Mama took a slow, deep drag on her tea and picked up the check. "You can do a lot better than that boy," she said.

I wait for the first stoplight I hit in town before I look in the envelope: four hundred freaking dollars, all of it in twenties. I came on this trip to solve a mystery, and it seems like I've only managed to make it deeper. Why the hell would a complete stranger offer me this kind of money? Even before I knew how much it was, I thanked him over and over and told him I'd repay him as soon as I'm settled, but he and I both know that I'll never get settled. This is payola, not a loan, and if he was buying himself anything, it was probably the back of my head. Besides, he didn't give me his full name or address, so how the hell would I ever find him again, even if I were so inclined? And what was he doing out at sunrise on that deserted road with four hundred dollars in his pocket, all in small bills? He had pulled out a wad, the sort of wad I didn't know men carried anymore, not even politicians in middling-sized Georgia towns. And he gave the whole of it to me based solely on the fact he'd once known my mother.

He'd even said he hadn't known her very well, although that's obviously a lie. Hearing she was dead wounded him. I could see the little flinch from behind the aviator shades, and yet he had asked for no details, had sought to know pitifully little about her life or her death. Granted, it's all pretty suspicious, but I do the math, and the math doesn't work. Mama got pregnant no more than six weeks before she left Graceland, it's the only thing that makes sense.

"Just promise me you won't sleep in the car anymore." That's all the man said as he handed me the money. "It isn't safe."

It's just past eight, and there's a long line at the drive-thru. I order sausage biscuits for both me and the dog off the dollar menu. Just because I'm flush for the moment doesn't mean I should blow it all at once, but at least this answers the question of how I'm going to get to Fairhope. As I'm waiting to pay, my eye falls on a building just past the McDonald's. A big sign says HEART OF GEORGIA CARDIOLOGY and across from it is the Macon Services for the Blind, the entrance to which is ironically well landscaped. In fact, it's the prettiest little patch of land I've seen since I rolled into town. And between these two fine institutions, with the name written in tiny letters, almost as if they're ashamed of their purpose here among so many noble causes, is a third medical office.

DNA Testing.

I look down at the seat beside me. If there's one thing I have in this car in undeniable abundance, it's DNA. The smell of Elvis is on the seats, and the smell of Honey too, and honey, and then there's the matter of this lipstick imprint on this cup. Could there be some lingering saliva on that straw? Leary was right, it's probably blood on this Kleenex, not chocolate, and almost certainly the blood of Elvis himself, rendered on his way home from the dentist office. Because that's the last place he ever drove to, you see, a bit of trivia that is well documented on all the websites. I look down at the Kleenex, with those tiny little flecks of blood.

That trip to the dentist was the last time Elvis was ever

sighted alive, at least by the general public. A photographer snapped him at about two in the morning, coming back into the gates of Graceland, riding in this very car. The lens had been pointed straight at Elvis and Elvis alone, giving the photographer a tight close-up of his face. There was no way of knowing who was driving or if anyone was beside him or crammed down in the back. It was the middle of the night for normal people, but around lunchtime for him, because day and night were reversed for Elvis, as anybody who has followed his tale well knows. He would awaken at sunset, which meant if he was on tour that his evening's performance in effect marked the beginning of his day, with time to party and decompress afterward. If he was home in Memphis, he would run any errands, such as this final trip to the dentist, after sunset, because a man as famous as Elvis couldn't get his teeth cleaned in the middle of the day. A riot would have broken out. The whole city was prepared to stay awake to service the needs of their favored son, from movie theaters to jewelry stores to car dealerships.

His entourage was held hostage to this strange rhythm as well, eating breakfast at midnight and going days at a time without ever seeing the sun. Hard to imagine Mama in that world too, even harder to imagine than her lolling around in the beanbag chairs of the Juicy Lucy. When I was growing up, Mama would come rapping on my door every morning at six thirty sharp, even on Saturday, telling me the day was wasting. Was getting up early her attempt to get back the 365 days of sunlight she lost during that year she lived with Elvis?

"That is one cool car," says the kid at the drive-thru window. I am sitting down so low that I have to reach up to give him the five, and he hands me the bag and my change with a kind of reverence. His voice drops, the way I'd imagine people start whispering when they enter the Sistine Chapel, because you just can't use a normal tone of voice when you're in the middle of something that's obviously holy, something that's just sitting there before you, sent from God on high to explain you to yourself. The kid flinches, like he's almost blinded by his own reflection in the hood, and I wonder all of a sudden if that was why Elvis did such a good job of breaking America's heart. Because he kept showing us ourselves, even when we didn't like looking at it. He kept showing us what happens when a poor boy from Tupelo, Mississippi, gets all the money and sex and fame in the world and still isn't happy.

"Yeah," I say. "Isn't it?" I've decided at some point my best defense is to acknowledge that the car is amazing, because to act nonchalant just gives rise to a whole new type of question. I take the two sausage biscuits, my coffee, and all the little planet-choking packets of sugar and cream and pull into a parking place. Lucy is going nuts with the smell of the sausage. I feed it to him in little pieces and study the building in front of me. Can paternity be determined from the saliva on an old straw? The blood on a napkin? I imagine Elvis pressing the napkin to his mouth, driving through the Graceland gate on that August night thirty-seven years ago, unaware he'd never drive out of them again. Unaware he may have fathered me as well, unaware Honey would take his car and flee all the way from the Mississippi to the Atlantic, looking for something she evidently was not destined to find, before finally abandoning the car and everything it represented in a shed in South Carolina. Where it would have stayed forever if Bradley hadn't needed his waders and I hadn't been the kind of girl who has absolutely nothing to lose.

I could drive to Atlanta and get some big-city answers. Take my bag of questions to the CDC and let them sort it all out. I glance down at the sack of trash in the floor of the passenger seat, even though I know anything within it likely only holds the DNA of Laura Berry Ainsworth, the one person whose identity was never in question. Lover to some, perhaps even to many. Mother to one. A funnel that the whole world rushed through in the summer of 1977, and as quickly as the idea rises, it dies. It's Saturday, early in the morning. There's a drop-off slot, I can see it from here. The Kleenex with the blood is the most important piece of evidence, along with the blood that courses through my own veins, but there's no way to put either of them through a shiny silver slot in a door of a bush-league medical clinic in Macon, Georgia. There's a law office right beside the DNA clinic, a liquor store on the corner. I guess you can make a day of it if you want to. Find out who your baby daddy is, sue him for child support, and get rip-roaring drunk.

But not at eight twenty on a Saturday morning.

"You ready to hit the road, boy?" I say, and Lucy whinnies as if to say *Yeah, the sooner we blow this Popsicle stand, the better*.

But leaving Macon is harder than I thought it would be. I get so lost I circle the city for nearly an hour, mostly because I'm still trying to avoid the interstate. At first I tell myself the whole thing is sort of a charming adventure. It's the back roads that give you the feel of a place, that's what Mama always said, but after my third wrong turn with no phone to help me, I'm happy as an Alabama pig to see a sign pointing to I-75. I get on it and drive slow, or at least as slow as a car like the Blackhawk can go. Lucy's curled up with Bradley's waders in the back, snoring and farting, and the envelope with the money is beside me on the seat. At one point I think I pass one of the billboards with my benefactor's picture, but his dark, sorrowful eyes are behind me in a flash and I'm half happy I don't know this man's name or what sort of office he feels entitled to hold. Better to think of him as just one more guardian angel of the road come to give me bad news and good money. And so I keep on driving until Macon, Georgia, is just a shimmer in my rearview mirror.

HONEY

August 19, 1977

ou've got to help me."

"And why is that? Why've I got to help you? We both know it's not mine."

The worst words a man can say to a woman, but I try not to let the fear show on my face. "What makes you so sure?"

"Because I had the mumps when I was thirteen. Has anyone ever told you what the mumps do to a thirteen-year-old boy?"

He looks toward the open door and frowns, like he's remembering something. Something unpleasant. I try to remain calm, but inside I'm shivering. This baby has to be Philip's. The timing is right and I can prove it, because I never outgrew my girlhood habit of keeping a diary. I still mark the start of my periods with a little star. I wish I had a diary like my old one with the pink hearts and the lock instead of what I write in now, which is just a plain blue spiral notebook from the grocery store. My old diary was small. It forced a girl to reduce her life to a series of tiny boxes, giving her just five lines to summarize who had hurt her and who had helped her, all the good and bad that can happen in a single day. It's a fine thing, I think, to be forced to edit reality. It turns your life into a haiku.

> *Back to the Lucy.*
> *Told him there's a baby.*
> *Mumps steal my best chance.*

I'd like to add a word, to put a *but* in the last line, so that it reads "but mumps steal my best chance." Unfortunately, that one *but* would destroy the unforgiving pattern of the poem. A haiku is a five-syllable line, followed by a seven-syllable line, then five more. I learned how to write them from one of the karate teachers at Graceland, a would-be country singer who'd left Pasadena with the name David but who had a vision somewhere along the road and arrived in Memphis calling himself Nin Tuch. I guess he thought it sounded more spiritual. Elvis renamed him at once. He'd call him "Nunchucks," and everyone would laugh, because that was the first rule of Graceland. Elvis makes a joke, no matter how corny, and everyone rolls around on the floor in hysterics.

"You had the mumps?" I repeat to Philip. I say it like I don't understand what that means, but of course I do. He's telling me that he's sterile, and that's why he laughed me off two months ago, as we lay tangled up in each other on this same dusty floor, when I finally got up my courage enough to suggest he use a rubber. Of course he had laughed. He's been carrying a Get Out of Jail Free card ever since he was thirteen.

But he must be telling the truth, because he's the very picture of nonchalance, smiling at me as he leans back against the refrigerator. It's broken, just like everything in this bar. There's a puddle of water at his feet and his arms are folded across his chest. He's not ever going to open those arms to me, much less to this baby. He's already written me off as a slut who's been with a dozen men, when the truth is there have only been two, and if this little heartbeat fluttering below my ribs wasn't set into motion by him, then it must have been the work of the other. I'm not sure how I feel about this information—in fact, I'm not sure how I feel about anything at all because my mind is busy galloping ahead. Philip had the mumps and therefore he can't be the father, and as awful as he is—I can see his awfulness now, standing right in front of me—he was still the better of the two options.

I start to say, "You took my virginity," but what would be the point? He wouldn't believe me, and even if he did, that simple statement—which would make the perfect middle line of a haiku, come to think of it, seven syllables—doesn't begin to tell the whole story. I wanted to be rid of my innocence. He didn't take it from me, I threw it at him, and if he hadn't been the one who happened to lie beside me on that magic carpet night, with the music so seductive and the air thick as a blanket, sooner or later I would have found someone else. I was tired of being the only virgin flying on the *Lisa Marie* and I stupidly imagined that sex would open some kind of door. That it would take me into a different room, to a different part of myself.

We were all still revved after the Saturday show when we came into the Lucy that night, just looking to chill for a few hours before it was time to fly to Jacksonville. Something in the air had felt special. Different. Someone had strung up Christmas lights, placed them all around the ceiling so that red and green pulsated and the music sounded better than usual, like I was hearing each song for the first time. I spent some of the best hours of my life in this place, but now, in full daylight, it seems so tawdry. The murals look like a child drew them, the rugs and blankets are grimy, and the mirror behind the bar is cracked.

But when I look at my reflection, I don't look much better myself. I spent last night in a rest stop, barely sleeping, scared of every truck that pulled in beside me, and before the sun was even up I was washing the best I could in the women's room sink. Pulling my hair back and putting on the only makeup I could find in the Blackhawk, a single tube of lipstick that had been rolling around in the floor. Marilee's lipstick, as it turns out and now, as the sun streams in and hits the glass behind the bar, I can see it was a mistake. My mouth is bright pink, tropical, right for a black girl but all wrong for me. With my ponytail and pale skin and that single slash of color across my face, I look like a child who got caught playing in her mother's bathroom drawers.

> *Light is so ugly.*
> *Shows the world that really is.*
> *Me as I am too.*

My extended silence must make him nervous, because Philip suddenly jerks into motion. He steps behind the grill, picks up the spatula, and begins scraping. Loud and systematically.

"You want something to eat?" he asks, tossing the words over his shoulder as he scrapes. It's a southern thing to automatically offer food as the solution to any problem. When I don't answer, he tries again. "What about a beer?"

"It's nine in the morning."

"So it is. And I don't guess a beer's the best choice for a girl in your condition at any time of day. I assume you're keeping it?"

"Of course I'm going to keep it," I say. "I don't know what you think of me, just because we met when I was traveling with Elvis, but that night—"

"That night was magic." Despite everything, it still feels good to hear him say it.

"The King and his court," Philip muses, opening the refrigerator and taking out a handful of jars and cartons, "come in their finery to our humble little village. Magicians and jesters, serving girls and princesses." He looks up at me, his face suddenly radiant. "I was honored when you noticed me."

He's cute when he smiles, and this pains me. The whole memory pains me.

"You trembled," I say.

"I trembled?"

"That night. When you took my hand and pulled me in the back."

"Well," he says lightly, "if you say so."

"Marilee didn't like you."

He chuckles and turns back to the burgers. "Does Marilee ever like anybody?"

He has a point. "She said you were the kind of man who leeched off people's souls."

"And yet she came here, didn't she? Sat down beside you on that very stool and ate a bowl of my chili. And Elvis was playing in the corner like a traveling troubadour . . . Do you remember what he sang?"

"No."

"That's funny. Neither do I."

"All I remember is that when he finished Marilee stood up and said, 'Well, I leave you all to your mess,' and she stomped her way back to the *Lisa Marie*."

"She wanted you to come with her."

"But I didn't."

"No," he says, swiveling away from the grill as neatly as a dancer. "In fact, if memory serves, you stayed the whole night." He's cooked me a double, or else he's planning to eat with me. Two patties are stacked on the spatula and they hover, almost reverently, in the air. He's serious about his food, even if nobody else around here is. In another life he might have been a chef, just like in another life I might have been a rock star in my own right, or a teacher or a pilot or Miss America or a nun.

Philip places both burgers on the grilled bun and adds a bit of his homemade relish, a concoction he makes every Sunday morning, using a recipe his grandma taught him years ago. It's one of the few things I know about him, one of the few stories we actually told each other on that dark and tangled night, but it shows what kind of man he really is, down deep in the heart. The stoners who eat here don't understand that the slow making of this Sunday relish is his personal sacrament. They see it as only one more sauce on a burger that is already dripping. They wipe it off their chins and keep consuming in that mindless, openmouthed way we all have. *Send me more pleasure*, we all say. *And please, Lord, send it now.*

"My family," he says kind of vaguely, pausing to wipe his brow with a paisley dishrag. "They own half the town."

"Right."

"Not the good half. More like . . . this half."

"Even so."

"Everyone expects me to make something of myself. My uncle used to be mayor. Did I ever tell you that?"

"We didn't talk much."

"No," he says quietly. "I don't guess we did. But what I'm saying is that I come from good people. They think the way I'm living now is a stage. There are . . . there are expectations that I'll give all this up at some point."

"And make something of yourself."

"Yeah."

He says it more like an apology than a brag and I know what he's really telling me. That he can't show up at Christmas dragging some nineteen-year-old girl who's a stranger to his people. Especially one carrying a baby who everybody knows can't be his.

"My life," he adds slowly, almost idly, "was written for me before I was born. I'm just turning the pages and living it, year by year. Do you know what that feels like, Honey—

"Berry. I'm Honey Berry. Actually I'm Laura Berry. From Beaufort, South Carolina. I have a name, you know. And a family of my own who expects something out of me."

He pauses with the ketchup bottle poised above the burger and looks at me with lifted eyebrows, but I shake my head. Bottled ketchup from a plant somewhere in the Midwest would be a defilement considering everything this man and I have been through together, and I have a decision to make. I can hate him for what he can't be and for all the things he's not prepared to do, or I can take this fine burger—which has been made with care and love, despite it all—and head on down the highway. "Bag it," I tell him.

"You're sure?"

"Yeah. If I drive straight, I can be home in two hours."

Philip nods. He looks simultaneously relieved and sorry.

"Here," he says, handing me the bag across the counter, along with a Styrofoam cup, which I didn't request but that he gives me anyway. I will be almost to the South Carolina state line before I realize that the cup holds milk. The goddess Lucy is smiling down at me from the wall. I never got exactly straight what she was the goddess of, or what kind of girl she has come to bless.

"It's on the house," Philip adds, and then he looks away, as if he's ashamed of himself.

I slide off the stool with the bag in one hand and the cup in the other. Stumble toward the door and out into the parking lot. My eyes water as I walk, but I tell myself it must be the Vidalia onions. Or maybe it's the heat.

PART THREE

Fairhope, Alabama

CORY

June 1, 2015

I'm proud to be a southerner, which isn't always a fashionable thing to say. Proud to be an American too, which is even less fashionable. I'm not talking about politics or money or history or about who did what to whom and when or why. I'm just talking about the feeling you get when you're heading west and the road is unfolding before you, like a gas station map. I'm talking about how it feels to get in a car and just ride.

Southern states are big. It's not like New England or the Atlantic Seaboard, places I worked earlier in my career, during that brief expanse of time when country music was so cool that all a girl had to do was stretch out her accent to get Yankee gigs. But when you're driving up north there's the constant illusion of progress, with Connecticut turning into Rhode Island and then here comes Massachusetts before you can hardly blink. But in the South, it's like you're traveling the same piece of land, over and over. The open space can hypnotize you.

I'm drifting through Georgia, weaving my way toward Alabama, and there's no evidence in the trash bag as to how Honey might have navigated this particular stretch of the trip. I spend most of the morning on the back roads, the two-laners. Every now and then the road swells, becomes somewhat wider, so that you can let the car that's been on your bumper for the last twenty minutes finally pass. Or maybe you're the one who swings out and accelerates, swooping around a tractor or the occasional logging truck. It's all real civilized and polite, like you're constantly opening the door for a succession of strangers. You go first. No really, you. I insist. Lucy and I stop in a little dollhouse of a town called Madison for lunch, then walk to stretch our legs. And it's during this stroll around the square that I do the math in my head and am forced to conclude that all this sweet meandering is costing me two extra hours in transit and at least one extra tank of gas.

After that it's back to the interstate, which provides mental entertainment of a completely different type. Reading the billboards is practically like having a conversation. I learn, for example, that La Quinta is a pet-friendly chain. This is welcome news, since we're going to have to find a place to stop for the night. Of course, saying that La Quinta is pet-friendly is no guarantee they'll be thrilled to welcome this particular pet, who sits up and howls at periodical intervals, for reasons I can't begin to guess. I furthermore suspect Lucy's going to be a bedspread chewer and curtain yanker. I'm basing this on the fact that sometime during the long trance of Georgia, he bit my guitar strap clean in half.

I've been singing as I drive and I've found myself building on the snippet of the song from the tape. The problem with the first line is that Elvis ended with the word *water*. A rookie mistake. Hardly anything rhymes with *water*, so I move the words around until the two opening lines end with *pier* and *down*, both excellent songwriting choices, words that open up a world of rhyming possibilities.

I like to compose while I'm driving, so it hasn't particularly bothered me that in this age of satellites and sound systems my radio and busted eight-track player are useless. In fact, the longer I drive, the less it bothers me that I don't even have a phone. Nobody's likely to be calling and it's even less likely that anybody would call with any news I'd want to hear. Gerry would only be screaming about how I've left him in the lurch on Memorial Day weekend and Bradley might want to know if I've shipped his waders yet. I haven't, although I should, especially in light of the fact that with any luck, I'll be spending tonight in some perfectly civilized interstate La Quinta, and will thus no longer have to use the boots as an anti-rape device.

"We need to find a post office," I tell Lucy. "Bradley doesn't ask anything of me, so it seems I should at least be able to do this one tiny thing. Especially considering I'm his only child."

Lucy climbs from the back to the passenger seat as if he knows I need to talk.

"I don't know why I'm an only child," I tell him. "Laura and Bradley were the kind of people who could've handled a bucket-load of kids, so I don't know why they stopped with just me. It's not like I'm any prize."

The dog whinnies, seems to nod.

"You don't have to be so quick to agree. But it is weird. They were twenty when I was born, which is young to have a baby, but even younger to stop having babies. I mean, Laura was obviously fertile and Bradley obviously liked being a dad. He spent every weekend volunteering for the athletic association and the band boosters. You're thinking there was some problem, probably on his side of the bed. I wonder if they got tested."

Lucy tilts his head, considering the issue.

"You're right," I say. "They wouldn't have bothered testing Laura, but if they tested Bradley and he came back sterile . . . Can you imagine what an awkward day that would have been? Proof beyond measure that I really wasn't his child, and I don't know if that ever happened, but if it did, Bradley's even more of a saint than I ever thought. Because he never treated me one bit different than a man would treat his blood daughter. Hell, he was better than 99 percent of the daddies out there. You'd like Bradley. He'd like you. He likes dogs. Dogs and kids."

Lucy looks at me out of the corner of his eye.

"Exactly. He deserves a lot better than me in his declining years, and the fact that I'm all he's got is proof there's no justice in this world. We gotta find ourselves a small town and a small-town post office and send him his boots."

An exit is coming up, but it doesn't say anything about a town. It just promises strippers and Jesus, two things that Alabama seems to offer in endless supply. A few miles back I passed a billboard with Jesus holding out his arms and asking, "Are you lonely?" and then right above it was a bunch of pouty-lipped girls saying, "This is all you need to know." Or maybe it was the other way around and the strippers are there to comfort the lonely and Jesus is all you need to know. It hardly matters. Last night's sleep was brief and shallow, so I'm starting to get careless. Each time I look down I see I'm driving too fast. Fifteen miles over the speed limit, when anybody but a fool knows only ten is prudent. It's like the Blackhawk is taking charge, like if I leave it alone it'll bird-dog its way back to Memphis on its own. Meanwhile every exit I pass has chain hotels and fast food and strip clubs and churches, but none of them says a damn thing about the US Postal Service.

"Here's the thing," I say to Lucy. "Now that I've had some time to ponder it, the notion of mailing Bradley his waders raises a different issue. Will the post office let me ship a great big package COD to Clearwater without a return address? Hell, I don't even have a box and it'll take a coffin to ship these waders. You've seen them. I don't want Bradley to know where I am or what I'm doing, and there's already a good chance he might put it together. He sent me out to Polawana, after all, and if he calls Bruiser's again and Gerry tells him I've taken off without explanation . . . then getting a pair of waders sent from Bumfuck, Alabama, will only cinch the deal."

Lucy yawns.

"No," I say, "you're wrong. Bradley's nice, but he's not stupid."

So maybe the waders will just have to come with me a little longer after all, at least until I hit the Gulf of Mexico and it's too late for anyone to try and stop me. Tonight I will find a clean, safe, ordinary La Quinta, one that looks just like a thousand other La Quintas and has a clean bathroom and a decent bed. A hot shower and good night's sleep can solve just about everything.

"That Philip guy back in Macon," I say to Lucy. "That politician. He knew my mama. He knew her just fine and you can tell by looking that he wouldn't have hesitated to despoil her. He's one of those guys who shoots first and asks questions later.

I know that kind. I just never knew my mama knew that kind, you know?" I glance down at the $268, which I've moved to the cup holder to accommodate Lucy.

"And you know why he gave me this money, don't you?" I say to Lucy, even though he's lost interest in the conversation and is almost asleep. "He thinks he's my daddy. I mean, he isn't. He can't be. The math doesn't work."

According to the stories they always told me, Laura got back to Beaufort in the heat of a Friday afternoon. She showed up while Bradley was having lunch and he swung her round and round under a cypress tree. They got married the very next day. Bradley wanted to invite the whole town, but Laura said no, let's keep it small. Her daddy did the service, her mama was on the organ, his parents were the only witnesses. There was no time to shop so Laura wore her prom dress, which just happened to be white. In the pictures, Mama looked terrified and Bradley was grinning ear to ear.

Saturday, August 20, 1977. The date of their anniversary is stuck in my head because I'm always counting forward from it. Counting forward to my birthday on February 24, and February's such a short month and I was born so close to the end that I've always wondered why Mama couldn't hang on just a few days longer, until March, when I wouldn't have been quite so obviously a bastard and she wouldn't have been quite so obviously a knocked-up girl in a white prom dress. But that's all water over the dam now, and the point is that I was always counting forward but never counting back. Counting back is giving me a whole new kind of mystery to ponder.

"If I was born in February, Mama must have gotten pregnant at the very beginning of the summer." I continue, ignoring Lucy's snores. "And she wasn't anywhere close to Macon, Georgia, in the summer of '77. I looked up the schedule online years ago and they wrapped up their touring in April, and that's too early. She was living at Graceland when she got pregnant, and there's no way around it."

I guess Philip didn't have time to do all that figuring. He just knew that the daughter of a girl he once slept with showed up on his doorstep asking questions and figured it was worth four hundred dollars to move her on down the road. But it's odd that we both were at the Juicy Lucy on this particular morning, and that he didn't even seem all that surprised to see me sleeping in his parking lot. It was almost like he knew I was coming.

"But that doesn't make any sense either," I say, still talking out loud even though I know Lucy's asleep. "I didn't know I was coming until day before yesterday, so there's no way anybody could have called and warned him. I'm just getting paranoid. It comes from spending too much time in this car alone."

And so I go back to playing the alphabet game, counting out-of-state license plates, and singing song lyrics in my head. Anything to distract myself, but my mind keeps drifting back to the way Philip peeled the bills off that wad of money, twenty after twenty. Real calm and methodical, like he always knew this day would come. Like he was paying off a debt that had accumulated interest over a long stretch of time.

A night spent in the Montgomery La Quinta has me feeling like myself again. The next morning, I put the three hours to Mobile behind me without any problem, and take the Fairhope exit, which throws me onto the same sort of swampy connectors that I'm used to from home. One bridge after another and clumps of reeds and circling gulls and a dead deer barely knocked off the pavement. It's impossible to make good time on roads like this. I take it slow and easy, but even so, I figure that by noon I'll be eating lunch at Doozy's Barbecue. Just like my mama did thirty-seven years ago. Fairhope was her pivotal stop. I feel it in my bones.

I pass a little white cinder-block building that proclaims itself to be the post office, town hall, library, recycling center, and DMV for a town called Wild Acre, Alabama. There wasn't much of an indication I'd entered any town at all, save for the fact the speed limit dropped from forty-five to thirty-five a couple minutes back. Since I got off I-10, I've been watching the signs like a hawk. The Blackhawk is such a noteworthy car that it's a miracle I've gotten this far without falling into the clutches of the law, and the last thing I need is to get pulled over by some Wild Acre cop.

I do a U-ey and turn back. The parking area is rutted, with maybe a handful of gravel scattered through the whole lot, and I bounce my way around to the back of the building. Lucy, sensing a shift in the energy of the vehicle, has already climbed into my lap. I'm snapping the leash on him when I notice a second cinder-block building, identical in size and shape to the first. Except this one has a hand-painted sign saying EDDIE'S followed by the words: WE FIX EVERYTHING.

Well that's quite a claim. Nobody can fix everything, but I nonetheless grab the busted eight-track tape and pick my way through the mud to the screen door, keeping Lucy in a choke hold as I enter.

Eddie turns out to be a black guy, about five decades younger than I would have guessed. Younger than me, which it seems more and more people are these days, and he's watching a ball game on a thirteen-inch TV with rabbit ears, which is balanced on a bar stool. He looks up as I enter and frowns at the dog.

"Define everything," I say.

"That dog doesn't bite, does it?"

"I've never known him to bite," I say, leaving out the part about how I've only had the dog in my possession for twenty-four hours and that during that time he did indeed make a lunge at the desk clerk of the Montgomery La Quinta.

"I got bit when I was a kid," Eddie says, getting to his feet almost apologetically as I slide the eight-track across the counter.

"This is a tape," I say, echoing Bradley's oft-stated claim that a person can never go wrong by stating the obvious. "I put it in an eight-track player and the player chewed it up. Anything you could salvage would be a gift."

Eddie picks up the cartridge and considers it from all angles. "I don't think I can fix it," he says.

"You sign says you can fix everything."

"Maybe it should say I can fix everything made in this century."

"Come on," I say with a pointed look at the television, which is at least as old as God. "I'm not expecting miracles. Can't you splice it, or whatever the word is? I'll take anything you come up with, even a snippet."

"Mind if I crack the case?"

"Be my guest."

He picks up a hammer and taps his way around the edges

of the cartridge, which obligingly splits at every corner. And once he has the top off I can see that a fair amount of the tape is still spooled and my heart lifts.

"I can't do much with these little giblets," Eddie says, one eye still on Lucy. "And if you expect me to connect the strips that have come off the spool . . . they might not end up in the right order. How'd you say it got damaged?"

"The player in my car."

He squints out the door and beholds the Blackhawk sitting in all its glory, glittering in the morning sun. I expect some sort of reaction, maybe a cavalcade of questions, but he merely takes it in and then shrugs.

"If the car chewed it up once, what's to say it won't chew it up again?"

An excellent point. "Is there anywhere in town," I ask, "where I might purchase an eight-track player?"

"Joe's Vintage and Salvage," he says promptly. "It's on Free-mason's Street in Fairhope. I'm not saying they'd have one for sure but they specialize in . . . vintage and salvage."

"Sounds fair. Look, I need to go next door to the post office for a minute. Do you mind if I leave my dog with you?"

He looks warily at Lucy. "It's Sunday. The post office is closed."

"So why are you open?"

"I wasn't open. I was watching ESPN Classic. The sign on the door was turned to Closed, but you came in anyway."

"The post office is bound to open tomorrow."

"That's Memorial Day."

"Ah yes. So it is. But the day after that is a regular old Tuesday and they've got to open eventually, don't they? What I'm asking is, do you happen to have some sort of big box laying around anywhere? Big enough to ship a man's pair of wader boots? You know, those boots that go up as high as your hips?"

I'm clearly the worst thing that's happened to Eddie in months. He looks at the dog and sighs, then he looks out the door at the car and sighs again. Then he says, "I think I have a weed whacker box laying around here somewhere."

"That would be perfect," I say. "You're a saint." This man is the Wild Acres, Alabama, answer to Leary Dupree, that much is obvious, and experience has taught me that men who promise the least usually deliver the most, so the more Eddie predicts trouble the more I'm starting to trust him. He goes in the back and returns with the box, dusty but ample in size. I loop Lucy's leash around the handle of a nearby lawnmower and fish around in my backpack until I find the last of the waffles I snitched from the La Quinta buffet. I throw it at him and he snags it in midair. He may not be the smartest or the prettiest dog in America, but he does seem to have real good depth perception.

"If I get these pieces together, which I'm not saying I can," Eddie mutters, ironing little bits of the tape flat with the tip of his finger, "they might not end up in the right order."

"You already said so. And that's okay. I wasn't planning to sing along with it."

"It's music?"

"I think it might be the last live recording of Elvis Presley."

"Elvis Presley?" he says, looking up, and he's so surprised that he's not even deterred by the sight of Lucy dragging the lawn mower around behind him like Santa's sleigh, zigging first one direction and then the other. "How'd you get your hands on something like that?" And then, almost immediately, realization begins to dawn across this features. "Is that Elvis's own car?"

"I think so. I just found it. My mama was one of his backup singers on his last tour."

"Like Marilee."

"Pardon?"

"Marilee Jones. She owns the Bay Restaurant. She was a backup singer for Elvis years ago and she's got a voice—"

"Is she black?"

"As much as I am. She's my aunt. Actually, she's my cousin's aunt on the other side, twice removed. But I always see her at Christmas, if you know what I mean."

I know exactly what he means, and lights are beginning to come on in the back of my head as well. "You say this Marilee Jones owns the . . ."

"The Bay Restaurant. It's a restaurant on the bay. Right on top of the water. She's the cook there too. Cook and singer and owner and everything."

"I believe I may have a picture of her," I say as Lucy lurches and pulls the lawn mower over, then turns in a snarling fury and tries to bite it. I rummage around in the backpack again and hand him the snapshot. Eddie takes one look at it and laughs.

"She lost the Afro a while back and I've never known her to wear a turquoise jumpsuit, but yeah. That's Marilee."

"The girl with her is my mother."

He glances up. "I can see that."

"Look," I say. "Thank you kindly for the box and I will reim-burse you for it, as well as any work you do on the tape, when I come back. You've been more help than you could possibly know. As for now, I've got to find the Bay Restaurant and Joe's Salvage and Vintage."

"Vintage and Salvage."

"Right. When do you figure the tape will be ready?"

He sighs again. He's a sigher. Of course, so was the politi-cian back in Macon and my mother too, and even Leary, come to think of it. Maybe there's just something about me that makes people sigh. But my head is clearing and I feel for the first time since I looked in Bradley's shed like I know where the next step is going to lead me.

"I was planning to go surf fishing. I was planning to knock off early for Memorial Day weekend."

"Then why are you watching ESPN Classic in your shop?"

"I live in the back."

"It won't take you two whole days," I say, and I know I'm wheedling, but I can't seem to stop myself. "Just give it five minutes here and there. Work on it at halftime."

"I'm watching baseball."

"Work on it between innings. Or when somebody gets hit in the head with a wild pitch."

"Whatever good I can do will be done by tomorrow," Eddie says. "But I can't promise you much."

"That's okay," I say, untangling Lucy from the mower and pulling him toward the screen door. "I haven't had much luck with men who make promises."

"Maybe you've been messing with the wrong kind of men."

"Now that, my friend," I say, pushing on the screen door, "is a distinct possibility."

If there's any place on earth any cuter than Fairhope, Alabama, I've never run into it.

The town is built up high on a bluff above the Gulf of Mexico and somehow—God knows how, it being at least fifty miles from nowhere—Fairhope seems to have fashioned itself as a bit of an artist colony. Or a mecca for rich retirees. I figure all this by the fact that the place is bustling, even on a Sunday morning. I have to circle the periphery of town twice before I find a reasonably deserted place to park. Then I work my way toward the main drag, which is lined with little storefronts that all have their doors open and music coming out, shops selling pottery or gelato or clothes made from hemp and other pricey, trendy things.

Lucy and I walk the length of Main Street, past the carefully restored houses with their broad porches and sky blue shutters. The trees are draped with Spanish moss, which I love, at least in daylight before it turns spooky, and three different houses have placed those little lending libraries full of free books out near the sidewalk. Mostly cookbooks, I note, when I stop to check one out, but I take a beat-up old copy of *Alice in Wonderland* for sentimentality's sake, since my mama used to read it to me as a child. And then church bells ring, reverberating through the cobblestone streets, and I find myself suddenly, briefly, momentarily—but sincerely—wishing I were the kind of girl who went to church.

I don't see Joe's Vintage and Salvage, which isn't surprising. It's probably the kind of establishment that can't afford to sit elbow to elbow with boutiques and wine bars. And I sure as hell don't see Doozy's Barbecue, which is probably located somewhere else as well. Somewhere like 1978. Eddie told me that the Bay Restaurant was on the bay, and it seems this street is heading just there. It's a steady, gentle slope downhill through the town, then you walk through a little park with benches and fountains, followed by a series of stone steps angling back and forth on themselves. I try not to let Lucy—who has gone apeshit with his first whiff of the water—make me stumble. By the second landing the trees part and I have a clear view of the gulf. The water sparkles, the midday sun bouncing off it like light off a mirror.

I'd noticed several rooms to rent as I walked, mostly homes with carriage houses out back, freestanding buildings they've rehabbed into rental suites. But since it's a holiday weekend, odds are they're all taken and, besides, any part of town this precious is undoubtedly out of my budget. Part of the problem is constantly feeling like I have to hide the car, or at least not go asking for trouble by driving it down the middle of Main Street. It seems like I keep abandoning it on scrubby little side streets, and then I'm constantly nervous. It would be an easy car to break into, the doors so big and loose that they almost invite you to run a coat hanger down the window or slip a jimmy through the cracks. So in the last two days I've gotten in the habit of taking everything of value out of the car every time I stop. Eddie's in possession of the tape now, but I have my guitar on my back, the strap knotted as best I can, and the remaining $268 is crammed in my bra, making me look misshapen. It felt like a fortune in Macon, but $268 would be gone in a poof if I decided to rent one of those little carriage house rooms and treat myself to dinner at one of the tapas restaurants I passed.

The steps leading to the beach are rhythmic. Ten, then you zig and walk down ten more. Over and over, I descend and turn, until I lose count how many times I've done it. Coming back up is going to be God's own bitch, but at least now, thanks to Eddie, I know why Mama came to Fairhope. She must have been bringing the other backup singer, Marilee Jones, home. There had been two girls leaving Memphis in the Blackhawk, and given the undeniable charm of the town, I'm betting that Fairhope is also where Mama stayed that extra night before moving on. I pause, panting, pulling Lucy up on the leash, and consider the view. So much of what I've learned in the last forty-eight hours has been bewildering, hard to integrate with the woman I thought was my mother. But it does make sense she would linger here. Fairhope is just her kind of place. I guess they didn't have the gelato and the free libraries then, but they had the Spanish moss and this flat blue water and it feels like home, only slightly better, and isn't that what we're all looking for—a slightly better version of home? I can see why if a girl was tired and scared and barely pregnant, that Fairhope would seem like the perfect place to start over.

I also think I can see the restaurant, halfway up the beach, perched up on stilts at the end of the pier. I pause at one of those periscopes they put in vacation places and fish a couple of quarters out of my backpack, simultaneously trying to contain Lucy, who's showing way more enthusiasm for the smell of the bay than you'd think a landlocked Macon coonhound could muster.

But the periscope works and after I swipe it wildly left and right a couple of times, nearly blinding myself with the glitter of the day, I finally figure out how to focus. It gives me a good look at the restaurant. Sea-green shingles and a low-sloped roof with a deck on all four sides and a choir of beat-up Adirondack-style chairs, clustered in groups, so that the patrons can take in the view from every direction. Lots of southern restaurants are designed to look like shacks. On my walk through town, I passed a self-proclaimed supper club with the whole patio enclosed with abandoned screen doors, which had been further embellished with cleverly coaxed patterns of rust. I've sung in plenty of places like that through the years, and I guess it's cute, if that's how you want to think of the South. God knows the tourists love it. But the Bay Restaurant—which it seems this place must be, even though there's no sign of a sign—isn't like that. It isn't faux old or faux poor or faux rotted. It's just old and poor and rotted.

We go down the last four flights of steps and walk across the beach, then pick our way to the pier. About every other board has been patched and replaced and I try to step on the fresh planks, more out of superstition than anything else. When I get to the restaurant, it takes me a minute to find the door. It truly is a perfect square, set within the perfect square of the deck, and I have to almost circle the building, going the wrong way and turning three corners before I find how you get in. I knock and wait. If the church bells were any indication, it must be around eleven fifteen. Odds are they aren't open yet. I shield my eyes and look out at the water, wishing I'd brought my sunglasses. The day is so bright that I'm already working on half a headache.

I knock again and step back. I've come too early. I may as

well sit down in one of the Adirondack chairs or take a walk on the beach, or go back to town. Maybe try and find a brunch place with outside seating and an omelet for less than sixteen dollars and just as I'm thinking this, the door is wrenched open.

I can only conclude that the woman on the other side is Marilee Jones. She's tall. She must have been swiveled down in some sort of Playboy Bunny dip in that old photograph with Mama. In the picture, she didn't look much more than three inches taller than my mama and me, maybe five five at the most, but now . . . somehow through the years she learned how to stand up straight and claim her full spine, because the woman before me is easily six feet. She has the rangy, self-possessed, quasi-lesbian look of a former athlete and she's barefoot, wearing a wash-worn dashiki and a pair of khaki pants. Her hair is cut short, so short she looks like a shorn sheep, and even though she's tossed the afro and the makeup and the turquoise jumpsuit, it's not hard to picture her onstage. This is somebody people would pay to look at.

"We're not open," she says. "Give me an hour." She says it neither defensively nor regretfully. Just with an absolute matter-of-factness, and I know from her tone that the Bay Restaurant is successful. She doesn't care if I come back in an hour or not, because plenty of other people will.

"I'm not here to eat," I say, and then I spill out the whole story. That I'm Honey Berry's daughter and that I have in my possession a Stutz Blackhawk that once belonged to none other than Elvis Presley. I'm beginning to suspect that my best move is to spew out the facts and then shut up and wait for something to happen, good or ill.

Marilee wipes her hands on a cloth that's hanging from her waist, pulls out a pair of glasses from the top of the dashiki, puts them on, and then slowly studies me from top to bottom.

She must have been getting ready for the lunch rush. She's been chopping and dicing for an hour or better, that's my guess, and the music coming at me through the door isn't the sort of track you play when the guests arrive, not that muted and inoffensive stuff that's only one step up from elevator music. What's coming through the door is James Brown, cranked to the max. Prep music, and she probably has a prep beer on the counter too, Sunday or not.

"You've got the car with you?" she says after she's checked me over and I've evidently passed muster. Looking like my mother has never opened so many doors for me as it has on this trip.

"Yes, ma'am. Parked . . . parked somewhere. Under a tree."

"And you're taking it back to Graceland?"

"Eventually."

"You want a beer?"

"Absolutely."

"All right," she says, glancing at a clock on the wall behind her. "I can give you twenty minutes. Is that dog with you?"

"Unfortunately, yes, ma'am, yes. I must confess that he is."

"I'll get him water," she says, then jerks her head at Lucy and says, "Lay down, dog."

To my absolute shock, Lucy does.

Marilee goes inside, the door slamming behind her in a way that suggests I'm not to follow. I lace Lucy's leash through the deck railing and sit down in one of the chairs, which reclines so sharply that the minute my butt hits the seat I'm thrown back, looking up at the bright blue sky. James Brown cuts off, right in the middle of "Papa's Got a Brand New Bag," and in the silence that follows I can hear the *schloop-oop* of the water beneath me, the slow and steady suck of a tidal bay.

Marilee had not flinched in the least when I said I was Honey's daughter. Once again, I have the vague sense I'm expected. Would Eddie have called her, given his aunt a heads-up that a girl with a chewed-up eight-track and a muscle car and a snarling dog was looking for some answers? Unlikely. And her face didn't even change all that much when I told her Mama was dead.

She already knew it. I don't know how she could've, but she did.

Marilee's back, with a mixing bowl full of water, which she plunks at Lucy's feet, and a Miller which she hands to me before sinking into the Adirondack beside mine. She's heavier than she looks. I can tell by the way the chair groans when it takes her weight, and that's the way it is with tall people. They can hide their bulk, while five pounds on me looks like twenty. She settles back and asks, "You said your name's Cory?"

"Yes, ma'am. Cory Beth Ainsworth. Most recently of Beaufort, South Carolina."

She turns her head and looks at me strangely, so I rush on. "The Ainsworth is for my father, or my adoptive father, I guess I should say. Honey's husband. His name's Bradley Ainsworth. I have to tell you, to be honest, that all this 'Honey' business is new to me. I'd never heard the name until three days ago. I grew up thinking my mother was just plain Laura Ainsworth, but finding the Blackhawk changed everything. Do you remember the Blackhawk?"

"Nobody forgets that car."

"I guess not," I say as Lucy noses the mixing bowl off the side of the deck. It teeters right on the edge, then falls into the bay. It seems like it takes forever before we hear the splash.

"I told you to sit down, Mr. Dog," Marilee hisses, and Lucy drops like he's been shot.

"I'm looking for two places," I say. "The first is Doozy's Barbecue." No response, so I go on. "And the other one is called Joe's Salvage and Vintage."

"Vintage and Salvage. I know it. What you need to go there for?"

So I explain about the eight-track disaster and how I dropped the whole mess in the hands of her nephew or cousin or whatever Eddie is to her and he said he would do what he could. It's beginning to dawn on me that I left the most valuable item I've ever owned with an absolute stranger. Because now that I've had time to think on it, I've decided that tape is probably worth even more than the Blackhawk. Elvis had a lot of cars, but as far as I know he only wrote one song. Marilee just nods slowly as I ramble on, neither confirming nor denying that it was her voice and Honey's talking to Elvis, although of course it was, and they must have been listening to the tape as they drove south from Memphis, otherwise why would it have been waiting in the player for thirty-seven years? I didn't see any other tapes in the car. For all I know, my mama listened to the same two or three bars of that song nonstop for three days, from the Mississippi River to the Atlantic Ocean.

"Do you know where I might find this Doozy's Barbecue?" I say when it becomes obvious that Marilee doesn't intend to comment on the news that I first destroyed and then abandoned the last recorded music of Elvis Presley. She's lifted her head from the slope of the chair and is looking out over the water, with a plastic beer stein full of what looks like sweet tea in her hand, but at my second mention of Doozy's, she slowly pulls her attention back to me.

"Well, you've found Doozy's," she says. "What's left of it, anyway. There's a piece of the pig sign inside, over the bar, so remind me to point it out to you later. That's where I worked, you know. Where I worked before I went on tour and after . . . after your mama and I left Graceland, all I could think was if I got back here, maybe Mr. Doozer would give me my old wait-ressing job."

"So she brought you here. Honey, I mean. She drove you down from Memphis."

She cuts her large, heavy-lidded eyes toward me and I see that I've offended her. "We drove each other down from Memphis."

"Right. I've been thinking all morning that Fairhope is exactly the sort of town my mama would have loved. The whole time I was driving, I was wondering why she ever came to Fairhope, but now that I've seen the place, I'm wondering why she would have ever left. I'm guessing Mr. Doozer gave you back your job?"

"That he did."

"I'm surprised Mama didn't want a job waiting tables at Doozer's too."

"Maybe she did," Marilee said with a snort. "But there were complications."

"Like her being pregnant."

Marilee shifts her weight in the chair. "Pregnant? Not so as I'd know about it."

"I was born seven months after my parents got married," I say. "They told everybody in town I was a preemie, but I weighed over nine pounds."

"You counted it out."

"Yes, ma'am. In fourth grade we had to draw a family tree and put all the dates on it. Weddings and births and that sort of thing, so there it was staring me in the face, the fact they'd married in August and I was born in February. Of course I was only a kid. They told me I'd come early and I believed them."

"At least for a while."

"I guess. But you know the funny thing is, I couldn't bring myself to turn in that family tree. I took the first zero of my life on that assignment. I guess even a kid knows on some level that there's no such thing as a nine-pound preemie."

"Nine pounds," Marilee says with a chuckle. "Little Honey must have looked a sight, carrying you at the end."

"Her stomach stuck out so far she always said she could set a saucer and teacup on it and use me like a table. But that's not the point. The point is—"

"The point is that Honey was pregnant when she left Graceland," Marilee says. "And that is news. News indeed."

I have the impression that she's lying. Still trying to hold on to some promise she made thirty-eight years ago. Because if Mama confided in anybody, it seems like it would have been

Marilee. But I've got no proof of that or anything else, so I decide to keep the conversation moving.

"Do you have any idea . . . who the father might be?"

"*The* father?"

"Do you have any idea who my father might be?"

She shakes her head slowly. I'm not sure if I believe her or not, but I've only been here ten minutes and I don't want to fall back into my old habit of burning every bridge right after I've crossed it, or hell, half the time I'm slinging gasoline while I'm still over the water, torching my own security right out from under me. I rush things. I always do. I ask the wrong question or, just as bad, I ask the right question at the wrong time. So I do myself a favor and let the silence stretch. Marilee and I sit and wait, listening to the slurp of the water and the distant church bells coming down from the town. The lunch crowd will be on its way soon.

"So your mama never told you anything," Marilee says softly.

"Not much. She told me she learned more about music in that one year on the road than in a lifetime before or after. But about living with Elvis?" I shake my head. "She wouldn't even have his records in the house."

Marilee stares me down at this. She's thinking something, and thinking it hard, but her face is one of those show business faces. It's expressive in one way, the mouth mobile, the eyes large and darting, and she waves her hands around like a hula dancer. But in another way she's blank, hard to penetrate. My mama was like that too. Both there and not there. I guess it's a trick they taught the girls at Graceland.

"You could have stacked up every Bible in Memphis, Tennessee," Marilee finally says, "and I would have sworn on every single one of them that Miss Honey Berry was a virgin."

Now this is pretty much the exact opposite of how the man in Macon portrayed Honey. *Your mother was a wild child,* that's what he'd said, pushing back his aviator shades with the tip of his finger. *She did it all and she did it all the time.* I suspect those words will be burned in my brain until the day I die. Either one of these two strangers is lying to me or Honey was as big an enigma to her friends as she was to her daughter. One of those women who showed a different side to everybody she met.

"If Honey wanted to stay here in Fairhope with you, maybe work at Doozy's," I say slowly, "why did you send her on her way?" I have to tread carefully. I'm on this woman's property and we are both aware that Marilee Jones owes me less than nothing.

"Doozy's was a black restaurant."

"It was 1977. Restaurants weren't segregated."

She pushes to her feet. "Maybe not legally. But we had our ways. Things that were just understood, that went without saying. You've got to remember this is the Deep South, not the middling South where you started from, or the shallow South up around Virginia. It makes a difference. Fairhope's as deep as you get."

To illustrate, she gestures toward the bay and she is indeed right, for if a voyager like me were to take two steps in any direction, she'd be in the water. *Picked up a boy just south of Mobile,* I think, apropos of nothing.

"Honey always said she'd come back one day," Marilee says. "She looked into this water and put her hands on her hips and swore to me that she'd be back."

"But you never saw her again."

"It's getting close to lunchtime. Want me to fix you something to eat?"

Those waffles from the Montgomery La Quinta breakfast bar are long gone and I definitely do want her to fix me something to eat. But I don't see anyone else coming down the pier, not a server or a line cook or anything, and it's hard to believe she runs this place, tiny as it is, all by herself.

"And your dog," Marilee goes on. "I'm guessing he'd like more than a bowl of water. Maybe a pork bone."

"That would be very nice. But you don't have to—"

"I'm thinking you should stay here a day or so," Marilee says, to my surprise. I've spent the whole conversation rocking from one butt cheek to the other in the deep Adirondack chair, getting ready to jump up at any point and retreat, so the last thing I expected is that she would ask me to stay.

"Hurricanes hit the gulf about every third or fourth year," Marilee goes on idly, as if this is a logical next sentence to say after just asking me to stay without adding any explanation as to why or where. "A major one got us in the fall of '79, and it was enough to blow Doozy's from the top of the bluff right into the water. They pulled the shell of it back to the pier, and dried it out the best they could, but things that get that wet are never quite dry again. You know what I mean?"

"Yes, ma'am. I know exactly what you mean. I grew up on a marsh."

"Mr. Doozer said he'd had enough," Marilee said. "Seemed determined to take the storm as a sign from above. Sold me the restaurant for a song and then I figured if Jesus had seen fit to fling Doozy's in the water, then the water was where it would stay. We still sell barbecue, of course we do, but we sell seafood too, any kind you want. As long as it's fried." She looks at me evenly. "So what's your pleasure? Ribs or flounder?"

"Whatever's easy. You don't have to fire up the grill just for me."

She shrugs. "We open at twelve thirty on Sunday, just time enough to let the good people get themselves down from church. It takes them a while, you know, to greet their neighbors and compliment the preacher on his sermon and walk that long line of steps. No need to rush things. Nobody's got anywhere to be on a Sunday afternoon in Fairhope, so twelve thirty works out fine."

"Do you live here?"

"My room's off the kitchen." She gestures toward a hook on the railing, then another screwed in the side of the building. "But I've got a hammock you're welcome to, if you're not above sleeping outside."

Sleeping outside sounds like paradise, especially here, at the end of this long pier stretched over the bay, with the steady breeze and the constant *schloop-oop* of the water. I don't know why she's doing this, any more than I know why the politician in Macon gave me four hundred dollars. I can only assume that my mother was a much-loved woman, although apparently loved in lots of different ways, some of them the kind it's best not to pause and consider.

"Ribs would be nice," I finally say. Bruisers doesn't serve

ribs. I've eaten enough fried fish to last a girl a lifetime, but ribs would be a treat.

"Then there you go," says Marilee, turning toward the door, and Lucy, who gets excited by any movement, made by anybody, for any purpose, leaps to his feet, tail wagging.

"I'm thinking you'll be shark bait before this day is over, Mr. Dog," says Marilee, and then she adds, so casually that for a moment I think she's still talking to Lucy, "People like music. They like a bit of live music while they eat."

"So they tell me."

"That instrument at your feet. You know how to play it?"

"Since I was four."

"You any good?"

I reach down and pick up the guitar. It's all a little awkward, because when Lucy chewed the strap and I retied it, it ended up too short, and now the guitar is sitting higher on my chest than I like.

I sing "Love Me Tender."

I don't know why. I may have spent a whole career avoiding the songs of Elvis Presley, but I sing him here in Fairhope, gentle and true, half slumped down in the chair, thrown back at such a strange angle that I don't even have all my air. But it's a croon of a song and I croon it, and I remember every word.

When I finish, I put the guitar down. We wait, without either one of us saying anything, without even looking at each other face-to-face, but I can feel Marilee smile.

"Yeah," she says. "Honey came back, all right."

HONEY

August 18, 1977

Elvis may have chosen the little girl who went sprawling at his feet with her white panties and knee socks and headband, but everybody at Graceland knew I'd have to grow up fast before I could come on tour. I'd have to learn how to glitter. So on my third morning after I was hired, the resident beautician came to the bedroom I shared with a handful of other girls.

Her first words to me were: "What color would you say your hair is now?"

"Brown?" I said. I figured it had to be a trick question.

"And do you see anyone else at Graceland with brown hair?"

No. No, I did not. Everyone in the room had shiny black hair, including the beautician herself. So I accepted right off the bat that my hair would have to be dyed to the same patent-leather shade, but I begged her not to tease it, at least not into one of those weird Elly May Clampett styles, with the ponytail low and hanging to one side. That look was still popular within the walls of Graceland, even though this was 1976. When it came to fashion, we were at least ten years behind the times. Twelve if you're talking LA or New York.

But it was an awkward situation. There's no nice way to beg a beautician not to make you look like her. Or to ask her not to make you look like all the other women in the room, especially when they're lined up on the bed staring at you, their identical ponytails curled over their shoulders like a row of question marks. It made me paranoid that so many people were watching my transformation, but I hadn't been at Graceland long and didn't yet comprehend the rules. I thought I was being monitored because I was there on approval and that someone—probably Fred—had told the girls to keep an eye on me and report back. I would understand soon enough that wasn't what was going on at all. It was just that nothing ever happened at Graceland. Only a few people came in and nobody ever went out. The girls were lined up on the bed watching because me getting my hair done was the only thing going on that day.

And there's no nice way to say, "We look like a bunch of walking cartoons and people laugh at us, except maybe in Vegas and the deepest part of the South." So I asked for an Afro, which the black girls were allowed to have. They stayed in a different set of rooms, on a different part of the property, and I hadn't even met Marilee at that point. But I'd seen her in the studio, with her hair radiating out in that proud halo, looking like an Ethiopian angel. I might not have known her name yet, but I knew she was what I wanted to be. Her bearing made her different. She stood up straight, even when she wasn't performing.

Of course, the very notion of little five-one, lily-white me with an Afro got the other girls rolling on the bed, giggling so hard that I figured the only way out was to laugh too and pretend I'd been kidding. Marilee would later explain that the true purpose of the famous Graceland makeovers—which everybody got within a week of moving in—was to help us look as much as possible like him. Kings like mirrors. Kings crave nothing as much as their own reflection, and so no matter how they might've entered, everybody left the gates of Graceland looking a little bit like Elvis. Even the old black cook and the redheaded guy from Ireland who fixed the cars.

Lucky for me, I had a head start. In that back room at the first wave of auditions, Fred had mentioned I resembled Priscilla—the shy, fresh-faced Priscilla who first came to Graceland when she was sixteen. Of course, saying I looked like Priscilla was just another way of saying I looked like Elvis, since she was his truest reflection, the perfect female version of his own face. I hesitate to put it that way. It makes him sound like a vain man, and he wasn't, not really. I think Marilee was right when she said Elvis spent a lifetime searching for his lost twin. From the moment of his birth, he'd felt like he was only half there.

In the end, the hairdresser compromised on the style, giving me a Gypsy cut with long layers of curls. It was the way Cher was wearing her hair at the time and she didn't tease it too much, no more than a couple of inches. I was made to understand that I didn't look quite like the others and that this was a risk. If anybody pointed out that I was spoiling the uniformity of the backup girls, then it was straight back to the styling chair for me. But when Elvis saw me the next day he just smiled and said, "Now don't you look pretty, Honey Bear?"

I knew I'd dodged a bullet with the hairdo, so I was an extra good sport all through wardrobe, submitting to the boots and capes and even to the makeup: the big, dark doll eyes and the shiny pearl lips. Between the glue on my lashes and the stickiness of the lip gloss, I could barely open my eyes or my mouth, and while there were those who claimed my transformation aged me ten years, I never once felt like a woman, not during the whole time I was at Graceland. I felt more like a stewardess on some movie airplane that's fixing to crash.

And I couldn't stand being fancy all the time. Once I talked one of the drivers into taking me out alone, muttering something about a "lady problem," words guaranteed to silence any man. He drove me to Kmart and waited in the limo while I bought flannel pajamas from the children's section. I was small enough to wear a girl's size twelve and I got pink ones with unicorns, and then bought a jar of Noxzema, which my mother always swore by, because I was afraid all that makeup was ruining my skin. After that, I persuaded the driver to next take me by the library, a place I doubt the limo had ever stopped before. I had no Tennessee library card, so I gave them my daddy's street address back in Beaufort, just putting "Memphis" on the end of it, and figured that by the time they realized such an address didn't exist, I'd be long gone. If I was stealing the books (in a way, I was), I justified it by thinking of how much Elvis had donated to the city through the years. Surely in exchange they could give one of his backup singers four measly books. I would read them at night, over and over, under the blanket in my unicorn pajamas until I practically knew them by heart.

I was learning a lot. I was learning the sort of things there're no words for. But what I would have welcomed, even though it was never offered, was instruction in the musical arena. I knew I was a strong singer, with gospel harmony in my blood, but I had virtually none of that elusive quality called stage presence.

"Teach me how to perform," I said to Marilee. What I meant was, "Teach me how to be you."

"What are you talking about?" she said, and as it would turn out, no stage presence was needed. We girls were rarely expected to dance around with synchronized moves—in fact, it was considered a major faux pas if any of the backup singers did anything to draw attention away from Elvis. The only time Fred ever yelled at me was a rehearsal where my eyes were itching from the false eyelashes and I kept rubbing my face.

"Nobody in Cleveland or Dallas is paying their hard-earned dollars just to look at you," he barked, and after that I found a thousand ways to itch without scratching. It was a good thing I'd been raised in the front pew of a church. I had plenty of experience keeping my face blank no matter what was going on inside.

Elvis and Elvis alone was the show, and as for the army of people standing behind him? Our job was not to entertain. Our job was to come in on the notes Elvis couldn't hit anymore. The highest and the lowest parts of a person's register are the first ones to go, because people's range narrows as they age, especially someone who'd lived as hard as Elvis. There were eight backup singers, four black and four white, and we stood in the shadows while Elvis claimed the lights. I finally figured it out by studying Marilee. She would keep her eyes lowered every second she was onstage, like she was carried away in some ecstasy of song, but through her eyelashes she was watching Elvis. The instant he began to fade, she would step closer to the microphone and increase the volume of her own voice.

And when she moved forward, we all did. Eight of us gradually rising as he declined, until the web of music was woven all around Elvis, virtually holding him up, shakes and tremors and stumbles and all.

San Antonio was the fifth night of the western tour. Elvis had started out strong for the two dates in Los Angeles, had faded a bit in Phoenix, then bounced back to give them his best show yet in Houston. No one in the audience in any of those places had seemed to notice that we were using new, easier arrangements of the old songs or that he was talk-singing his way through half of them. He was pale and puffy, and he mumbled the familiar lyrics, but he still was Elvis. Just seeing him take the stage was enough for the crowd. Even the newspaper reviews had been kind.

But something was wrong in San Antonio. Fred had canceled rehearsal and the sound check, saying that Elvis had to rest. We were five days into a three-week tour and already his stamina was failing. No one said it in so many words, of course. The whole time I was at Graceland, I never heard anyone admit that Elvis had limitations in any category, or that the bad days were getting more frequent, and worse.

Performers are a superstitious crew, who like to do things in a certain sequence, every time. We were used to the sound check, then the rehearsal, eating, then dressing, then the vocal warm-ups and the prayer. But on this particular night, none of that was happening. Nobody had seen Elvis all day. Fred paced around backstage with a face like thunder, muttering about how we just had to get him onstage and keep him upright. They'd brought in chicken and three-bean salad and chocolate silk pie, but nobody was touching any of it.

The opening act, a girl group called the Belle Tones, would generally perform from eight to eight forty-five, with Elvis showing up backstage sometime in the middle of their set. But in San Antonio eight forty-five came and went with no Elvis, and Fred had sent word to the Belle Tones that they would have to stay onstage. The rest of us whispered even harder among ourselves. Was Elvis even there yet or was he still in transit? Had he somehow gone missing entirely?

He finally showed up at nine fifteen, with the crowd out front growing restless and the Belle Tones so desperate for material that they were singing church hymns. He seemed steady enough on his feet, but he blew past us all, including Fred, without any explanation, striding straight onto the stage and sending the crowd into a frenzy.

"Come on," said Marilee, grabbing my hand, because there was nothing for the rest of us to do but scramble onstage behind him, with the band members dragging their instruments and amps and the singers moving the microphones around as fast as we could. Elvis walked into the spotlight and slipped his arm around Ruth, the lead singer of the Belle Tones, and then he joined her in the chorus of "Love Lifted Me."

The crowd was roaring. Everyone in the audience was not only on her feet—for the Elvis faithful, at this point, were almost exclusively female—but pushing toward the stage like they thought this was Woodstock. The abruptness of Elvis's arrival and the fact he sprung himself upon them without any of the usual fanfare and introductions seemed to have whipped them into more than the usual fervor.

"We didn't pray," I whispered to Marilee. Normally the white girls stood on one side of the stage and the black girls on the other, but that night in San Antonio, we'd all just grabbed the nearest microphone and set up wherever we could.

"What?" she said. She was the only one among us who didn't seem to be in a complete panic.

"We forgot to pray for the show," I whispered again. Elvis and Ruth were singing beautifully together, although as far as I knew they had never rehearsed any sort of duet, and it seemed like this might be one of those nights when he was intact. Spectacular, even. Because there were times when Elvis could still effortlessly fill the biggest room in the world with his personality.

The song ended and he wiped the sweat from his brow with the long silk scarf that was dangling from around his neck. He almost always did this, making a great ceremony out of dabbing his forehead and then flinging the scarf into the audience; pretending to be surprised every time when all the fifty-year-old women would trample one another half to death trying to get to it. But maybe it was a bad sign that he was sweating already, after his very first song. We were all looking back and forth at one another, trying to figure out what it meant that he was singing well but acting crazy. The Belle Tones all but ran off the stage, without any bows or good-byes, and the rest of us huddled closer. We were circling the wagons like a bunch of pioneers.

It didn't fall apart all at once. Evidently inspired by the energy of the audience and the success of his opening number, Elvis went into a sequence of gospel songs. All the musicians were knocking their sheet music around, looking for the score, and Marilee hissed at the backups to just moan the word *Jesus* over and over. But Elvis's voice was sweet and strong that night, and he gave the crowd plenty of the "yes, ma'ams" and "thank ya'll very much" stuff they'd come to expect. And then, after finishing up "How Great Thou Art," he suddenly threw in a few karate moves.

The karate was a sore point between Elvis and Fred. Fred thought it was foolish, but Elvis said the crowd expected it, which was probably true—and even that they insisted on it, which probably wasn't. But Elvis had forty-two years' worth of experience in doing exactly what he wanted to do while convincing himself it was all for the sake of someone else. The second night in LA he had kicked high and then screamed. The audience thought it was part of the act. A warrior cry. But he had really torn a muscle. The next night in Phoenix he had dropped to one knee and been unable to get up. Two of the guitarists had moved in and yanked him to his feet, throwing in enough air chopping and yelling to make it seem like a staged fight and not a rescue. The audience had once again roared their approval.

So karate was always a risky addition to the show, and that night in San Antonio, we were already off our usual game. We'd started late, we hadn't prayed, and we were singing the songs all out of order. As he went into the first karate sequence, everyone onstage was holding their breath. One of the bassists laid down his guitar, just in case he'd have to catch him. Marilee got all us girls going in a sort of background doo-wop, ready to sing over the top of whatever happened next. But as prepared as we all were, it was still a shock when Elvis spun and kicked, both of his feet actually leaving the floor for a split second, and a pistol came flying out of his waistband and sailed across the stage.

It landed at the feet of the rhythm guitarist. I think his name was John and I don't remember much about him, except for the fact he didn't like guns. He was the kind of guy who kept to himself, which was unusual, because we all tended to do everything together, and by "everything" I mean everything Elvis wanted to do. We ate when he was hungry and slept when he was tired and if he sneezed, twenty-five people put on a sweater. But John was the only one of us who didn't race golf carts or shoot rifles or practice karate, or eat and sleep along with everyone else's schedule. There were rumors he had even voted for McGovern. The guys said it was only John's extreme talent that allowed him to live like a loner and still stay in the fold. So of course the gun came straight to him. It was that kind of night. He just stood there looking down at it, with an expression of numb horror. It had left Elvis's waistband with enough force that it was still spinning, skidding its way toward the bass section like a bottle in a kid's kissing game. John, God help him, kicked the damn thing and it took off again across the stage in the other direction. Hit the bottom of the drum set and ricocheted off, and this time came to rest pointing straight at me.

But there was no time to think about the symbolism of any

of that, because Elvis had stopped his karate moves and returned to the mike. He was covered in sweat, and since he had thrown his scarf so early, he had nothing to wipe it with. He blinked his eyes, brushed his forehead with the cuff of his jumpsuit, and broke, a cappella, into "Jailhouse Rock."

"Jailhouse Rock" was one of the few songs that required actual choreography, which we did as a tribute to the scene in the movie. All the girl singers stood between the microphone stands, with our hands gripping them like they were jailhouse bars and did an old sixties dance move, a sort of modified jerk. And while we scrambled into position, Marilee stooped down and scooped up the gun and slipped it, fast and easy, behind an amp. I felt the breath gradually begin to return to my body.

It seemed to take a million hours but eventually the show was over. The curtain was pulled. No finales tonight, even though we could hear the audience on the other side chanting, wanting more. Elvis turned, every part of him glittering with perspiration, and said, "Who has my Derringer?"

"You had no call bringing that thing onstage, Mr. Presley," Marilee said. She was one of the few people who could talk to Elvis like that. She retrieved it from behind the amp and handed it over to him. "Honey Bear 'bout got her feet shot off."

Elvis twirled the Derringer once, like a gunslinger, and stuck the gun into his pants. "Ya'll need to be more careful," he said.

There was a four-week break between the western tour and the southern tour. We went back to Graceland, supposedly to rest and regroup, but everybody was tense because Elvis's behavior was getting stranger every day. One night at dinner he stood up and said he felt like recording, and so we all stood up too and headed for the studio, leaving our steaming plates of spaghetti behind us. But when we got there, that wasn't right either. We hadn't been at the mikes more than ten minutes when Elvis said, "Call Nunchucks."

Both the karate studio and the recording studio were in the same building, out back from the main house, behind the garages and the swimming pool. None of us were dressed for karate. We'd come down to dinner in whatever we'd been wearing, bathrobes and bathing suits mostly, not planning to go out and sing, much less start rolling and kicking on those padded red mats. But Elvis gave the word, and someone picked up the phone and called Nunchucks. I'd never met him at that point. Had heard plenty of rumors, but had never actually seen the man until he walked in two minutes later, wearing only a pair of blue cotton judo pants.

"Well then," said Elvis. "'Bout time."

I had never felt lust before. I didn't know the word. Well, maybe I knew the word but I'd never been able to match it to an actual feeling. All I know is that I took one look at David Beth and my stomach lurched. There weren't any rainbows or unicorns. It was a sickening sensation, almost like someone had punched me, like I needed to sit down. But I was also aware that some whole new phase of my life was starting and that it was 'bout time. David's chest was long and slender, ropy like a ballet dancer's or a swimmer's. *Elegant,* I thought, the word rushing into my mind from nowhere. *What stands before me is an elegant man.*

I knew what people said about him. They thought he was full of himself and they resented how much time he spent alone with Elvis. They called him a poser, which was really saying something at Graceland, where everybody was pretending, either trying to be something that they weren't or trying not to show what they really were. And even in that moment, as my stomach was falling and my knees were still heading south, I could see their point. I could see that he was learning as he went, that all his fine talk about martial arts and poetry and Asian philosophy was little more than bluster. He was starting to get a sense of what he could be, but he wasn't quite there yet, and maybe that's what I liked about him. He reminded me of myself.

Elvis turned and bowed to him. "Welcome, Master."

Now that was something. Elvis bowed to no one. Well, maybe the audience. I had seen him lower his heavy, corseted body to one knee at the end of the show, as if he were waiting for the audience to knight him, or accept his proposal, with all of us standing behind him with bated breath, hoping like hell he had the strength and the balance to get back to his feet. But bowing to the audience was an ironic thing, part of the act, and on that summer night that Elvis bowed to David Beth and called him "Master," it felt completely different. The whole room went silent.

"You know everyone," said Elvis. He didn't seem to pick up on the uncomfortable vibe around him. Elvis always had this ability to live entirely inside his own skin, utterly unaware of the wider world. That might have been the source of his power.

David looked right at me. "I don't believe I've met this young lady."

"That's Honey Bear," said Elvis. "You're going to teach her, right?"

"It will be my greatest pleasure," David said, bowing low. So Elvis bowed to David and David bowed to me and when he looked up our eyes locked. For the first time since I got to Graceland, I wasn't just some South Carolina preacher's daughter swimming in waters that were way too deep for her. I wasn't just Laura Berry with dyed hair, trying to fit in, trying to keep up. For the first time in my life, I felt like Honey.

"She needs to learn some self-defense," said Elvis. "Every girl here does. 'Cause I'll tell you something. This old world is full of bad boys."

So it is, I thought. *And I have the feeling I'm going to enjoy it.*

Within the week, I was turning everything I saw into a haiku.

Soap on the counter
It smells like rain in summer.
The girl washes away.

Open the closet
Only one hanger waits there.
Leaving again soon.

Okay, so I didn't say they were any good. I only said that I made them up, compulsively and mindlessly. But during that four-week break between the western and summer tours, I fell in love. Managed to convince myself that David Beth was a poet and a warrior and a philosopher and everything dark and mysterious that I'd taken to the road to find.

"I don't want to be your first," he told me one night after one of our long sessions of kissing and groping and tussling around on the red karate mat. "I would never invite such heavy karma."

I didn't ask him how he knew I was a virgin just by looking at me, but the point is, he meant what he said. Whenever we were alone together, he was always able to pull back just before the point of no return and his control over his own desire only made me desire him more. Got me thinking that maybe, somewhere deep inside, he really was a spiritual creature.

"But somebody's got to be my first and I want it to be you," I said, wiggling under him. Trying to drag him toward the same edge I fell over every time we were together. "I want you to make love to me."

"This is making love."

"You know what I mean."

He smiled. He liked it when I begged. "Be patient."

I was trying, but none of this was anything like the polite little dance I'd done in the backseat of Bradley Ainsworth's car. That had been thirty minutes of kissing, five minutes above the waist, one hickey given and another received, maybe thirty seconds below the waist before I'd sit up straight and declare, "It's time to go home." But there was no sequencing to the lovemaking of David Beth—he would sometimes pull himself off me in the midst of our wild grinding and spend the next full hour simply tracing every line of my face with a fingertip. It was the first time I was the one who wanted something that was being withheld and it drove me a little bit insane.

"It is not my destiny," he said, "to unlock this particular door."

I should have known that all this gobbledygook about destiny was just his way of saying he didn't love me. That I might have been his favorite distraction for the summer of 1976, but that's as far as it went. To be a girl's first implies something he wasn't feeling. That came with a certain sense of responsibility that he wasn't willing to take on.

That said, he made it clear he had absolutely no problem with being my second.

When we came back from the southern leg of the tour and my fateful stop at the Juicy Lucy, where Philip Cory had gladly shouldered the task that he refused, David sensed the change in me immediately. We got back to Graceland on a Tuesday, slept all day Wednesday, and were back in the studio by Thursday. Elvis was recording a cover of the Gary Puckett hit "This Girl Is a Woman Now," the sort of melodramatic soap opera garbage that he kept working into the end of the southern tour, even though everybody but him knew that he was better than that. The Gary Pucketts of the world should be covering him, not the other way around, but when Elvis got to the part about "She's found out what it's all about," David, who had come in late and was leaning against the wall, caught my eye and smiled.

It was tacky, I can see that now. I can see a lot of things now, even those I'd rather not. But in that moment, all I could do was flush red to the roots of my hair. Not with embarrassment, but with anticipation.

Here's the joke—one of them, anyway. I hadn't found out

what it was all about. I'd lost my virginity in a café, behind a bedspread hung as a curtain, half wedged into some sort of storage pantry that held beer and grits and hamburger buns. I'd been caught up in the moment, but when the moment was over, I'd stood up and caught a reflection of myself in the ice maker door. I looked utterly unchanged. So I told myself, "Well, that's done," and I was relieved, relieved the way you are when you've taken your SATs or had a tooth pulled. And if the sex itself had been a letdown, I told myself it was because I didn't love Philip Cory. Not like I loved David Beth.

But the important thing is that the deed was done and David knew it. He stared at me all though the song, so intently that I got flustered and came in late, ruining the harmony on the chorus. I'd never done that. When it came to the recording studio, I was meticulous. If we needed a second take, or a third, I always made sure it wasn't because of Honey Berry, and now even Elvis turned and looked at me, lifting his lip just a little in that way he had, that knowing little smirk.

"You feeling all right, Honey Bear?" he said.

But I'll have to give David this. Philip Cory had been all smoke and mirrors, all blinking lights and pulsing bass. But David Beth knew how to make things romantic. A few days after we got back from the southern tour, he took me outside, to a checkered tablecloth at the very edge of the property, and he'd brought a disc of Gouda cheese and a bottle of wine. A bright pink wine called Almaden that came in an earthenware crock. The wine was so cold that I shuddered when I tasted it. Trembled as it rushed across my tongue, but I swore to him that it was glorious, even though all the preacher's daughter in me could think was *This is the blood of Christ spilled for you.*

Needless to say, there was poetry for the occasion—poetry and wine and a canopy of trees, and if afterward I still didn't feel quite as changed, quite as transformed as I wanted to be, this time I knew that I only had myself to blame. I don't know much about sex, even now, but I do know it isn't magic. It can't take you anywhere you don't know how to get to on our own. And when David hovered over me, in that moment I'd been waiting for since June, he looked deeply into my eyes and said, "You did what you needed to do, right?"

"Everything," I told him. I was talking about that night in Macon, on the gritty floor of the Juicy Lucy, when I'd submitted myself to a stranger posed just above me, in this same position. "I did it all."

It didn't occur to me until six weeks later that I had completely misunderstood his question.

CORY

I work through both lunch and dinner and that long Sunday afternoon stretch in between. Not just singing and playing, but also hopping off the stool to bus tables when it was called for, and scooping Marilee's red vinegar slaw into little plastic cups. An astounding array of people have passed through the Bay Restaurant in the course of this particular Memorial Day weekend, so I've tried to make myself useful wherever I could. At one point, carrying in a tray load of empty beer glasses, I saw the Doozy's sign, which blew away in the hurricane, now mounted over the bar, just as Marilee claimed. So I can mark two items off my list. The Juicy Lucy and Doozy's, both down.

But I feel good. It was a day full of the sort of mind-numbing work that makes you strangely happy. The kind of day when you're too busy to worry or doubt or even think.

Eventually, all the customers clear out. The old lady working the register has gone, along with the half-witted waitress who I suspect accidentally gave away a lot of beer for free. It's just me and Marilee back on the deck, in the same two chairs, only now the sky above us is navy.

I feel better about taking her hospitality after my afternoon of hard labor, more like I've earned something rather than just taken it. Marilee has brought Lucy another bone, kicking a couple of his little turds off the deck without comment, and she's also carried one of those big, blanket-style Mexican hammocks out and dumped it in the corner. My bed for the night, I guess, and God knows, I've had worse.

"So," she says, settling back in with the same stein of tea and picking up the conversation as if we'd never paused it. "Did you like the ribs?"

"Best ever," I say, which is the truth.

"I learned how to make that dry rub in Memphis," she says. "People down here soak their barbecue to death in sauce."

"People back home soak it to death too."

"There's a hundred ways to do barbecue," she says. "Just like there's a hundred ways to praise the Lord. You ever been to a Renaissance fair?"

It's another strange shift in conversational direction, but luckily the last few days have disenchanted me with any former value I might have put in linear thought. Besides, I was one of the people whom the waitress kept bringing beers to, so I'm pleasantly buzzed. Looking out over the water with my dog, and my sixth—maybe seventh—beer of the day, I feel fine enough that I don't care that this conversation doesn't make any particular sense.

"I've not only been to a Renaissance festival," I say, "but I've been hired on as a troubadour. Worked them in Savannah and Charleston."

"Well, that's what Graceland was like," she says. "A traveling fair. Did your mama ever tell you?"

I shake my head. "She didn't like to talk about Graceland."

"Elvis was the king," Marilee says, "which goes without saying. And there was only one queen and she was gone and that hurt him bad. Real bad. So bad nobody was allowed to talk about it. There were other girls—some of them stayed for years—but they were never more than . . ."

"Concubines?" I venture when she runs out of steam.

She frowns.

"Serving wenches?" I try again, and this time she nods.

"Closer," she says. "Do you understand what I'm trying to get at?"

I don't but I take a stab. "Elvis was constantly surrounded by people but he was still lonely?"

To my great surprise, that's exactly the answer she's looking for.

"Yes," she says. "He was lonely in that way that only the best kind of people are. The people who care and can't stop themselves, the ones who can't kill the nerve no matter how hard they try . . . they all live lonely." She pushes to her feet and goes over to the corner of the deck, where she begins to sort out the tangle of my hammock, all the ropes and cords. I could help her. I should help her, but I'm afraid it will break the spell.

"He had everything," she says, looking down at the snarl of cloth. It's getting dark. Someone somewhere should go and turn on a light. Marilee fastens the top part of the hammock to the corner of the deck and then adds, more to herself than to me, "Had everything in the world, but it still didn't add up to enough."

"Do you ever miss Graceland?"

She shakes her head without looking up.

"Do you ever miss singing?"

"There are lots of ways to sing," she says. "Cooking's singing. I like to say I'm making music in people's mouths."

I nod. I can't vouch for her fried seafood, but the barbecue of Marilee Jones is a holy thing, some combination of a Memphis dry rub and an Alabama soak and the last of Doozy's secret recipe, plucked from the bay.

"Best barbecue I'll ever have," I say again, which is an outrageous thing for a southerner to claim, the equivalent of standing up on an altar in front of God and everybody and promising to be true to one man until the day you die, even knowing that the possibility of better barbecue will always await you five miles down the road.

She finishes attaching the hammock to the deck and drops back down in the chair.

"How did you and Honey get the car?" I finally ask when enough peaceful time has passed that I think it's safe.

"He gave it to her."

"Elvis?"

She gives me a pained little nod.

"When I called Graceland they put me on the phone with some guy named Fred. He said Elvis gave away a lot of cars, but he'd never give away a Blackhawk."

She laughs, takes a swig from the stein. "Fred's still alive? I bet he and I are the only two left who remember the old days."

"Not quite. I met a man in Macon, Georgia. I knew to go there because I was following the trash in the car. You know, trying to find all the restaurants where Mama must have stopped for food on her drive home. There was a cup from a place called the Juicy Lucy. This man found me sleeping in the parking lot and it turns out he used to own it."

Marilee nods, still not surprised, and I'm beginning to wonder if anything I could say would shock her or at least shock her bad enough that she would let it show. "That would be Fantasy Phil. Yes, ma'am. If a girl was following a line of trash, it would take her straight to him."

"He said he used to be the cook."

"That's one word for it."

"He's a politician now. I saw his picture on a billboard. Just a glance. But when I met him, I said, 'You're running for office, aren't you?' and he didn't deny it."

"That doesn't surprise me. Hamburgers and promises. Phil was always feeding the people one thing or another."

"Well, he gave me four hundred dollars, out of a clear blue sky. I didn't ask him for it. But when I told him I was Honey's daughter, he pulled out a pocketful of money and handed every bit of it to me. Do you have any theory as to why a man I'd never seen before would do such a thing?"

"I'd imagine you're the one with the idea."

"I think he thinks he's my daddy."

Marilee leans back and sighs, but for once it's not the sigh of someone who's exasperated with me. It's the sigh of a woman who's worked a hard day, who has sawed ribs and boned fish and dodged wave after wave of grease splashing out of the hush puppy fryer. The sun is going down over the water, a rare sight east of the Mississippi, and she pauses for a minute to take in the final smear of gold and rose across the horizon, even though she's presumably witnessed thousands of gulf sunsets during her years in Fairhope. This slow, silent contemplation of nature . . . taking the time to really stop and look . . . it's the first time she's done anything that remotely reminds me of my mother. I guess Marilee's also trying to make up for all those days she spent in the dark.

"Just for the record, money or not, I don't think I'm itching to claim that man as my daddy," I say, after the silence has stretched past the point of comfort. "He made me a little bit uneasy, and by the way you called him Fantasy Phil, I'm guessing he might have been a drug dealer."

"Now why would any of us need to know a drug dealer?"

"A band on tour might—"

"Because Elvis didn't cotton to drug dealers," she snaps, and I wonder whose reputation she's still trying to protect after all these years.

"I know," I say. "I read about it. He got the local police force to deputize him and he liked to ride along on vice busts. And President Nixon made him head of some sort of enforcement agency. An honorary post, just an excuse to give him medals, but I've seen the pictures."

"That's not exactly right, but close enough."

"If you don't mind me saying so, him being so antidrug, fraternizing with the vice cops. It seems like the ultimate in hypocrisy. I mean, when you consider how he died."

"Most lies are nothing more than people telling you how they wish things had been."

Now that's something I'm going to have to remember. It's a

kind view of the world, and one I might shortly be able to use to my advantage.

"I know Elvis had no tolerance for street drugs, and that he used legally prescribed pharmaceuticals," I say. "I understand that he died on the right side of the law." Marilee looks mildly pained by my word choice but I soldier on. "All I'm saying is that there was such a big entourage that traveled with him. You said yourself it was like a Renaissance fair. A bunch of musicians and dancers and roadies and security, and they might not have all had the same scruples." Or the same obliging doctors either, but there's no need to add that part. I have to tread carefully with Marilee. She seems to be one of those people who leads you right to the door of something, but gets mad when you step over the threshold. "So I'm thinking that maybe Fantasy Phil supplied people like them during the tours? I saw the Juicy Lucy. He took me inside. The whole thing looked a little suspect. And it was a regular stop, I figure? Phil made it sound like the *Lisa Marie* had flown through Macon more than once."

"Well, now, isn't that head of yours slammed full of thoughts?" Marilee drains the last of the tea from her stein. "Does your dog eat corn bread?"

"He eats whatever I give him. Sometimes he eats things I don't give him."

"What made you name a boy dog Lucy?"

"It's a long story."

"Aren't they all?" She stands up and disappears back into the restaurant, returning within seconds with a basket of cold hush puppies, which she sets in front of Lucy. She can't seem to sit still. Maybe I'm making her nervous. Or maybe she's just one of those compulsive workers, one of those people who can never rest as long as there's one more thing to do. She's a mother to the world, that much is clear to a blind man, and I'm surprised she didn't take Mama under her wing. I'm surprised that she instead cast her out onto the long and heartless highway. Of course, Marilee claims she didn't know Mama was pregnant, and I guess she didn't. If she'd understood how deep the girl's well of desperation truly was, this whole story might have had a different ending. I might have been born in Fairhope. I might have grown up right here on this half-rotted pier.

"Phil had an eye for the young ones," Marilee says when she settles back into the Adirondack chair. "So it wouldn't surprise me to hear he tried his luck with Honey, but trying ain't getting. I thought your mother was pure as the driven snow when she headed out of here back in 1977, but you've done the numbers and nobody can argue with numbers. She must have laid down with somebody, and I guess it could have been Fantasy Phil."

"He told me she was wild."

"She wasn't wild. If he said something like that, it's just proof of how little he knew her."

I'm relieved. He may have given me four hundred dollars, but I don't like the idea that the man in Macon, hereafter to be known as Fantasy Phil, could truly be my father. Not to be a snob or anything, and heaven knows I've made my own selection errors throughout the years, but I don't like the notion I was conceived in a kudzu-choked pot palace, spray-painted with pastel mushrooms, located behind the airport of a middling southern town. Conceived by two people too stoned to know what they were doing. Such a scenario fiddles with my sense of destiny.

"I don't suppose there's any chance . . ." I say, but then I can't think how to finish the question.

"Any chance of what?"

"That Elvis himself might have—"

"No, girl, not a one. He was too sick by that time and his mind was running in directions . . ."

"He was only forty-two." Forty-two is young. I'll be forty-two in five years.

"So that's why you came here?" Marilee says softly, her words coming out of utter darkness. Night has fallen, just like it so often does, without me noticing. "Because there's a part of you that's been thinking all these years Elvis Presley was your daddy? Thinking if it's true, your whole life will start to make sense?"

"It's possible."

I hear her shake her head. Actually I hear her earrings rattle. Two big hoops, silver and hanging halfway to her shoulders, the only ornamentation Marilee Jones chose on this particular day.

"He was too broken," she says, "and besides, Elvis had lines he did not cross, and even if they didn't make any sense to other people, they made sense to him. He had his own religion. He made it up in his head as he went."

I guess some of those lines were like riding along with cops to drug busts, I think, *even when he was likely stoned himself at the time*. But I don't say it. Marilee's still trying to protect something and I guess I am too.

"It's possible," I say again, more for myself than for Marilee.

"Anything's pos-si-ble," Marilee says, breaking the word into as many syllables as she can. She thinks I'm silly. Thinks I'm eighteen years older, but still just as silly as my mama was, passing through here from another direction, a lifetime ago.

"Thank you for giving me the hammock."

"Loaning it, not giving it."

"Understood."

"Should be a good night to sleep out," she goes on, a statement that is beyond argument. The evening air feels like velvet and stars are beginning to peek out, enough coming early to promise a canopy within the hour, and the sound of the water has me drowsy already, along with the beer. "I'll put the dog in the back bedroom with me."

"Are you sure? Lucy doesn't seem like the kind of dog you bring inside."

"Don't seem like the kind of dog you leave outside either. He might leap off the deck in the night and then what would we have?"

"A hanged dog."

"I don't think either one of us wants to wake up to a hanged dog."

"I'll take him down the beach and walk him one last time," I say. "But first I've got to ask you . . . could Mama have been with somebody else from the tour? Like Fred?"

Marilee chuckles, genuinely amused. "Fred was a thousand years old even back then. He must be two thousand now. You say he's still at Graceland?"

"He said he was some sort of historian. He's got a fancy title."

"When you get there, make him pay."

"Excuse me?"

"For the Blackhawk. Before you hand over the keys, make Fred pay you for it. Elvis gave that car to Honey free and clear and that makes it your inheritance."

The thought of demanding payment for the Blackhawk never occurred to me, which I guess is proof I really am a silly fool. "The whole time I've been driving, I keep thinking that if the cops catch me, I'm fucked."

"Don't talk like that. Your mama wouldn't like it. Besides, you found that car on family property and possession is nine-tenths of the law. So you make them pay you good." Marilee sits back with a deep, closing-time sigh. "You owe Honey that much, at least."

As I was crawling into the hammock that night I started thinking about the time my mama tried to teach me how to sing.

Or maybe I should say the time she tried to teach me how to sing like her, because music was always in our house and I learned it natural as breathing. I could pick out chords on a guitar before I could pick out words on a page. But I had a lower natural pitch than Mama, a narrower range. Whenever I'd sing along with the radio I always came in just a little under the melody and I liked that about myself. I thought it gave me distinction, made me more salt than sugar. I wanted edge. A sort of Delta-dirty, bourbon-soaked sound.

I guess all I'm saying is, I didn't want to sound like my mother.

Oh, she was the better musician, no doubt about it. You can't spend a lifetime singing backup and leading church choir and teaching piano to tone-deaf children without knowing everything there is to know about how a song works. She was the one who had thought and studied, who'd broken it all down and put it back together again. But I was the one who was going to be a star.

And I would have sworn she knew that too, right up to the Christmas of my last year in high school when she looked up over breakfast one morning and said just as cool as if we'd discussed it, "I've put you down for lead angel in the pageant."

From my point of view, there were about a hundred things wrong with that statement. For starters, I was almost eighteen. Just a few months shy of the age she'd been when she took a bus to Memphis and got herself pregnant with me. So I wasn't a child, I was a breath away from being a woman fully formed. She had no right to "put me down" for anything.

Much less for lead angel. Lord. The lead angel closes out the pageant with "Ave Maria."

"I don't have those notes," I said.

She smeared jam on her toast. Smeared it hard, like she was mad, but she didn't look up at me when she answered.

"You most certainly do have those notes," she said. "Or you could have them. Anytime you choose to claim them."

"I don't go that high."

"It's not that high."

"What do you mean, it's not that high? It's 'Ave Maria.'"

She folded the piece of bread taco style, like she always did before shoving it into her mouth. "We'll see," she said.

Yes, we certainly would. Mama could be as stubborn as crabgrass, but I could too. Despite what she thought, I was entirely too old to be wrapped in a bedsheet and have coat hanger-and-tissue-paper wings strapped to my back. Besides, singing high . . . well, I can't say exactly what I thought singing high meant. Being a good girl and going to church and keeping your legs closed and ending up disappointed with what all that virtue had bought you . . . probably something like that.

I'm older now and I've seen a lot more. I know there are worse things to wind up being than Laura Ainsworth. Lots of them. My mama's life had dignity and purpose and there were people who loved her—starting and ending with Bradley, who looked at her the way no man's ever looked at me. That's something. It's a lot.

But in the winter of 1995, all I could think was that, yeah, we'd just see about me strapping on those coat-hanger wings and being lead angel. I had worked for my lower register. The gravel in my voice was hard won and I wasn't about to give it up, not even for my last Christmas pageant.

So in the church, during the first rehearsal, I deliberately blew it. I cracked on the money note, even though it hurt my pride to see everybody else in the choir shudder.

Mama was standing in front of us, behind her podium. She had her glasses on.

"Try again," she said.

"It's out of my range," I said.

"Cory Beth, I'm asking you to try again."

So I tried again and cracked again and then, an hour later, when everyone was packing up and getting the hell away from the tension in that choir loft, Mama looked at me cold as ice and said, "What do you think you're trying to do?"

It was a question that could have applied to several aspects of my life. She and Bradley had been scraping together dimes and dollars for years, but I'd announced to them that I had no intention of going to college, or even taking the SATs. I spewed out some nonsense about a gap year, even though I think all three of us knew good and well that if I got a chance to veer off the path they had planned for me, that the detour would likely last my whole life.

"That snarling thing," Mama said, taking off her glasses and rubbing her temples. "Going below the note. You're going to ruin your voice if you keep trying . . . trying to be what you weren't meant to be."

She had a point. Twenty years of trying to pitch too low has wreaked havoc on my vocal cords and left me where the hoarseness that I once affected is now my natural sound. Life's like that. Full of jokes. Pretend to be whiskey and burlap for long enough and one morning you wake up to find that's what you really are. You couldn't go back if you tried.

"But maybe," I told my mama back then, in that empty church, "my voice is more like my father's. Has anybody ever thought of that?"

Mama hesitated. She must have known I had my doubts, but I'd never raised the issue so directly.

"I've got nobody else to be lead angel," she finally said. "You know what we have in this choir as well as I do. It's not like there's anybody else waiting in the wings."

"Is that a joke?"

"Why would it be a joke?"

"You know, an angel . . . waiting in the wings."

"That's not what I meant," she said, and she pulled her purse off the front pew and started digging around for a Goody's Powder. I felt bad. I'd given her another headache, not the first and not the last, and besides, Mama cared about those church Christmas pageants. She wanted them to be good. And for a moment I wondered, out of nowhere, what we'd be like if we weren't mother and daughter, if we were just equals and friends. I've known some girls who claimed to be friends with their mothers, even a couple who have sworn their mother was their best friend. They say it like it's something to be proud of, but it just makes me think they must not have any real friends or they'd know better than to say such a foolish thing. You can't turn milk into water.

"I'm not trying to give trouble, Mama," I said, which was such an outrageous lie I'm surprised the cross on the wall behind me didn't come loose right that moment and fall on my head. "Honestly, I'm not trying to be stubborn. I just don't have that note. I don't have the breath."

Mama did the last thing I expected her to do then. She smiled and let it go. "Now, my sweet girl," she said, "you and I both know that note's on layaway for you. Somebody's been paying on it for years and you can pick it up anytime you're ready."

That's what she said. That was my mama. The woman was always a mystery to me. Every step I ever took toward her just ended up leading me further away, and every time I tried to escape her I just wound up back in my own front yard. There's no point in pretending otherwise, at least not now, when I'm looking over Mobile Bay, lying in a hammock made out of a Mexican blanket, my beer buzz slowly setting, just like the sun. I told myself that I was taking this trip to learn who my father was, but it's occurring to me that I'm taking it to find out who my mother was. Really was. Not just the choir director Leary remembers or the wild child Philip claimed to know or the virgin Marilee Jones sent on her way. Certainly not my best friend, although as it turns out, at least when it came to my singing voice, Mama was right.

When the time came for me to hit the high note in "Ave Maria," I cleared it with an oceanful of breath to spare.

For the second time in three days, I awaken with a man staring down at me. I jerk and the hammock sways, and when he extends a hand to stabilize me, I realize it's not a complete stranger. It's Eddie, the man who can fix anything.

"I've got something for you," he says as I scramble out of the well of the hammock and onto the deck. I'm disoriented, partly from eight hours of swaying suspension and partly from yesterday's beers. My mouth feels gritty and stale. I have to pee. I need to brush my teeth and have a big mug of coffee. Then my gaze falls on Lucy's empty leash and for a moment I panic, until I remember that last night, after our walk, Marilee took the dog into the restaurant with her.

"The tape," I say, trying to swim my way back to the here and now. "You fixed it."

"Somewhat. A little bit. I can't promise that—"

"I know. You can't promise that the pieces are in the right order. Can you give me a minute to pull myself together? Would you like a cup of coffee?" It's not really my place to offer this kid something I may not be able to deliver, not even something as simple as a cup of coffee, but surely Marilee has a drip pot in the kitchen somewhere.

He nods and sits and as I head inside, I parenthetically notice the bag in his hands. It's suspiciously big if all he's brought me is an eight-track, but for now I pick up my backpack and stumble in through the screen door, heading for the ladies' room. As I brush my teeth and change my T-shirt and scrub off the old sunscreen and put on some more, I can hear Marilee moving around. She's talking to someone—either Eddie or Lucy, I guess—and I'm happy to smell that she's already got coffee brewing.

Through the propped-open screen door I can see they're all out on the deck, including the dog. He likes it here. It might be kinder to leave Lucy in Fairhope, assuming Marilee will agree to take him, rather than to force him back into that cramped little backseat and haul him on the next leg of this journey to nowhere.

"Want me to wait for the coffee?" I holler out the door.

Marilee hollers back. "I think you need to come out right now and hear what this boy has to tell you."

That doesn't sound good.

I ease my way back out and pull up the chair beside Eddie's, making everybody wince with the sound of scraping wood. He's holding a poster. One of the kind they used for outlaws in the Wild West saying "$10,000 Reward for Armless Hank the Bank Robber" or some such foolishness. I didn't even know they made posters like that anymore.

"Cop came by this morning," Eddie says. "Asked me if I'd

take this over to the post office when they open Tuesday so they could put it on the bulletin board."

"Oh God," I say. "I knew this was coming. I'm a wanted woman."

"Actually, you're a missing woman," Eddie says, handing it over, and that is indeed the word at the top of the poster: MISSING, in big black letters, along with my name, age, height, and weight, or at least the height and weight I gave the DMV the last time I went in, which is somewhat accurate if I'm standing up real straight in heels and have just had two solid weeks of stomach flu.

And then there are three pictures. The first is taken from my driver's license, which of course is horrible and in some ways as big a fiction as the height and the weight, but it's kind of a relief to see that the picture looks nothing like me. It's generic. The face staring out at the world could be any middle-aged white woman with dark hair in all of America, and God knows there are plenty of us.

As if the FBI realized this, they added two more pictures to the bottom of the poster.

These are the real problem.

One is a picture of the Blackhawk. Not only that, it has Elvis standing beside it, although someone has put a big black pixel box over his face. Which is stupid, since it's obviously Elvis, leaning against the long shiny hood of an extraordinary machine with the high columns of Graceland visible in the background, wearing one of those white jumpsuits with a shoe-lace closing in the front and an attached cape. Who the hell else could it be? It's either Elvis or an Elvis impersonator—those're pretty much the only two options.

And then there's a picture of Mama. Not the photo of her and Marilee, but one very similar to it. She's dressed in full backup dancer regalia, with an explosion of jet black curls and a big smile. It's an odd thing, I guess, that someone somewhere must have thought a picture of my mother would help the cops track me down, and the even odder thing is that they're right. I guess I may as well stop saying I'm not like her, because I am and this poster proves it. I look more like my mama than I look like myself.

"The cop came in with no regard for the fact it's a holiday," Eddie is saying to Marilee, who nods soberly. "He asked me if I'd seen her and I said no, so now I've lied to an officer of the law."

"Thank you," I say to Eddie. "But don't take it to the post office. If that cop comes back, tell him you lost it."

"Child," Marilee says sharply. "You can't ask this boy to state a damning falsehood for you, and besides, it wouldn't matter a hill of beans if he did. If they brought this poster to the Wild Acre post office, then you can rest assured they've brought it to every post office in the South and you're likely on the news as well. Besides, you sang on this very deck all day yesterday and what? Maybe a hundred people saw you then?"

"At least," I say miserably.

"You got a ball cap?" Eddie says. "Pull it down and hide your face." He's being a champ, considering he doesn't even know where I'm going or why. But I get the sense he's enjoying the drama of the whole thing.

"I've got a ball cap," I say. "But my face isn't the problem. The problem is that they've got a picture of the car."

Marilee is chewing on her lip, deep in thought, and she

doesn't even say anything to Lucy when he jumps off the chair and wanders over to pee on the leg of a picnic table. It's not his fault. The clock over the bar said nine fifteen. Somebody needs to walk him.

"Where's the car now?"

"Parked somewhere under a tree. I think it's called Free-mason's Street."

Eddie whistles. "That's no good."

"What was I supposed to do with it?" I ask, rubbing my temples. I'm in for a headache today. One of the big ones.

"You had this car for thirty-eight years . . ." Eddie says.

"Who told you I'm thirty-eight?" I say. It's a stupid thing to be concerned about, in light of the bigger picture, the literally bigger picture, which is now sitting in my lap, but I've been assured I can pass for thirty-two. Repeatedly assured. Granted, most of these assurances have been made by drunk men looking to get laid, but even so . . .

"Nobody told me," Eddie says levelly. But if it's a '73 Stutz Blackhawk, that car is better than forty years old. That's a long time to hold on to a valuable car. What made you decide to take it to Graceland now, after all this time?"

"I've already explained that," I say, although maybe I explained it to Marilee. Or Fantasy Phil. It's getting hard to remember who I told what to. "I just found the car. Bradley sent me to look for his waders and I found the car."

"Exactly where had they stashed it?" says Marilee. "And why do you keep rubbing the side of your head? Are you fixing to come down with one of those sick headaches like your mama used to get?"

"At the lake property Bradley's owned for years. If you want to get there, first you turn off the paved road and then you turn off the dirt road. It's that far back. They kept the car in a shed by the marsh."

"And you'd never once looked in that shed before?" Marilee's tone is skeptical. For the first time since I showed up yesterday, I can see she's doubting the story I'm telling her.

"No. Why would I? Bradley told me that shed was full of boat parts. And I'm not sure I would have gone in two days ago," I said. "But Bradley—that's my daddy—"

"Why do you call your daddy Bradley?" Eddie asks.

I rub my temples. "Because that's his name, number one. And because maybe he's not my real daddy, number two. But he sent me to get his waders and he said they were in the shack, not the shed, and so I was to look in the shack, not the shed, and he said that about three times for emphasis . . ."

"Sounds to me," Eddie says, "like a real good way to get a person to look in a shed."

"Just what I'm thinking," says Marilee, and they're right, of course they are. Bradley more or less left town and sent me to find the car. Why, I can't say. I guess he's done the math too. Maybe he's as sick of the lies as I am.

"But for Bradley to call the law and report me missing . . . that makes zero sense. Why would he send me to find the car and then turn me in for taking it?"

"I don't know," says Marilee. "But I do know what you're going to do next, which is go in that back bedroom and pull the shades against this sun before you start throwing up your coffee all over this deck."

"I'm not sick," I say. "Not very. I can get rid of it with four Extra Strength Ty—"

"You're sick and that's clear as glass," Marilee says. "Go in there and lie down."

"Even if you didn't have a sick headache," says Eddie, still trying to fix things, "you wouldn't need to start out anywhere on Memorial Day. Every road near the coast will be swarming with cops. It'd be smarter to wait till tomorrow morning when the holiday weekend has passed and everybody's guard is down. In the meantime, we can move the car to behind my shop. Put a tarp over it."

"Thank you," I say, and for some reason my eyes fill with tears. Maybe it's the headache, maybe it's the poster with the pictures of me and Elvis and Mama and that big word MISSING right across the top, a statement that is accurate in more ways than I can begin to count. Maybe it's just that all these strangers are being so very kind. "I don't know why I'm acting foolish. It's just that I've made some mistakes in life, you know, cut some corners. But this is the first time I've ever been in trouble with the law."

"You're not in trouble with the law," Eddie points out. "You're just missing. And even if the cops do catch up with you, they're gonna give you the benefit of the doubt. You're a pretty white woman. Bad stuff doesn't happen to pretty white women."

"Are you kidding me?" I say. "Pretty white women end up raped and strangled on the eleven o'clock news every night."

"And that's why it's news. Because they're pretty white women. If something bad happens to an ugly black man, that ain't no news to anybody."

He's got a point but I'm in no mood to admit it. I'm still too upset thinking about my picture being on a missing poster. Bradley would never do such a thing. He couldn't stand the shame. In fact, if Bradley walks into the Clearwater PO and sees me and Mama and Elvis all hanging up there on the wall, he'll have a heart attack on the spot. "At least you got the eight-track fixed."

"I wouldn't say fixed. I'd say—"

"We got to find something to play it on. Marilee, do you have an eight-track player?"

She shoots me an incredulous look.

"Then I have to get to Joe's Vintage and Salvage," I say.

"Don't bother," says Eddie. "I called over there before I came, and to the Goodwill too. There's not an eight-track player left in Fairhope. Anywhere in the world, most likely."

"Forget that tape player," Marilee says decisively. "We need to get some aspirin and eggs into you before that headache takes hold and, Eddie, you've got to walk this dog before he shits any more on my deck. And then we've got to move that car and cover it with a tarp and we've got to cover you with a tarp too, Miss Cory Beth Ainsworth, or at least put you to bed back in my room where nobody will see you. Tomorrow, first thing in the morning, while it's still dark and everybody's in bed sleeping off Memorial Day, you start out bright and early for Graceland. That's the plan."

And it's a pretty good one, but I still hear myself talking. "I want to hear the eight-track," I say.

Marilee nods. "And so do I. But we'll have to listen to it in the car."

"That car is what chewed it up the first time."

"The gears just jammed up from a lack of use," Marilee says, and then she looks at Eddie. "You got oil?"

"Not with me."

"We can use frying oil."

"Wait a minute," I say, even though my head is screaming. "We can't squirt a bunch of Mazola down the mouth of an eight-track player in a priceless car and put a priceless tape in and just hope it all comes out well. I'll take the tape to Graceland and turn it over to them scot-free before I do that. They've got somebody there who will know what to do, especially when I tell them it's got Elvis on it, Elvis singing some song nobody's ever heard."

I look at Eddie. "We can at least get some WD-40 at a hardware store, right? Something that'll work better than cooking oil?"

Marilee has picked up the cartridge and she's turning it over and over in her hands, her fingertips grazing the edges. "When you get to Graceland with this tape," she says softly, "you need to tell them what you have, not ask them what you have. You hear what I'm saying to you?"

I nod. "So they won't screw me on the money."

"Among other things."

"You think Phil's the one who told the cops I'm missing, don't you?"

"That's not what I said."

"You didn't have to. But why would Fantasy Phil give me four hundred dollars and send me on my way and then decide he wanted me back? It doesn't make any sense."

"Nothing about his name struck you as strange?"

"I don't know his name. Not the whole name. I saw his picture on a billboard but I was past it before I got much more than a glimpse of his eyes. I didn't even know the Fantasy Phil part until I got here and you told me."

"I'll get the eggs going," Marilee says, pushing to her feet. "If we don't get some food in you fast your knees are going to buckle right out from under you. Eddie, take that dog to do his business."

"Why's his name Lucy if he's a boy?" says Eddie, unweaving Lucy's leash from the railing. He seems to be getting over his fear of dogs, or at least this particular dog, but I can't seem to pull my eyes from Marilee. Even though my head is pounding worse, and I think it may be too late for the eggs and Tylenol to save me. I know these headaches. I'm getting ready to lose a whole day of my life, possibly two. Eddie chuckles and snaps on the leash, then starts dragging Lucy down the deck. Even though the dog clearly needs a walk, he keeps pulling back toward me, enough so that Eddie has to put some muscle into getting him moving. I guess I really can't leave him here, no more than I could give him to Leary. He's my dog now. Probably has been since the moment he jumped over my lap in that rest area.

I wait until they're both out of earshot, then I say to Marilee, trying to keep my voice low and even. "What makes you think some politician from Macon, Georgia, is coming after me? Especially when we both know he paid good money just to get me out of his sight?"

"You showing up like that got him in a panic," she says. "He paid you fast and maybe he started thinking about it later."

"You weren't there. You don't know how it happened."

"I know enough to know you scared the shit out of him."

"I doubt that very seriously. He seemed more like the kind of person that keeps all his shit up inside of him his whole life."

"Maybe so. But if I had to guess who's coming after you, I'd guess him."

"And why would he do that?"

"Because that man's full name is Philip Cory," Marilee says. "Now how do you take your eggs?"

HONEY

Something's wrong with our song. Bad wrong, but it's not what Marilee thinks it is. She says it's because we got a man to sing a woman's story, but the trouble goes way deeper than that.

Daughter and water. It's off, and not just because the words don't make a perfect rhyme.

Marilee wants me to throw the tape into the nearest Dumpster. I told her I would. Put my hand on an imaginary Bible and said, "I swear."

But this tape . . . it was just the three of us in the jungle room and he kept putting his head back against the carpeted wall. He looked awful. Bloated and sweaty, and he was messing up the words. And Marilee said, "You need to go to sleep, baby. You need to do whatever it takes to get yourself to sleep."

Three days later, after he'd truly done whatever it took to get himself to sleep, when Marilee and I were in the car and barreling south from Memphis, one of us pushed the tape in. We listened until the bitter end, to the part where Elvis stops singing and Marilee says, so soft and gentle, that he needs to sleep. And she added, "Put yourself in the hands of Jesus. You and I know there's nothing down here worth sticking around for."

When Marilee heard her own words coming back to her, she panicked. She slammed on the brakes and pulled off the road and started looking around her, all wild, even though we were just sitting on this nothing road in north Mississippi, without another car even in sight.

"I'll drive," I said, but she shook her head.

"It sounds like I'm telling him to take his drugs," she said. "Don't you understand? Sweet Jesus, on this tape it sounds like I'm telling the man he may as well go upstairs and kill himself."

"That wasn't what you meant," I said. "Everybody was always telling him to take his drugs." And this was true. An unmedicated Elvis was like living with a bull, or with a 250-pound toddler, and there wasn't a person at Graceland who didn't at some time or another urge the man to dose himself and let us have some peace. "And everybody knows what you meant by putting it in the hands of Jesus. You've got a hundred people who'll swear that's nothing more than the prayer we used to say before showtime."

But even while I was trying to reassure her, I knew why she was worried. Her words could be twisted so easily in a Tennessee courthouse. An angry mob was probably already assembling outside the gates of Graceland, demanding to know who among us had killed their King. We all felt guilty and, in a way, we were all guilty. I daresay as they were pushing him out of Graceland on the gurney with the sheet over his face, everybody lining the halls was thinking back to what he or she might have said. Or what they didn't say, which is worse.

We might all have failed him in one way or another, but only Marilee's voice was on the tape. Clear as day, recognizable to anyone who'd ever met her, more or less urging Elvis to leave one world and go onto the next.

So it was natural she'd panic, but that was yesterday, the most awful day in the world, when we were driving through Mississippi. And today is a new day. We've made it to Fairhope. Marilee's home.

And she's safe here. I know she is. I saw within five minutes of pulling into town that no matter what condition Marilee Jones might scrape up in, the people of Fairhope will open their arms and take her back. This town won't ask her any questions, at least not the sort Beaufort is getting ready to ask me. By ten o'clock this morning she'd gotten back her old job, working in the kitchen at a place called Doozy's Barbecue. I'd sat on one of the swivel stools at the counter and watched her march straight toward the kitchen, pushing back the swinging doors like she owned the place. And when Mr. Doozer, the sort of man who looked like he'd been born unhappy, started giving her lip about running out on him six years earlier, she just tied on her apron, said, "Hush," and fried up a bunch of eggs for her and me. Mr. Doozer gave me the fish eye and at first I thought it was because we were eating six of his eggs without payment, but later Marilee said it was because I was the first white person who'd ever sat at that counter.

"I didn't know you knew how to cook," I told her.

"You've only seen a sliver of me," she said with that little half-snorting, half-laughing thing she does. "Just the part that came to Graceland. What you don't know about Marilee Jones could fill a Bible." And I have no doubt that's true. We've lived shoulder to shoulder for the last fourteen months, touring and singing and eating and peeing together, playing cards and teaching each other dance steps and fixing our hair, but we don't know beans about what the other one was like before Graceland. BG, that's how I'm going to measure my life from now on, I guess. BG and AG. Before and after Graceland.

We go walking out to the pier after her shift and I swallow my pride and ask her if I can stay. She could teach me to cook, or at least I could waitress. I all but beg, and yet she just smiles and turns her back on me, and in a way I can't blame her. If fate and geography were different and I was the one who was already safe at home, then who knows? I might turn my back on her.

"Get going," she says. "Hit the road."

"You don't mind me taking the car?"

"He gave it to you, didn't he?"

I look down at the water swirling beneath us. *Water* and *daughter*. They don't rhyme, but they're all we seem to have.

"I'll be back someday," I tell her.

"Let's hope not." She hugs me and slaps my rump. "Now get. Go find that baby a daddy."

CORY

The rest of Sunday is no more than a blur. I gulp the Tylenol and force down an egg or two, then fall immediately asleep on Marilee's bed. I'm dimly aware of time passing, of clanging pans and slamming doors, and people laughing on the deck. When I finally open my eyes, the worst of the headache is gone.

Nothing's left but what Mama used to call that echo pain, a sort of low-level soreness, like something came in and stretched my head and now I'm just trying to settle it back to its previous size. I'd thrown a towel over the curtain at the window before I lay down, trying to keep the room as dark as possible, but the towel must have gradually slid out of place, because when I roll over and slowly open my eyes, a rectangle of light has broken through to the floor. It's dim. Looks like I've slept most of the day away.

My bladder is ready to burst, so I struggle to my feet and push open the door. The restaurant is empty, except for Marilee and Lucy that is. Both of them are at the same table, with Marilee sipping coffee.

"She lives," she says.

"Where is everybody?"

"Where they should be on the morning after Memorial Day weekend. In their beds."

It takes me a minute to put together what she's saying. "I was out for the whole day and the whole night too?"

"It's just after six, Tuesday morning. Do you feel like driving? If so, we need to get you on the road."

"Let me brush my teeth."

When I get out of the bathroom Marilee has my stuff packed, with the guitar balanced uneasily on top of the pile, and a tuna salad sandwich folded into a paper bag. I put the backpack on, take the bag and a cup of coffee while Marilee wrangles the guitar and Lucy. We pass the hammock on the deck, and when I thank her for sleeping outside last night and giving me her bed, she just says, "Hush."

It's like she understands the echo pain. Maybe it's something she remembers from my mama. We walk down the pier, the beach, and up the steps without speaking. I don't even ask her where we're going. Well, I guess I sort of know that. She and Eddie must have moved the car at some point and she's taking me back to his place to claim it. Only I'm not sure how we're going to get there until finally, all three of us panting from the climb, we make it back to the landing at the top of the stairs and I see a pickup truck with DOOZY'S BARBECUE painted on the side.

It's a strange little hybrid world she lives in. Her business is half Doozy's and half Bay Restaurant, half pig and half fish, and she lives in the back of it and she's half a star and half a drudge.

It's rare to see anyone work the way Marilee Jones works, running the whole place. She seems to be running the whole town. I could tell by the way Eddie fell in with whatever she said that Marilee has a lot of sway in Fairhope, that getting out and coming back has earned her more respect than it ever earned Honey in Beaufort.

We climb in. Lucy sits between us. Letting a dog of his limited mental capacity ride back in a flatbed is out of the question. As she pulls from the lot into the road, Marilee is humming something, half under her breath. The melody sounds familiar and I start to ask her what it is, but then it hits me. And for once in my life I'm glad I had the sense to hush.

HONEY

So I hug her and say good-bye. I love Marilee, probably as good as I love anybody in this world, and I do promise, but even as I'm saying the words, I know there's no way I'm throwing out that tape. Deep down in her heart of hearts, I don't think she really expects me to. If she wants our song destroyed, let her pitch the whole thing into Mobile Bay herself.

But she doesn't. She gives it to me—along with the car, and the jar of tupelo honey, and this road map, already folded to the great state of Georgia.

I accelerate as I leave town. Dare some Alabama cop to try and stop me. Throw the tape away? Right. Like I'm going to do a fool thing like that.

This tape is all I've got left of Elvis.

Hell. It's all I've got left of me.

CORY

It's a relief when Eddie comes out of his shop carrying WD-40 instead of Mazola, and it belatedly occurs to me that they were kidding about the cooking oil last night. That's one of my first signs I'm getting a migraine, along with rubbing my temples. I start failing to understand when people are making a joke. Eddie climbs into the back of the Blackhawk without asking, even though this means Lucy is going to sit in his lap and kiss him senseless the whole time. I start to congratulate him for making so much progress on the dog thing, but when Marilee gets in the passenger seat, she has the tape in her hand and that distracts me. Eddie says he's already lubed it up once and thinks it's okay, but we have to go through the whole disclaimer thing one more time about how he can't vouch for the condition of the tape or what the tape player might get a mind to do. Finally, more to shut him up than anything else, I take the eight-track from Marilee and cram it into the player.

We all wait.

Nothing. Nothing for a while. No chewing, which is good, but no sound either. Then a couple of little thumps and a scrap of music. Honey's voice, just a word or two of it. The aborted strum of a guitar. A couple of more thumps. Marilee asking if this is a good place to set something. Another bit of song, enough to know for sure that it's Elvis. A line and a half, then silence. We wait for at least a minute, none of us speaking, then I hit eject. The tape slides right out and everyone exhales in unison, even the dog.

"The first time I tried to play it, your voice—" I start, but Marilee has heard enough. She seems to remember the day precisely, the way she seems to remember everything from that era.

"We were in the jungle room," she says. "He recorded there sometimes. Did your mama tell you that? But no, you say no, you say she didn't tell you anything. It was about noon, so everybody else in the house was asleep. That's the first thing you learn at Graceland. If you want to hide something, you gotta do it in full daylight."

"I'm sorry I couldn't get you more of the song," Eddie says. I cut him off at once.

"Did Elvis write those lyrics?" I ask Marilee.

"If he did—" says Eddie.

"I know," I say. "It would make it worth a fortune. Elvis wasn't known for writing songs."

Marilee doesn't say anything. She just sits still and square in her seat, like she's gone to church.

"It was his song, right?" I ask.

"Yeah. It was his."

"Was there ever any more to it? Or just those first lines?"

She hesitates. Just a little too long for my taste. "That's all."

"But it could still be valuable," I say. "The sad thing is that he made a mistake right off the bat with the lyrics. He ended the first line with 'water,' and there's no logical word that rhymes with 'water.' You could say 'squatter' or 'rotter,' but they're not exactly lyrical."

"What about 'daughter'?" Marilee says, still staring straight ahead over the low sloped dashboard of the Blackhawk.

"'Daughter'?" I say. "It's not bad, but it's not—"

"It works if you don't mind it being a soft rhyme," she says. "Elvis always slurred his words when he sang, you know. That made it easier for us to go with soft rhymes."

"Us?"

"Him, I mean. Since he's the one who wrote it."

She's lying to me. Maybe she's been lying to me since the moment when I first walked down her pier. Not the straight-in-your-face kind of lie or the I'm-going-to-screw-you-over kind of lie, but the gentler sort. What Bradley calls a Christian lie. The kind where what you say is true enough but you stop short of telling the whole story because the whole story is complex, and inconvenient, and it might piss all over somebody's future or break somebody's heart.

"What do I owe you?" I say, turning to Eddie. "You said you'd fix it and you did."

"You don't owe him a thing," Marilee says. "I'll pay him for his time with pork and shrimp." She cuts me off before I can thank her. "Consider this tape my gift to you," she says, and she pops open the door.

"With any luck the cops are all home in bed," says Eddie. "You'll be in Memphis by afternoon."

Marilee shakes her head. "You need to take 98 to 45 to 78," she says to me. "Say it back to me."

For a crazy minute I think she's talking about record speeds but then I realize she means roads.

"Take 98 to 45 to 78," I repeat.

"Seriously?" says Eddie. "Then maybe she won't be in Memphis by afternoon. I know we said she needs to stick to back roads, but 98 to 45 to 78 is a ride. Well, girl, you won't miss a swamp anywhere in the state of Mississippi, that's for damn sure."

"It'll take her through Tupelo," Marilee says, still staring out straight ahead like she's seeing some road that's not there, her profile as calm as a queen on a coin and still giving no sign as to how she feels about being back in the Blackhawk after all these years. How it feels to hear her voice on that tape along with Honey and Elvis, carrying her back to a time that I still don't know if she loved or if she hated.

"Oh God," I say. "Tupelo. That's right. There's a receipt from Tupelo I found when I cleaned out the car. You and Mama bought something there for a dollar ninety-five."

"Honey."

"What'd she buy?"

"Honey's what we bought. A jar of tupelo honey from a roadside stand on Highway 45."

"Why?" I say. "Because of her nickname?"

"Tupelo's the best honey in the world," says Eddie.

I ignore him. "Do you remember the name of the stand where you got it?"

Marilee shakes her head. "Roadside stands don't have names."

"Tupelo's not exactly on the way," I say, pointing to the map crumpled up at Marilee's feet. "Why did the two of you go through there? Surely not just to buy honey. Honey's all over the state. Were you looking for Elvis's birthplace?"

Marilee snorts, but still doesn't turn her head. "I'd already seen it, what there was to see. Just a little shotgun house. Nothing to stop for there. His folks were as poor as white folks were allowed to be."

"But the baby's grave is in Tupelo too," I say. "Jesse? His twin brother who died."

Marilee suddenly reaches up for the leather strap and begins to heave her weight out of the car.

"I have to get back," she says. "I've got three hours until the lunch crowd."

"That clock on the dash isn't right," I tell her.

"Never was."

Part of me wants to get on the road, but on another level, the fact that she's moving panics me. She's already half out of the car and Eddie has pushed up the seat, getting ready to follow her. Within minutes I will be back on my own. I catch her shoulder and she turns.

"Why're you sending me through Tupelo? Not to see a birthplace or a grave or some roadside stand selling honey. There's something else you're still not telling me."

"Your mama would have my head on a platter if she knew I'd said even this much."

"Maybe so, but your head's safe enough. Mama's dead."

"That she is." Marilee says, pulling herself to her feet. "So I may as well tell you we carried him as far as Tupelo, crazy out of his gourd with drugs and talking nonsense the whole way. Your mama said she felt sorry for him. Felt a sense of duty despite all he'd done with her and to her. We left him in a cheap motel with a bucket of ice and a Bible on the bedside table, and we turned the television to some golf game, since that was the only channel that wasn't talking about the death of Elvis. 'Find him something peaceful to wake up to,' that's what Honey said, 'because the world's gone crazy.' Why she cared so much about what that trifling white boy woke up to is beyond me. But I guess she still loved him, despite it all."

"Loved who?" I say. I'm desperate, because I know I'm getting ready to lose Marilee for good. I can see it in the set of her shoulders, the way she turns from me and this car, pointing her feet back in the direction of Mobile Bay. She'll go back to the pier and wash my sick sweat out of her sheets and she'll give Eddie a dozen big southern farmhand-sized lunches in exchange for fixing my tape and keeping my secrets. She's a decent woman and she'll do the decent thing. For me, just like she did for my mama. But she gives me one more tiny scrap of the wrinkled, chewed-up truth for the road. She throws it back over her shoulder, just as casual as you throw a dog a hush puppy, throws it as she's walking toward the flatbed truck.

"David Beth" she says. "Everybody called him Nunchucks. If I've done my counting right, he's the one who's most likely your blood father. We left his sad ass at a Rest-A-While in Tupelo in August of 1977, and far as I know, it's still there."

PART FOUR

Tupelo, Mississippi

CORY

June 3, 2015

I feel it happening all around me—the sense that I'm sinking, that something's getting deeper. At some point during the last three days, the car must have driven over that invisible line between the South and *The South*. I've watched the social acceptability of Georgia slowly give way to the anxiety of Alabama and then the complete throwing-in-the-towel-ness of Mississippi.

I sort of envy Mississippi. It must be a relief to be the undisputed worst at everything. To have it all counted up and documented and put on a graph, so that the whole world can see your failure, and there's no longer any point in pretending. When I started out this morning, I would have said I'm like Alabama, near the bottom but not totally bottomed out, always looking around the room trying to find somebody more fucked up than me. The drunk girl ragging on somebody drunker, the person three months behind on the rent sneering at the person who's four. Nothing's any meaner than a loser who still has just a little bit left to lose. But now I'm thinking it might be better to admit that I'm more like Mississippi and to just let my life fall at my feet with a thunk.

I pass a yard that has a flag lying on the ground in front of a tombstone that reads RIP AMERICA and then right beside it, on a slightly more hopeful note, somebody's put a wheelbarrow with another sign reading Melons for Sale. So all the clichés about the angry South are there, but it's also true that now that I've slowed down and taken my time to really look, the road before me has become a fairyland. The trees vault high and grow together, touching branch to branch over the road, turning it into a leafy green tunnel with sunlight waiting at the end. And once I'm through that tunnel I find myself crossing a huge expanse of marsh, the cypresses standing like soldiers knee deep in the sparkling water, and still I keep driving, with Elvis coming at me through the speakers, his voice sad and low and holy.

"He was," my mama said once, "a beautiful man." I don't remember in particular what prompted the statement. She didn't say his name. She didn't have to. All those years when I was growing up, she so rarely said the words *Elvis* or *Graceland*, and yet somehow they were all around us, whispering from every corner. Whispering my name as much as hers. The longer I drive, the more certain I become that Mama must have called Marilee when she got sick. Maybe she even called Philip too, and that's why neither of them was surprised to hear that she was dead and why they weren't particularly surprised to see me coming through either. They knew I existed, and probably knew that I would shortly find the Blackhawk. They had been true and purely warned that Cory Beth Ainsworth was the sort of stubborn girl who would get in that car and drive it west no matter what anybody tried to tell her. Because the more the co-incidences add up, the more I'm forced to admit that there's nothing coincidental about any of this. Even after Mama turned back into Laura there must have been a little bit of Honey left in her, and the Honey part set up this whole thing. Maybe she even had Bradley's help. What am I saying? Of course she had Bradley's help. The man's gone to Florida every spring since I can remember and never once forgot his waders, not until now.

The car was always waiting in the shed. Waiting for the moment when Mama was too far gone to be hurt or shamed, wait-ing for the moment when even careful, slow-moving Bradley was willing to unleash the truth. My mind flashes back to one summer day, maybe twenty-five years ago, when we were all at the cabin and Bradley had taken me out fishing. He and I were in the rowboat, drifting down the marsh, and it was getting dark and he said the tide was turning, so we started rowing back to the cabin. It had rained the day before. The river was swollen and dark, the color of chocolate milk. Bradley was doing the bulk of the rowing, like he usually did, and I was dragging my hand through the water, like I always do, for there is something in me that loves the sensation of the marsh slipping between my fingers, the truth of it both there and not there even in the same instant. We were almost back when we saw her. Mama was coming out of the shed, walking up that steep hill fast, not looking back. The word *scramble* would not have been inappro-priate to describe her movements. That's how fast and how awkward she was, and I said to Bradley, "What was Mama doing in the shed?"

He said "Look." He pointed. He said there was a hawk, a big dark one, flying high above the trees. Did I see it?

Of course I didn't see it. There wasn't any hawk to see. He just knew that I liked them, that all he'd have to do is say the word and I'd be distracted, leaning back and shading my eyes, forgetting all about Mama coming out of the shed and walking so fast. I guess she must have visited the car sometimes, on those rare occasions when she had a moment alone. The car's a Blackhawk and he told me to look for a black hawk and maybe that means something too, something I still don't understand.

Dinner was late that night, which dinner hardly ever was. We were a well-organized family. We ate at six thirty on the day the *Challenger* blew up and also on the day my grandparents were killed by a drunk driver, just as they were pulling out of the church parking lot. We ate at six thirty on 9/11 and every Christmas Eve of my life. But on this particular day it was nearly eight before Mama called us in, with no explanation as to why. Bradley and I pulled up on the shore, fishless like we so often were, and it occurs to me now—belatedly, like everything seems to occur to me, for I am God's own fool, a Mississippi girl to the roots of her soul—that when Bradley took me fishing, his intention never was to fish. It was the time we had alone, him and me, drifting on the water. We rarely talked, but the silence was companionable, and I guess it gave Mama something too. A chance to go deep into her own mind, to find whatever shards of Honey might still be left there. Evidently on this particular day our fishing trip gave her the chance to pay homage to the Blackhawk, sealed up as tight as a memory can be.

I struggle to pull my mind back to the present, to the reality of this hot Mississippi day. I've been driving steadily but not too fast. A sign says that Tupelo is thirty-four miles away and I've made good time, all things considered. Eddie was wrong. I'll be there comfortably by lunchtime, back roads or not, and I'd like to pee but there's no place to, and then my eye falls on a billboard, another stinking billboard with just a man's face. But this man isn't running for political office, he's aiming for a different kind of glory. David Beth, the sign says. Pastor of Pinnacle Church and host of the Pinnacle Radio Ministry, and I swear I would throw my head back and scream if it wouldn't wake up the dog.

Did my mother ever fuck a man who didn't end up on a billboard? Am I destined to drive through life with every sign that heaven intends to send me on an actual goddamn sign?

David Beth. A pastor. A radio preacher. The second candidate for the role of being my biological father. The lowest of the low, but at least he's still in Tupelo, just as Marilee predicted.

David Beth. He kept his name or maybe more to the point, he dropped the "Nunchucks" and went back to his original name. He looks buffed and polished and phony as Vegas, but still a little bit handsome. *My daddy's hot,* I think, and I look up into his face for so long that the Blackhawk, easing its way up to sixty like the Blackhawk always wants to do, edges off the pavement and begins to rumble a warning. I get it back on the road, but I wake up Lucy in the process and, even worse, I draw the attention of the car behind me, which swings out and rides parallel to me for quite a while, long after David Beth fades from sight. It makes me uncomfortable, a car swinging out to pass on a two-lane road as curvy as this one, and taking its sweet time about it. It refuses to cut around me, even when I give the Blackhawk the brake. In fact, the car very pointedly flanks me for a handful of long seconds until I finally look over and lo and behold, I see what I've feared since the moment I left Beaufort.

A cop.

He rides parallel but he does not pass and he does not turn on his siren. The car is too close for me to see the writing on the door, to figure out if this cop is state or local and exactly what depth of trouble I'm in. Then suddenly it accelerates and pulls away and I see that I've been accosted not by a legitimate officer at all, but rather by a joke of a cop, a parody of law enforcement.

The emblem on the side of his door reads GRACELAND SECURITY. Hell, he doesn't have a siren. He probably doesn't have any authority either or at least not here—not thirty miles from Tupelo and probably ninety miles from Memphis.

And yet he lifts his finger. He lifts his pudgy cop's finger off the steering wheel and points toward the side of the road. I take my foot off the gas and start looking for a place wide enough to pull over without being on the lip of the swamp.

I find it in the parking lot of an elementary school. I cut off the engine and glance down at the missing-person poster in the passenger seat beside me. Not much point in hiding it now.

He won't ask for my license or registration. He's not entitled to such and he and I both know it. This man is no more than one beat up from mall security, and at least three beats down from the sheriff's deputy of whatever godforsaken county I've managed to drive myself into. And yet he strides slowly up to me, adjusting his manhood as he walks, and I wonder why on earth he's here, so far from Graceland, but of course part of me knows the answer, even as I'm asking the question. When I left Beaufort in this car, I flipped a domino. Set off a whole chain of events.

I stare straight ahead as he approaches. The sign in the schoolyard says something about sixth-grade graduation. There's an upcoming bake sale. A track meet. Congratulations go out to the winner of their spelling bee, a girl with an Indian name. Well, good for her. Good for all of them.

He leans down. I look up.

And he says, "Are you Cory Beth Ainsworth?"

And I say, "Yes, I am. But you know that already, don't you?"

He smiles. It's not a bad smile, all things considered. Not mean or even sarcastic. He says, "I believe you may be in possession of our property."

I don't make a fuss. There's no point. I called Graceland of my own free will and told them I had the car. I put a bunch of coins in a payphone and dialed the number on my arm and proudly, stupidly announced the fact to a man named Fred. Marilee described him as old, and Marilee is no spring chicken, so apparently this Fred is prepared to live forever. He once harassed my mother and Marilee and now he seems hell-bent on harassing me.

"I'm only trying to get the car back to Graceland," I say, which is more-or-less somewhat true. "That has been my full intent since the beginning of my journey. But I will admit that I was hoping to spend some time here in Tupelo first."

"Of course you are," says the man. "Tupelo's important." He

is possibly the first person in history to ever utter this sentence and yet I find myself nodding.

"I know you've been looking for me," I say, handing him the poster. "Or I know you've been looking for the car. I was in Fairhope, Alabama, and the local police brought it around to the post office . . ."

This pleases him.

"We cooperate," he says, "with local and state authorities on all sides of the lines."

He says "the lines" with such great pride that I can only assume he means the state lines between Tennessee and Mississippi and Alabama. Or hell, possibly farther. For all I know, posters showing me and Mama and Elvis and this car are spread all over the country. Maybe even the world.

"Perhaps," the cop adds, "the Fairhope officer was so thorough because he's hoping to someday hold a position with us." He says it like working Graceland security is the absolute height of law enforcement, like right now every cop in America is fighting and scrapping for his job.

Three days ago I would have snapped back. I would have said something smartass, made some attempt to put this guy in his place. But I remember what Eddie told me, that I'm white and female and reasonably pretty and that there's power in all that, so I smile. I give him my best pretty white girl smile and I say, "I eagerly await my arrival at Graceland. It's the shame of my lifetime that I've never been. But please don't make me go quite yet. Not when there's so much in Tupelo to see."

"Like what?" he says. He knows damn well like what.

"Well, there's the house where Elvis was born," I say. "That's a given. And I want to go to the church of David Beth. I believe the sign I passed awhile back said he was the pastor of Pinnacle Church."

"Why do you want to see David Beth?" he says. He's fat. Close to fifty. Has a crappy job that he thinks is a good job and I've seen a thousand men like this, working the same bars that I have, from Cape Cod to Key West, towing cars and bouncing out drunks and bumming free drinks and hitting on girls way above their station. I know how to play them as well as my guitar. But for some reason I trust this Graceland cop, whose badge says Dirk, so I take a chance on the truth.

"Because I'm looking for my biological father," I tell him. "And I have reason to believe he may be the pastor of Pinnacle Church. I won't leave Tupelo until I find out, and frankly, it would be easier if you helped me. Helped me with all of it. I need someone who can really show me the town."

He's flattered, just like I hoped he'd be, but still he hesitates. "I'm from Memphis, not Tupelo."

"Of course you are. But you've been here a dozen times, haven't you? And you work at Graceland so you know everything there is to know about Elvis, from birth to death. I bet you're qualified to lead every tour yourself. I bet you know things they don't even tell the regular tourists, the behind-the-scenes stuff."

"I'm supposed to take you in," he says.

"And you will. I promise. We'll head to Memphis straight after this. But what difference does it make what time of day we get there?"

He's tempted. He sways back and forth on his legs, which are planted wide apart.

"Come on," I say. "I'm only asking for an hour or two. Show me around." But still he's still kind of fretful, so I play my trump card.

"Maybe you'd like to drive the car?"

Only one event of note has ever happened in Tupelo, Mississippi, so it's not hard to figure out where our tour will begin. Dirk pulls right up in front of Elvis's birthplace in the Blackhawk and even manages to parallel park the thing. He's as eager to show it off as I was to hide it, and I pull in behind him. I'm driving the Graceland Security car, with Lucy riding shotgun beside me. He's already licked the passenger-side window blurry.

I'd seen pictures and was prepared to be underwhelmed, but still . . . the little frame house where Elvis was born is shockingly small, no bigger than a train car. If it wasn't for a single marker in the yard—one of those plain black-and-white historical signs—you'd shoot right by the place without a glance.

"Here you have it," Dirk says. "Humble as a manger. Just one of many shotgun houses that the cotton pickers all lived in during the thirties."

Marilee had used the same term, but I didn't understand it. "Why'd they call them shotgun houses?"

" 'Cause they're built so skinny. Laid out with one room behind another. The notion was that you could stand in the front doorframe and shoot a gun down the hall and it'd go clean out the back door without hitting a thing. But this is where Elvis took his first breath."

"No hospital?"

"No, and you can see why not. Vernon and Gladys Presley were hardly more than kids themselves when the time came, and dirt poor."

"Midwife delivery?"

"Yep."

"And Jesse Garon was first, born dead."

Dirk nods. "They say the midwife almost lost Gladys too, that the blood and the pains wouldn't stop. Of course she hadn't seen a doctor the whole time, so they didn't know she was delivering twins, not until—"

"The second boy came. Elvis Aron. They were too poor to even afford another A."

He stiffens. "You think this is funny?"

"I assure you that I don't."

He looks at me skeptically, but continues. "It was January. The ground was frozen hard. So hard they couldn't bury their first boy for better than a week. They say he lay that whole time on the kitchen table in a little shoebox."

"Good God." I would have sworn I knew all the Elvis stories, but this bit about the shoebox catches me unaware.

"So of course the surviving child—" Dirk breaks off.

Entered the world fucked up beyond belief is what I think, but I say, "He must have been a very cherished baby."

Dirk nods. "And with Gladys nearly dying in the delivery, I guess they knew he'd be their only one from the start."

Like me, I think, but of course I don't add that. It's just strange that this is the first time it's really hit me, this particular similarity between Elvis and myself. Both born to parents barely out of their teens, born to be only children, always special and always alone.

"Elvis learned to sing in the Assembly of God Church on Adams Street," Dirk says, pointing down the street. "We'll drive by there next, even though there's not much to see. Less than this. They say that when his parents took him to service, he used to crawl under their feet and walk down the aisle, clapping his hands to the beat of the gospel music. And one time when he was a toddler, he slipped clean away from them and went up into the choir. Nobody knows why. He was too little to know the words, or how to sing, but he just seemed to know that's where he belonged."

"Wouldn't you know to find me in my father's house?" I say.

"You know your Bible."

"My granddaddy was a preacher. I didn't have any choice but to know my Bible." And of course everybody who's read anything about Elvis knows how he'd slip away from his parents and hide in the choir. I've always wondered if he told that story to so many reporters because it's so similar to how Mary and Joseph found Jesus talking with the rabbis in the temple. It makes Elvis seem likewise chosen from the start, with a destiny too large to outrun or ignore.

Dirk is in full tour-guide mode now. "And when he was twelve his mama scrimped and saved and bought him his first guitar. After he got famous, whenever any interviewer would ask him about that first guitar, Elvis would always tell them—"

"*What I really wanted was a bike,*" I say. Actually Dirk and I say it in unison and he turns to me, surprised, the word *bike* half ending in a laugh.

"So you know your Elvis too," he says.

"Maybe not everything, but yeah, I've done some reading."

"But even with all that you swear you've never been to Graceland?"

I shake my head.

"I'm only asking because you look kind of familiar."

"Everybody says that."

"Do you want to go inside?"

To my surprise I don't. "I'm not sure I can take it. It'll only make me sad."

"I shouldn't have told you about the dead baby on the kitchen table," Dirk said. "Women don't like that part of the story."

"And men do?"

This stops him for a minute. "No, come to think of it, I don't guess anybody likes that part of the story. But I'm sorry if I offended your sensibilities." He almost says *ma'am*. I can hear it implied.

I shake my head. "I'm not sad for the boy who died," I say. "I'm sad for the one who lived."

We drive by the Assembly of God church and then Dirk tells me how when we get to Memphis—he says "we"—that we'll have to take time to go past Sun Records. In 1954 Elvis paid them four dollars to record his first demo. They saw he had talent and signed him on the spot, but nobody knew what to do with a white boy who sounded like he was black. This was Tennessee, after all, and more than sixty years ago, and the airwaves were as segregated as the water fountains. So Sun Records put what they considered to be a black song, "That's When Your Heartaches Begin," on the B side and a white song, "My Happiness," on the A side and sent the record to every radio station in Mississippi, no matter what their formats, figuring that they'd let the audience make the call.

Only both the A and the B sides went to number one and from then on, Elvis always had both black and white backup singers whenever he would record or go on tour. It was an acknowledgment of the twin roots of his musical power. Proof he was the first artist to sing like all of America, not just half of it. Proof that he had come to bring us happiness and heartache in the same spin of the turntable.

Dirk tells me this as we drive around. I already know most of these stories, but I let him tell me again. At some point we ditch the Graceland Security car in the parking lot of a Walmart and he looks at me with a question on his face. I shake my head. He can keep driving. The Blackhawk is making him so happy that it would be cruel to take the keys back, and, besides, even though he's mostly only telling me things I've read a dozen times before, I'm enjoying the sound of his voice. Part of me has been making fun of him, but I'm just as big an Elvis nerd, reading every Wikipedia article and every trashy tabloid claiming he's still alive. In fact, I'm warming to Dirk more every minute. There's something in his way that feels easy and familiar, like we've met in some previous lifetime, and so I'm not even surprised when, over a late lunch at a meat-and-two diner, he finally breaks down and confides that he's Fred's son.

"I grew up at Graceland," he says. "More or less."

"Do you remember my mama? It's okay with me if you don't. She was only there for a year."

He nods, wiping a smear of gravy from his mouth. He's having meat loaf with limas and mashed potatoes. I'm having pan-fried chicken with okra and stewed tomatoes. Both of us asked for corn bread but, without discussion, we also both wrapped it in a napkin the minute it came, intending to take it to Lucy, who's waiting in the car. We got him water in a Styrofoam cup and he's okay for now, but as the day gets hotter, as Mississippi days invariably do, we're going to have to come up with a new solution. And there's not a La Quinta in Tupelo. I've already borrowed Dirk's iPhone and looked.

"I sure do remember Honey," Dirk says, balling up his napkin. "She was sweet. Is that why they called her that?"

"I think it was more her last name: Berry. Elvis started calling her Honey Bear."

Dirk nods. "Sounds right. I was eleven or twelve when she came, something like that, and I had a crush on Miss Honey something awful. She took the time to talk to me and not everybody did. I mean, I was just Fred's son, just a pimply kid trying to pick up a dollar or two helping the gardener, so most of Graceland didn't take the time to say boo to me. But your mama . . . one time we went in the kitchen and she even made cookies."

"Let me guess. Oatmeal raisin."

"How'd you know that?"

"That's the only kind she knew how to make."

"Yeah," he says, taking a swig of the wine-dark tea. "Exactly. She fixed me oatmeal raisin cookies, only the cook came in and found us and didn't like it one bit." He smiles with the memory. "She even took a swing at your mama with a cast-iron skillet and told her to leave that stove alone, 'cause that's how it was at Graceland. Everybody was supposed to stay in their place. Cooks cooked. Singers sang. Yard boys didn't eat in the kitchen."

"My mama was—" I say, but then I stop myself as the waitress approaches. It seems to me that she more than takes her sweet time refilling our glasses and I know she's curious about us, just like everybody in the diner probably is. When we came in, Dirk in his Graceland Security uniform and me in my ripped-up jean shorts, we must have seemed like an unlikely pair. And then we asked for water in a to-go cup, but when the waitress tried to put a lid and a straw on it, Dirk told her not to bother, that we had a dog in the car. And he glanced out the door as he said it, so of course she did too, looking right at the Blackhawk parked in the handicapped space, with half a coonhound hanging out the driver's-side window, barking his head off at anybody who came within fifty feet.

The waitress gawked, but she gave us the water, which Dirk took right out to Lucy, and I'm sure that ever since then, as this girl goes from table to table about her business, she's been pointing us out to everybody in the place, making sure anyone who managed to miss our entrance is twisted in their booths to check us out now. I tug at my shorts, even though my legs aren't visible under the table. I need to change clothes at some point and probably should do it here, in the diner bathroom, even though that'll just give them one more piece to chew over. The woman who entered the bathroom dressed like a hooker and came out dressed like a lady. Or at least as close to a lady as I'll ever be able to come to. I bought a black knit shift for Mama's funeral and I can't think why I shoved it into the bottom of my backpack in the rush of packing, but now I'm glad I did.

I wait for the waitress to retreat, holding her pitcher of sweet tea in one hand and her pitcher of unsweet tea in the other, then I lean over the table and finish my story.

"My mama was pregnant when she left Graceland."

Dirk leans forward too. "Carrying you?"

"None other." I wait for him to say something, but he doesn't. He just feigns an unnatural amount of attention to his lima beans. Finally I say, "It's just like I told you. I have to know."

He pulls the iPhone out of his pocket. Punches at it with his chubby fingers and finally, after a pause so long that it makes me nervous, he says "Everybody is entitled to a sense of their own personal identity."

"Exactly. That's the point of this whole trip."

He shakes his head. "I didn't come up with that off the top of my head. It's the motto of the Express Paternity service, located exactly 2.4 miles from this very diner."

"Express Paternity? Seriously? That's the name?"

He nods, still squinting at the screen. "I assume you've got something to go on? Something more than a hunch and a car?"

"I've got a Kleenex with the blood of Elvis on it."

He freezes, finger in midair. "Whatcha mean, the blood of Elvis?"

"He went to the dentist, didn't he, on the last day he drove the car? And he must have bled, you know how you do sometimes, when they clean your teeth rough or fill a cavity, and he must have wiped his mouth on a Kleenex while he was driving back to Graceland. It was sitting right there in the cup holder when I found the car."

Dirk puts the phone down and his eyes, which are that washed-out shade of Levi's blue and prone to bulging, bulge out even more. "So you're thinking—"

"Not so much anymore. It's what I thought at first, but the longer I drive the more I've come to terms with the fact it's not likely Elvis is my daddy. It doesn't look like he and my mama were ever that way. But I do want to go to Express Paternity. If it wasn't Elvis, I have an idea who it might be."

"Do I even want to hear this?"

"Probably not. Get your corn bread and let's call for the check. We're going to Pinnacle Church. I need to get some DNA from David Beth." I feel myself nodding as I'm speaking. I've been calm and patient through our morning-long tour of Elvis's youth, both because I like Dirk and because, despite my smartass talk, I really was interested. But now we've paid tribute to the King and had our meat-and-two lunch, and it's time to get on to the real purpose of my visit.

"Lord, girl," Dirk says, his eyes growing wide as he wipes his mouth. "Are you sure? Why would your pretty mama ever have taken up with a mess like David Beth? You ought to hear him on the radio. He starts out talking about Jesus and pretty soon he's talking about Buddha and Oprah and hell, sometimes he says something about the Arabs too, and the Japanese, like they're all sitting up in heaven in one big room. And he looks a fool on those billboards."

"He probably is a fool. Most people are. But that doesn't mean he's not my daddy."

Dirk picks up the phone again, squints at the screen. "Express Paternity claims it can run the test off of blood, feces, saliva, bones, hair, chewing gum, or semen."

"Chewing gum or semen? Seems like we got a lot of options."

He waves for the check. "Save your money, darlin'. Lunch is on me."

HONEY

August 16, 1977

"Are you sick yet?"

"You make it sound it's a sure thing that I'm gonna be sick."

Marilee taps her hands lightly against the steering wheel. "They say it's a good sign if you are. Means the baby's taken root. That it's going to stick around."

"I'm not sure I want it to stick around."

"Oh yeah. Yeah, you do."

I don't know exactly how we got from Memphis to Tupelo. We didn't open a map or consult each other on the direction. It's like the car came here of its own accord, nothing more than a horse headed back to a barn. The sun, which was just peeking at us in Memphis, is fully up now.

"So what are we going to do with him?"

"I don't know."

"Don't ask me to take that skinny, Buddha-quoting white boy to Fairhope."

"Well I sure as shooting can't take him to Beaufort."

Marilee glances in the rearview mirror, then bites at her lower lip like she's starting to say something. Probably about how if the man passed out in the backseat of this car really is the father of my child, that's all the more reason I should drive him back to Beaufort. Rehabilitate him and then marry him or perhaps, given the circumstances, marry him and then rehabilitate him. The sequence of things hardly matters when you're in a mess as bad as this.

"All right, then," Marilee says. "If you don't want him and I don't want him, it looks like we need to find a hotel. See if you can lay your hands on some cash."

It's a good idea. Elvis was a renowned stasher of money, always leaving twenties tucked here and there, under every ashtray, crammed low in every pocket. It was like on some level he always knew this day was coming, only he thought it might be him who'd have to leave Memphis in a rush, taking just the clothes on his back and the gas in his tank. So while Marilee adjusts the visor against the morning sun and continues to drive steadily east, I began to riffle through the car, running my hands under the seat cushions and flipping open every little gold cubbyhole on the dash or the doors. I come up with eighty-four dollars, a middling amount, neither here nor there. My purse is back in Graceland, not that it would have provided much in the way of riches even if I'd thought to grab it, and I bet Marilee's is too. We don't even have our driver's licenses.

"Are you absolutely sure you don't want to carry that boy to South Carolina?" Marilee asks again. She can't quite seem to let go of the idea.

"Are you kidding? My daddy's a preacher. He'd take one

look at David and spit in the dirt. And my mama wanted me to marry my high school sweetheart. Told me to my face I'd never do better than Bradley Ainsworth."

There's a long pause while Marilee contemplates all this. Finally she asks, "Was she insulting you or complimenting him?"

I've never thought of it that way. "It felt like she was casting stones at me, but maybe you're right. Maybe it was just her way of building up Bradley. You know, saying I could search the earth and not find a bigger heart . . ."

"So he's got a big heart, this old boyfriend?"

"The biggest."

"And he still loves you?"

"Probably. His letters say—"

"Letters? He's still bothering to write you letters after all this time?"

I nod, rubbing my temples.

"Then there's your plan," Marilee says, in no particular tone of voice. That's one of her strengths, the way she can say something absolutely matter-of-fact, like a TV reporter, without giving you a single clue how she feels about it one way or another.

"I don't have a plan."

"Sure you do. Maybe not in the front of your head, maybe just in the back. But some part of you knows that if you can just get yourself back to Beaufort, your good old reliable high school sweetheart will make a fine daddy for your baby girl. Better than this load of trash we're hauling in the backseat, that's for sure."

It's a rush of words. A long speech for Marilee, who's never been much of a talker. And she's probably right, at least about Bradley making a better daddy than either David or Philip ever would, and maybe she's even right about how the back of my mind has been churning since the first day my period was late. I knew I was pregnant almost from the start. I've always been one of those girls who goes twenty-eight days without variation, just like the textbook. You could plant the crops by me.

For some reason I can only think of one thing to say in response. "This baby I'm carrying might be a boy."

"Nah," she says, and she laughs. "Somewhere deep in your heart, you know dang well it's a girl. You even put it in the song."

"I wrote those lyrics before I knew I was pregnant," I say, and I peel a twenty off the fold of bills, kind of quick and subtle, and slip it into my bra. I don't think Marilee sees me.

"Besides," I rush on, since I'm nervous about stealing the money from the fold and thus from Marilee, even though we both know I have a lot farther to go and she'd probably understand, "I've got to find this baby a daddy, and it's easier to find a daddy for a boy."

I say all this like it's fact, but the joke of the situation, if there is a joke in the situation, is that I don't particularly like boys. Never have. If I could choose, I'd rather have the baby girl Marilee predicted, but I've got to be practical, and there's no denying that the world greets boys with way more enthusiasm than it greets girls. It's okay for a man to show up unannounced and unexpected, to just walk into the room carrying nothing but himself. Everybody smiles and waves, because you can never have enough men in the world. But women? The universe is already drunk with girls. Nobody needs any more of us, and this bud of a baby inside of me is starting life with enough disadvantages. God will at least let it be a boy.

"Now why do you go and say a thing like that?" Marilee asks. "Because you think a man can't hold a daughter just as close as a son? Lord. You lived better than a year at Graceland and you still think that?"

"No, I guess you're right. He loved that little girl. There were times when I thought his little girl was the only thing on earth he could still love." We're coming up on an exit with a sign saying they have a Holiday Inn, but for some reason Marilee blows right past it. If anything, she speeds up. So I ask the question I most dread asking. "Will she be okay?"

Marilee hesitates, just long enough that I know she's remembering the exact same image I am. A nine-year-old, her hair drooping down in a messy ponytail, walking around Graceland in the middle of the night saying, "My daddy's dead, my daddy's dead." Saying it over and over until somebody finally had the presence of mind to take her downstairs and make her a milkshake.

"Not for a while," Marilee finally says, pulling the visor even lower. Because the sun is relentless and brutal, and it seems like maybe we're driving straight into the hottest day God ever made. "But eventually, yes. Yes she will."

From the back, David stirs, makes a sound more animal than human.

"So we'll take the next exit," Marilee says. "The first one that has anything."

I look in the backseat and nod. We don't have a choice.

Within a mile we see a sign for a Rest-A-While Inn and pull off. It may have had a sign on the interstate, but as it turns out, the hotel isn't particularly close to the interstate. We drive three or four miles through pure country until we come up on it, perched in the middle of a cracked parking lot. I would say this is the ragged side of Tupelo, but for all I know, every side of Tupelo is the ragged side.

Marilee pulls in and looks at me. I still have sixty-four dollars in the palm of my hand.

"You better get the room," she says.

"Why me?"

"You think we all need to parade in there? A black woman and a white woman and a half-dead, foaming-at-the-mouth white man, and we all three of us pull up in a fifty-thousand-dollar car at a no-tell motel at seven in the morning with a couple of wadded-up twenties in our hands, and tell them we're looking to take a room? You think that's not going to get the desk clerk calling the cops?"

She's got a point. After his brief spasm of consciousness, that singular growl, David has turned to his other side and appears to be sliding back into hibernation. So I get out, cash in hand and praying they don't ask for any kind of identification, and walk up to the scarred wooden door.

Welcome, it says, and a bell chimes as I walk into an empty room. Every surface is dotted with African violets. They're the last things I expected to see. They remind me of my mother and I think, once again, how disappointed she is going to be in me if I ever make it back to Beaufort. Her daughter who took off claiming she was going to be a star and who is now coming back nothing more than pregnant and broke.

There's a TV behind the counter, black-and-white and

turned to a Memphis station. TRAGEDY AT GRACELAND says the banner underneath the picture.

I raise my palm and start to ding the little dinger to try to pull somebody up from the vinyl curtain, and that's when I see her. She's huddled in a folding lawn chair behind the desk, staring at the TV screen with such intensity that she hasn't even noticed my presence. When I say, "Excuse me," she jumps.

Her hands are full of toilet paper and there's a roll beside her on the floor. She's been crying. Crying for hours, no doubt, all alone in that folding lawn chair, unable to look away from the TV. She stares at me as if she's having trouble focusing, as if she's a person emerging from a movie theater in broad daylight or just waking up from a dream.

"Did you hear?" she says. She wipes tears and snot and hair from her face with a long, limp strand of the toilet paper.

"Hear what?" I say weakly. Of course we knew that the news about Elvis would get out, but I don't think that until that very moment it had occurred to me that the news about Elvis would be the only news on TV. That the whole world would come still, just for a moment. Would pause on its axis and debate turning back the other way.

She shuffles out from behind the counter. She is a heavy woman, her feet shoved deep in her slippers and turning out to each side, like a ballerina's or a penguin's. Middle-aged, plain, and life has beaten her down in a hundred more ways than I could even begin to list. I've seen this woman, or plenty just like her, at every stop we made on every tour. This woman is willing to pay two weeks of hard-earned wages just to sit a few rows closer, just to have a chance of catching his scarf. Marilee and the others and I would stand back, in our safe place at the rear of the stage, and smirk at these women. Somebody was going to have a heart attack one night, that's what we always said. Go belly up halfway through the concert, die of pure bliss at the foot of the stage with Elvis's silk scarf in her hand.

Only now this particular woman is standing in front of me and she doesn't seem ridiculous at all.

She extends her pudgy arms toward me in a hug. "What are we going to do?" she asks, her voice a whisper. "What are we going to do without him?" Through the big glass window over her shoulder, I can see Marilee struggling to get David out of the backseat. He is sagging, going limp in her arms like a war protestor, and she looks toward the door in desperation, wondering what's taking me so long.

"I don't know," I whisper back to the woman. "I don't think any of us are ever going to be right again."

CORY

The receptionist is not pleased to see me. Even in my funeral dress and wearing the lipstick I fished out of my backpack, she still finds me unfit to stand within the walls of the Pinnacle Church. The lobby is understated, tasteful. It feels more like a hotel. All around us slender, blond women are walking back and forth in their little high heels. Their hair has been professionally blown out and their jackets are bright jewel colors.

"Do you have an appointment?" the receptionist asks, even though we both know I don't. From the skeptical look on her face, I can tell that she's afraid I'm a journalist. Journalists, I gathered in my quick flurry of research on Dirk's iPhone, have not been friends of the Pinnacle Church.

"Not exactly," I say. "But I think Mr. Beth might want to see me."

"Pastor."

"Pastor Beth. Could you just tell him that Honey Berry's daughter is here?"

She frowns. Mama's cartoon of a name has put her off, and the whole thing might've ended before it began if Dirk hadn't stepped forward at precisely that minute, coming up to the desk to stand beside me. He had insisted on escorting me in, even though we can't leave Lucy alone in the car for long. When we passed a bank on the way in, it showed ninety-two degrees, and yet Dirk had seemed to sense, better than I had, that I might need a man in uniform to give me an air of legitimacy.

The only trouble is, as he stepped forward, so did the bouncer for Pinnacle Church. They look almost identical, their khaki shirts straining across their stomachs, their expressions sour, and I have no idea who trumps whom in this situation— whether a Graceland security guard outranks a Pinnacle Church security guard, or what Dirk plans to do if they turn us away. For somebody who was sent here to apprehend me, he has turned from enemy to ally pretty fast.

"I believe the pastor was a friend of my mother's," I say again to the woman behind the desk. Like mine, her eyes are flicking back and forth between Dirk and her own hired muscle and, also like me, she seems to have no desire to find out what'll happen if these two start wailing on each other. "Tell him my name is Cory Beth Ainsworth and my mama was Honey Berry."

"Sit down," she says. "Someone will be right with you."

I nod at Dirk, who nods at the other cop, who nods at the receptionist, who nods at me. Dirk heads back out to Lucy and I move over to a group of chairs. Nice chairs. Solid, covered in a pastel plaid, and the flowers on the table before me are real, not silk or plastic. The rug beneath my feet is soft and deep and there's a sort of water fountain babbling away in the corner.

They do things right at Pinnacle, at least if the lobby is any indication. But there's also a portrait of David Beth hanging just across from me and I study it, looking for my face in his. I don't see it, which isn't surprising. There's no room for David Beth in my features, or any other man either. Everyone in Beaufort always said that I looked like Mama had spit me out whole.

"Miss Ainsworth?"

The voice doesn't boom. It doesn't threaten or frighten. Whatever kind of preacher David Beth has become, it isn't that kind. His voice is civilized and low pitched. Persuasive. Maybe some diction coach taught him how to sound so pleasant when his radio show first caught on, or who knows, maybe he always had it. The pastor's bio on Dirk's iPhone said he "hailed from California," and people from California often have this sort of nowhere-in-particular kind of voice.

He is standing before me, his arms spread. Evidently he thinks I'm going to stand up and hug him.

This is not how I thought this would happen. I suspected that I'd be granted entrance the minute I said my mama's open-sesame name, but I imagined being ushered in through some back door, with the whiff of shame trailing down the hall behind me. There'd be whispering. Shadows. For if the daughter of a dead lover shows up nearly forty years after the fact, she's generally come for only one reason. And not the sort a megachurch preacher would welcome.

But here David Beth is, standing before me, his arms open, beaming broadly like he's witnessing the second coming.

"I was grieved to hear of your mother's passing," he says as I stand and give him one of those awkward side-to-side hugs. We don't fit well. Our hipbones clank and I knock his chin with the top of my head.

"You know she's dead?" I whisper. I try to study him out of the corner of my eye, but the man in the flesh gives no more clues than the man in his portrait. Just as his voice is both friendly and formless, so is his face.

"I knew she was very ill," he says. "When we talked, I had the sense it was close to the end."

"Talked?"

"On the telephone. She called me . . . I guess it's been a year."

"And were you surprised to hear from her? Surprised that she just popped back in from nowhere after all that time?"

He shifts his weight, turns more squarely toward me, although he doesn't step back like a normal person would. We are still standing unnaturally close and he knows how to make and hold eye contact, this man. He knows how to stand with his legs grounded beneath him and put a hand on each side of a person's shoulders and look them right in the face without flinching, and as he does all these things to me, a chill runs down my back. Radio is too small to hold David Beth, at least for long. He has charisma and he knows it. TV is next. Politics after that. There's something Bill Clinton–like about him. The brilliant good old boy. Sexy but sincere. This man could go far.

"Honey said she had some loose ends to tie up," David says. "Some forgiveness that she both sought and sought to grant." He smiles suddenly, the professional solemnity giving away to an even more carefully rehearsed joy. "And she predicted that you might be coming."

"Did you know I existed? Not just when Mama called you from her deathbed but way back when, before I was born? Did she tell you she was pregnant?"

"Yes. She informed me of such on the day that we left Graceland."

She informed him of such. That's a damn cold way of putting it.

But yet at the same time I have to admire the guy's style, for during this whole strange little conversation, I haven't once dropped my voice. I'm not shouting, but I'm not whispering either, and this lobby is asses-to-elbows full of people. The security guard and some sort of camera crew, setting up for God knows what, and all those thin blond women going clickety-clack back and forth across the marble floor. But he does not flinch or try to shush me. He does not even step away. When one of us finally breaks this strange dance, it's me.

"Let us talk in private," he says, and it seems as if he is offering the privacy for my sake, not his. I'm shaking but he has an eerie sort of calm, and I remember that the Wikipedia article on Dirk's phone said that Pinnacle is a church not only without denomination, but without any clear political affiliation as well. He is neither red nor blue, this man who stands before me. Neither old school or new age. He quotes Jesus and Buddha and Gandhi and Oprah and he is Jewish by birth and yet he somehow gets away with it all, even here in the middle of the Bible Belt.

"So she predicted I might be coming?"

"Mothers know their daughters, I suppose," he says, and then he smiles, showing off the best that Mississippi cosmetic dentistry has to offer. "But, as I said, if you'd like to follow me, we can continue this conversation in my office."

"Thank you, Mr. Beth," I say. I say it weakly, aware I'm already halfway down some sort of slippery slope, the same one my mother slid down so long ago. For even in the middle of everything I've heard about him, even in the middle of his own confession that he knew Honey was pregnant and let her go anyway, even though that means he knew I existed and has done butt-nothing about it for thirty-seven years . . . there's something charming in this man. Something that makes me want to put my head on his shoulder here and now, even though I know I wouldn't be the first woman he's talked right out of her truth, and the odds are I won't be the last. "Or should I call you David?"

"You can call me Pastor," he says. "Everyone does."

"They left me lying there in the hotel bed," he says. We are sitting on a couch now, on opposite ends and facing each other. Even though his private office has a large and intimidating desk, he chooses to position himself beside me rather than stepping behind it. It's part of his game, I suppose. A way of saying *I own everything within sight and I could intimidate you, if I wanted to. But I don't want to. Instead, I will sit beside you on this couch, both of us turned with our legs half drawn beneath us. Equals. Friends.*

He chuckles. "They left me unconscious and fully dressed, right down to my shoes, although somebody had the mercy to leave a cup of water and an open Bible on the nightstand. It was probably the work of your mother. I was strung out. We all were."

"Because Elvis died."

He places his index fingers together and brings them to his chin. Like this is some game of charades and he's trying to make me say *philosopher*. Come to think of it, he'd struck pretty much the same pose in the portrait in the lobby. "I think anyone who'd spent much time with the man knew his days were numbered. We'd all seen him in bad shape, not just once, but a hundred times. But we had also seen him come roaring back a hundred times. It's an odd thing, isn't it? How you can know on one level that a tragedy is inevitable and yet still be surprised when it finally happens?"

I nod, and he goes sailing on.

"Some people say it was the drugs that killed him," David continues. "And some people deny they had anything to do with his death. But I was there, Miss Ainsworth, and believe me when I say that there's no doubt. Elvis died of an overdose."

I start to speak, but once again it would seem my contributions aren't necessary to keep the conversation going. This man asks questions, but he doesn't expect anyone else to answer, or venture an opinion of their own. It's a preacher trait. My grandfather had it too. Maybe that's why Honey fell for him so hard. No girl can resist a man who reminds her of her daddy.

"He mixed up quite a cocktail on the last night," David says. "A combination of uppers and downers, a heaping handful of pills. I remember looking down in the palm of his hand and thinking they looked like candy. Like M&M's, and we washed them down with Jack Daniel's, Elvis and I."

"So you were with him," I finally manage to wedge in. "Right before he died?"

"Perhaps I was the last person who saw Elvis alive," David says. "Except for Ginger, the particular young lady he was with at the time. From what I understand from the newspaper accounts, he woke her up when he got out of bed to go to the bathroom and she asked if he was okay. Something trifling like that. But I was the last person who really talked to him, who had a genuine conversation."

"You know that for sure?"

He smiles. "Who can say anything for sure? But I like to think so. The important thing is that Elvis was in a serious mood that night. He wanted to discuss philosophy. The nature of the divine, to be precise. He believed each human soul was put on the earth for a very specific purpose; that we all had been entrusted with a holy task that we were to carry out during our lifetimes. And that is what we discussed, until the wee hours of the morning. We had that sort of relationship, Elvis and I."

He's a self-satisfied bastard, I'll give him that, but I'm trying to get the sequence straight in my head. "So Elvis went to the dentist with Mama and Marilee, and when he got back to Graceland the two of you washed a handful of drugs down with Jim Beam and you talked about God. Then he went to bed with Ginger, and at some point early in the morning he got up and went to the bathroom and he died."

He nods. "It was Jack Daniel's we drank instead of Jim Beam, but otherwise, yes, that's exactly what happened."

"If you knew it was such a dangerous dose, why did you take it?"

He presses his fingertips together again and I find myself staring at them. Odd fingers. The second one is longer than the third. "I have spent a lifetime, Miss Ainsworth, asking myself precisely that question. It was such a large handful of pills and I gobbled them so willingly, not even asking what they were. I was a young man, twenty-seven, with everything in the world to live for. I certainly wasn't inviting death, not even on a subconscious level. And yet I took this ridiculous dose, passed from his palm to mine like a communion wafer, followed with a swig of dark brown southern poison, which I once again quite willingly swilled, straight from the bottle. Despite a lifetime of contemplation I've never been able to understand exactly why. Perhaps it's as simple as the fact we were all trained to do whatever Elvis did. I suspect your mother told you that much, that his every whim fell upon us like an edict from on high. Or perhaps on some level I knew a deeper calling was awaiting me somewhere."

He shrugs. "I only know," he says, "that Elvis and I took the pills, drank the bourbon, and spent the next few hours talking of God."

I sort of believe him. It's odd, but no odder than any of the other stories about what happened at Graceland on that final night. I know that the book Elvis was reading when he died, the book he took with him to the toilet where he would spend his last earthly minutes, was titled *The Scientific Search for the Face of Jesus.*

"It seems significant that you did exactly the same batch of drugs as Elvis," I say. "And yet he died and you lived."

"Yes," David says with sudden enthusiasm, and his hands fly out in an elegant gesture. Someone has coached him for television. Or maybe it's the old karate teacher in him. He knows how to make every move count. "Of the two of us, I was the one who was spared, and that is precisely the fulcrum on which it all tilts. I have told this story to so many people through the years, Miss Ainsworth, but somehow they have almost all managed to miss this key idea. You are very much like your mother. I saw her in your face, of course, the minute we met, but now I see her in your mind. For when I woke up in that dreadful little hotel where Honey and Marilee left me, this was the first thought that seized me. That Elvis and I had partaken of the same communion, that we had been led to exactly the same abyss, and yet he tumbled into it but I did not. Why do you guess that might be?"

It's startling to have this man who both asks and answers his own questions suddenly show so much interest in my opinion. I'm startled right into silence for a second and my first impulse is to point out the obvious: that Elvis was already aging and sick, already on the lip of that abyss, and so of course he'd fallen, while the younger, stronger David had managed to hang on. That's an honest answer and probably the closest we have to the right one. But something tells me that I'll get farther down the road with flattery—flattery of the most outrageous cosmic kind. So I say, "Because Elvis was right in saying that each man was put on earth for a reason, chosen for a specific purpose? God needed you to remain on earth for some special work?"

"Precisely," says David, dropping his hands and leaning back into the cushions. "That is the first thought that occurred to me when my eyes fluttered open in that awful little hotel. That Elvis was dead and I was alive, and you know what they say?"

"The King is dead. Long live the King."

"Precisely," he says again. He thinks I'm stupid. He likes me.

He likes stupid people better than any other kind. He's nothing but a puffed-up fraud and yet I know he's also telling me the truth. Or at least more of the truth than anyone else has ever managed to tell me, both since I've left Beaufort and before.

"It must have been a burden," I say. "To have been the one who lived when the other one died."

"You are so very perceptive," he says with a shake of his head. This is a strange chess match, me sitting here on a couch across from this man who might be my father, each of us trying to out-flatter and out-bullshit the other. "For 'burden' is just the right word, and that's why I went on a bender, I'm afraid. When I woke up and everyone around me was running back and forth, screaming that Elvis had died in the night, the first thing I did was not rush to his aid but take even more pills. I wanted to go back to sleep. Perhaps a part of me truly did want to die. But your mother and Marilee picked me up and they threw me in the back of the car and I suppose I shall forever owe them for that decision. They could have left me there for the police to find. They could have left it all to come down upon my head, for Elvis was hardly dead an hour before the witch hunt started brewing. The press . . ."

He gives a delicate little shudder. "Everyone was looking for someone to blame and it could so easily have been me. I might have had to face the world known only as the man who had given a fatal dose of drugs to Elvis Presley. Can you imagine what my life would have been like then?"

He doesn't expect an answer, so I don't bother giving him one. Instead, I look around the room. It's well done, just like the lobby. At the back of the office there are two open doors.

Through one I can see a bedroom, and through the other one a bath. He spends most nights here. He lives where he works. He is a man who, as they say, is "married to his calling."

"And so I woke up in a Rest-A-While Inn on the outskirts of Tupelo," he continues when it's obvious I have nothing to say. "I'd pissed myself more than once and it dried on my pants. I'd thrown up and it had dried on my shirt. The TV was turned to sports but I reached for the remote and started turning the channels." He smiles, and for a moment looks young and impish, like the boy my mama must have loved. "But wouldn't you know it? Elvis was dead on every damn one of them. And then I found the news channel and saw the date and realized I'd been asleep for three days. Three solid days. It didn't seem possible. But my mouth was dry as a desert, so I drank the water your mother had most kindly left me and then I got up and stumbled to the bathroom and tried to clean myself as best as I could. It was useless. And then I sat there on the edge of the bed with the remote in my hand and I started surfing the channels to see what the world knew.

"The tabloids were closer to the truth than anybody. Even now when I'm walking through a Walmart and I see a *Star* magazine or a *National Enquirer* saying that aliens invaded North Dakota I stop and think, 'Who knows, perhaps they're right.' Because the honorable news sources were falling all over themselves to say that drugs were not a factor in Elvis's death, and those cheap pickup newspapers were speculating on exactly what drugs he'd used. One or two of them came quite close to getting it right." He ducks his chin and smiles at me again. "You're not going to believe what I'm going to tell you next."

"Don't be so sure. I'm a very gullible girl. Try me."

He laughs, throwing his head back. "I detect a willing spirit in you, underneath all that smart talk and cynicism, so I'll risk the truth. Honesty is such a slippery thing, is it not?"

"Sometimes it's easier to tell the truth to strangers than to the people we know."

"Indeed it is. But I have the funny feeling I do know you, even though we've just met."

Because I'm your daughter, you asshole, I think, but I say, "Perhaps we met in a previous lifetime."

He nods. "Perhaps so, but to return to the story at hand, let me say that the more I regained consciousness on that strange, long-ago day, the more I sensed that the spirit of Elvis had come inside of me sometime during that lost time in which I had slept." He puts a hand on his heart. "I felt him. I knew that I had his strength and mine too, and I came through the grace of God to understand that when there are two spirits and one departs, that the person who is left behind has somehow double the power, as if both souls exist inside one body . . ."

"Like when Elvis lived and his twin brother died."

This flummoxes him. But only for a moment. "Who can say? Perhaps Jesse's sacrifice was what made Elvis Elvis, perhaps their two spirits merged and became stronger than either one of them could have managed on his own. Let me tell you what life has taught me, Miss Ainsworth: People don't become special just by accident. It isn't some throw of the genetic dice. They are special for a reason. And if his brother's death was what gave Elvis his extraordinary talent and charisma, can't you see how the power would be even stronger within me? Because

I hadn't just incorporated the soul of a newborn baby, I'd taken on the gifts of Elvis Presley himself. Do you understand what I am telling you?"

"That there are aliens in North Dakota?"

I wait for him to get angry, but he doesn't. He just smiles at me, and the smile is a little sad. Someone else has recently looked at me just like that, but in the moment I can't remember who. I'm just thinking that this man before me went on a three-day bender in a Rest-A-While Inn and somehow concluded that it was the equivalent of Christ rising from the tomb.

"I hurt for you," he says. "Because you are one of those who must see to believe."

"Actually, I'm one of those who has trouble believing even after I've seen."

"But you do understand what I'm saying to you."

"Yeah. You're telling me you think you're as big as Elvis."

"Oh, my dear child," he says. "I am much bigger than Elvis."

I ask him if I can freshen up, that stupid phrase. As I expected, he points me toward his private bathroom and I go inside, shut the door, and stand for a minute in the darkness, trying to pull myself together. When I finally flip on the light I see the bathroom is huge. Nearly as big as my trailer, bigger than the shotgun house from this morning, with mirrors on every wall. It has one of those showers that takes up half the room and has multiple showerheads and a bench where you can sit and steam yourself. I start there.

There's a disposable razor resting among the bottles of

Aveda bath products, and this is surprising on two levels. First of all, Pastor Beth seems like the sort of guy who'd order one of those fancy vintage razors online, not pick up a pack of disposables in Walgreens, and second, most men don't shave in the shower. I stand flat-footed on the marble, the thin plastic razor in my hand. Is there a woman somewhere who also uses this bathroom? Maybe even another man? I can't see the man known as Pastor bringing some paramour here, but then again, stranger things have happened and nobody batted an eye when he escorted me into his private rooms and then closed the door, even calling out that we were not to be disturbed. There's a snip of hair between the blades, thick and black, much like the hair on David Beth's head, so maybe he shaves his back or his chest or something. Hell, I don't know.

I only know I have exhibit A. I step from the shower and begin to run water in the sink to muffle the sounds. I pull open all the drawers until I find the rest of the pack of disposable razors, then pull out one and replace it in the shower. There's an extra toothbrush too, still resting in its box, and I break it out and swap it for the one resting in a cup beside the sink. The new toothbrush is a different color, which is unfortunate, and I have no idea if David Beth is the kind of man who notices these things. But I've come too far to back out now, so I cut off the running water and check the trash can for discarded Kleenex or dental floss.

All I come up with is a Q-tip. But I have the toothbrush and the razor too, and I wrap all three in toilet paper and zip them into the side pocket of my backpack, then step back into the pastor's study.

He's seated behind the desk now. It's a signal. We are moving from the friendly, conversational, shooting-the-breeze part of this interview to the serious part. The money part.

He waves for me to sit across from him.

"How did you find me?" he asks.

"You don't exactly keep a low profile. I counted eleven billboards with your face on them in a ten-mile stretch."

"Of course," he says. "I misstated my question. I shouldn't have asked how you found me, I should have asked how you knew I was the one you should be looking for."

"Marilee Jones gave me your name. I spent the last two days with her in Fairhope."

"Marilee. I should have known. How is she?"

"Strong and fine and reasonably happy. At least that's how she seemed to me."

"Not surprising. A hurricane couldn't knock down Marilee."

"I went through Macon too. Saw Philip Cory."

"And should that name mean anything in particular?" His expression wavers for just a second before immediately returning to his megawatt smile. "Ah yes, I think I see. And that is so like your mother. She named you Cory Beth, the last names of the two men who might be responsible. Hedged her bets a bit. I hope you don't judge her for that, the fact she really couldn't say for sure. The times were so different then."

"It's weird. Weird that you all stayed exactly where she left you and weird she was able to find you, after all this time. How do you think she did?"

He shrugs. "Facebook. What else? She said you were the one who set her up with an account."

"I did. To help her pass the time in hospice." I remember how she took to it, spending far more hours on that stupid laptop than I ever would have guessed and how one day when I walked in, she'd looked up at me and said, "A computer is a time machine, isn't it?"

David is looking at me quizzically, his head dropped to one side. "The other man . . ."

"Philip Cory."

"You say you stopped to see him too? What was he like?"

"He gave me four hundred dollars."

"An odd amount." He presses his hands together again in that childish pose. Here's the church and here's the steeple. "It seems too much to give a stranger and too little to give a daughter."

"I thought so too."

"But then again, you're a grown woman. How old are you, exactly?"

"Thirty-seven."

"Yes, of course. Do you have children of your own?"

I shake my head. "Not a husband or kids or even a real job. I'm a musician."

He nods thoughtfully. "Of course, I don't have to tell you that since you're thirty-seven, there's no need for parental support. No need for college. But don't worry. I wouldn't leave you utterly high and dry. There are discretionary funds in the budget for things like this."

Things like this? I'm a "thing like this"? Maybe Pastor Beth really is a miracle worker, because he's certainly done the impossible here. In the five minutes since I emerged from the

bathroom, he's got me praying that I'm the daughter of a Georgia politician.

Now he's pulling a checkbook from a drawer, clicking a
pen. I have a sudden vision that he's going to write me a check
for $401. Just enough to beat Philip Cory, because he's the sort
of man who has to beat everybody, and also because he likes the
idea of an odd amount. Enough to guarantee I'll thank him and
move on, but not enough to imply culpability.

"Don't you have the slightest curiosity?" I ask him, and I'm
ashamed to say my voice breaks on the word *curiosity*, almost
like I'm getting ready to cry. "Any curiosity at all as to whether
or not it's true and I'm your daughter?"

"But of course you are my daughter. Anyone who comes
through these doors seeking help is my son or daughter."

"Give me a fucking break. You know I'm talking about being
your blood daughter." I look at him there, his pen hovering over
the checkbook, frowning like he's try to do some sort of spiritual
math, and I know a better woman would stand up and tell him
where to stick that checkbook and flounce out the door. That's
what my mama would've done. In fact, that's probably exactly
what she did do, thirty-eight years ago. She just walked out on
this guy empty-handed and without looking back, even though
she was younger and more scared and in even worse shape than
I am now.

"Mama told you she was pregnant that last night at
Graceland, didn't she?" I say. "That's probably why you did
those drugs with Elvis. You know you were responsible and you
didn't want to face it. And when you woke up in that hotel room
all those years ago, you knew good and well you had a child on

the way. But you never called her once, in all those years. Never tried to find out if she'd had the baby and if it was healthy. Whether I was a boy or a girl."

"You must understand . . ."

"I understand just fine."

"I'm not sure you do. I had a destiny. I knew it. And anything that distracted me from that destiny was against the will of God."

"Anything like Mama and me."

"I'm not suggesting that you and your mother were against the will of God. Of course not. But it was not my calling to move to some small town in South Carolina and run a karate school while Honey taught piano and the two of us tried to eke out some meager living on the marsh. It wouldn't have been fair to either me or her, and it certainly wouldn't have been fair to the child in question. Raising you was not the task God put me on this earth to do, and I think you're beginning to see that, even though the look on your face in this particular moment, if I might say so, is very unpleasant. It's a shame it isn't Wednesday or Sunday, when we have our regular services. If you could observe my work in the pulpit, it would all be clear to you."

"You think you're too good to be a daddy."

"It has nothing to do with you. It's just that fatherhood is for ordinary men."

He rips the check out of the checkbook and hands it to me. I'm ashamed to tell you that I take it and that I look at the amount. A thousand dollars, pure and simple, no questions asked, and precious few answered.

I hand him back the check. "I need cash."

"I assure you a Pinnacle Church check won't bounce."

"You're probably right, but I don't have a bank account. At least not out here."

He slides open a drawer. "I may not be able to come up with a thousand in cash."

I nod. I don't trust my voice.

He digs around. Opens one box and then another. Winces at some point, although I'm not sure why. And finally comes up with $320. He hands it to me along with the check and says "Keep it all. You'll find your way home eventually."

Will I? I stand up, fold the check and the cash, and stick the whole mess into my pocket, then heft up my backpack, with this man's saliva and hair and earwax tucked inside of it.

"It's kind of ironic you should end up a Mississippi preacher," I say as I turn toward the door. "Considering you were born a Jew."

"I'm still a Jew," he says, "at least in a cultural sense."

"But you're a Christian and a Buddhist and a Rastafarian too."

He smiles. "I suppose I am, and don't forget the Hindus. That's why your question about blood—while understandable under the circumstances—ultimately doesn't matter. We are not our biology. We are all more than where we were born, and whatever particular sperm and egg randomly happened to unite. Remember this, my child, even if you choose to ignore everything else I've told you. In the end, people are whatever they choose to be."

HONEY

We can't just leave him here."

Marilee looks like she's going to lean back and slap me. "Of course we can. Don't go soft on me, not now. Why did you think we were giving up better than half our money to get him into this hotel if we weren't going to leave him here?"

"Maybe we can just let him sleep it off. We can't let him wake up alone with no car or money."

Marilee purses her lips. "We promised Fred we'd get him out of Memphis and we got him out of Memphis."

"He's sick."

"If he was going to die, he'd have died before now."

"How can you be so sure?"

"Because he took the same thing Elvis took, and it killed Elvis fast. And if Jesus ever stops to ask me my opinion of the last twenty-four hours, I'll look him right in the eye and tell him he took the wrong one home to heaven and left the wrong one in this sorry-ass bed, and I won't even blink when I say it."

I look at David, lying flat as a corpse with the cheap flowered bedspread pulled over him. We should try to get his clothes off. At least take off his shoes.

"I'm going to get him a bucket of ice," I say. "And a sandwich. So he'll have something to eat when he wakes up."

"Suit yourself," Marilee snaps. She pulls the Gideon's Bible out of the drawer of the bedside table and sits down in the room's single chair. I take the plastic ice bucket in my hand and step out the door onto the sidewalk. I look first one way and then the next, but I don't see an ice machine. It's probably in the lobby, along with that wailing woman and her African violets and every TV channel in the world all proclaiming the death of Elvis, and I don't think I can face going back in there again. And as for a sandwich . . . I look up and down the road in both directions, but I don't see a fast food place or even a service station. How on earth does this hotel survive, here on the outskirts of nowhere?

"Okay, so maybe not a sandwich and maybe not ice," I tell Marilee, coming back into the room. She's reading what looks like the tail end of the book, somewhere back in Revelations, probably looking to see how many signs of the end of the world we've amassed so far. "Maybe I'll just leave him a cup of water. And let's turn the TV to something nice for when he wakes up."

She stands with a sigh, plopping the Bible onto the bedside table and picking up the remote. I go into the sad little bathroom and fill a plastic cup with water, and when I come back she has the TV turned to golf.

"It's the only station that wasn't talking about Elvis," she says. "Now, enough. We gotta get going."

At the doorway I pause. I think about looking back, but I don't. *This is the last time you'll see him,* says that voice in my head. The one that seems to talk to me even when I wish that it wouldn't.

> *Here in Tupelo*
> *Our story ends and begins*
> *Middle still to come.*

No good. I'm trying to say something, but that isn't it. I try again.

> *Good-bye to this man*
> *Father of my unborn child*
> *Too bad he's out cold.*

Even worse. Marilee is walking across the parking lot toward the Blackhawk. She glances back. "What are you doing?"

"Making up a haiku."

"Haiku your ass over here," she growls, climbing into the driver's side without asking.

I get in. Pull the seat belt around me, and we begin to back out.

"It might be Philip Cory's," she tells me. "Just as easy could be."

"I know."

"And you'll find your way back. Eventually."

Back from what? I think, but I don't ask the question out loud. I know Marilee is trying to buck me up, but I can't face this conversation. Not now, when we're driving away from the motel where I'm leaving the first man I ever loved. David is trash. I know that and I don't need Marilee pointing it out, regular as a clock, every mile from here to Fairhope. He was trash, but I loved him, and as it turns out, leaving a pile of trash in a Tupelo motel hurts just as much as bidding farewell to a prince.

I lay my head back against the red leather seats. They're soft. I've always loved this car. It was always my favorite, of all the cars Elvis drove, and I think it was because of this leather. I rub my cheek against the smoothness.

"There's one more thing to do," Marilee says. "Before we leave Tupelo."

I glance over at her. "And what's that?"

"I'm taking you to see the baby's grave."

CORY

"You know what that preacher had the balls to say to me? He said he was bigger than Elvis."

Dirk grabs his chest and staggers around like he's been shot. "He did not."

"Oh, but he did. I don't know if there's any point in going to Express Paternity after all. I looked at his hands while he was talking and they . . . they looked just like mine."

To illustrate, I hold my hands out. I show him my abnormal index finger, nearly as long as my fuck-you finger, and the only thing on my body that doesn't look like my mama. The only thing on my body that looks exactly like David Beth.

We're walking Lucy around the well-manicured grounds of the Pinnacle Church. He's already crapped three times. The first one, I picked up with a Kleenex from my backpack and threw in a trash can. The second one, I kicked pine straw over. The third one I just ignored.

"But you got the evidence," Dirk says.

"I got a razor and a toothbrush and a Q-tip."

"And we have the blood from the dentist," he says, turning the dog slow and easy back toward the car. "I don't reckon you thought to get anything from that Philip guy in Georgia."

I shake my head. A church bell rings from somewhere, even though Pinnacle doesn't seem to have a steeple. It's four o'clock. Whatever we're going to do, we need to get going.

"You may as well take what you've got to Express Paternity," Dirk says, as if the chimes gave him the same thought. "They say it takes three hours, but you can call them tomorrow and see what they find. Or hell, maybe they run extended hours, who can say. Do you want to see Jesse's grave?"

"I didn't think there was anything to see."

He shrugs. "You can find it if you're know where to look. It's on the east side of town, a little place called Priceville Cemetery, and there's a marker that reads 1935–1935."

"Is it grand?"

"Grand? No. Not at all. It's small." He brightens. "But there's a marker in Jesse's honor at Graceland, where Elvis is buried with his parents, out in the Meditation Garden, and that, my friend, is absolutely glorious. Wait until you see it. You'll fall to your knees."

"But they never moved the baby."

"No. Not the actual body."

"That's sad. Thinking of him lying there all by himself, his little baby skeleton curved like a cat."

Dirk opens the door of the Blackhawk and Lucy jumps right in.

"We got no way of knowing if he's curved like a cat," he

says. "But what we do know is that we've got less than an hour to get you to the DNA testing place and then I gotta get back to Graceland."

"You're going back without me? That shows a lot of trust."

"I've been thinking I need to go in first and smooth the way with Pop. Get him used to the idea of who you are and what you deserve. Because you deserve something. Something good. Not just gas money and a kick in the ass."

We're backing out. I don't ask him where he's going because he seems to know. A quick stop at Express Paternity, a circle through the Walmart to get his Graceland cop car. Then he will drive back to Memphis and I will not be far behind him. According to Dirk's phone, there's a La Quinta on the south side of Memphis, not more than three miles from the gates of Graceland, and that's where Lucy and I will spend the night.

"You're a decent man," I say to Dirk as we roll out of the gates of Pinnacle and turn back toward the highway.

"So's my daddy, at least once you dig a little. Remember that tomorrow when he starts to give you shit. Because he will."

I nod. "Marilee said to make him pay me for the car. But I think I have something even more valuable." I wait for a stoplight and then I push the eight-track into the slot and Dirk listens. He hits repeat and listens to it again, and then again. It's only twenty seconds of sound, maybe not even that much, but it's my future and he and I both know it.

"Elvis wrote that piece of song?"

"Elvis and Marilee and my mama."

"Memphis is full of recording studios."

"So I've heard."

"And Sirius has an all-Elvis station. It broadcasts from the grounds of Graceland."

"I know."

"I'm saying this, because . . . What you've got there is gold, girl."

We ride for a few minutes in silence. Dirk navigates the streets of Tupelo like a pro and within minutes we pull up in the parking lot of Express Paternity. It's nothing fancy. Just a strip center medical front, the sort of place where you go if you manage to get yourself knocked up in Tupelo, Mississippi, and you don't know how or why.

"You got a voice," he says. "I heard you singing to the dog in the church parking lot when we were waiting for him to take a crap."

"Thank you."

"You sing harmony like your mama?"

I shake my head. "She tried to teach me, but I never got the knack. It may have been the biggest exasperation of her life. She kept me in the church choir till I turned eighteen, and every long car trip we ever took, she'd be on me again, determined she was going to teach me how to pick apart a chord and hear every individual note. Finally we both had to admit it. That maybe I was born to be a solo act."

"It's not such a bad thing, is it? To be the one with the star voice?"

"Depends on who you ask."

He rolls down the window. It's a sign that he and the dog will wait here in the car. Because I need to take my sack o' DNA into Express Paternity and give them my own blood as well. I look at the clock, even though I know it's broken, and then at Dirk's watch. I've got twenty minutes.

"Where you reckon you got that star voice?" he asks idly. "Who gave it to you?"

Just a few days ago I would've told you Elvis gave it to me, I thought. But that was four days and a thousand miles ago.

"Nobody," I say. "I gave it to myself."

An hour later, I'm on my own again, with just one more stop to make in Tupelo. I drive up and down Highway 45 until I find a roadside stand. Probably not the right roadside stand, not the same one where Mama and Marilee stopped, but close enough.

I ask them for tupelo honey.

The guy working the place is a talker. He starts telling me how tupelo honey isn't really from the town of Tupelo, despite what everybody thinks. They harvest it somewhere in the panhandle of Florida, from some magical swamp, and it is terribly special stuff. He tells me how they prime the hives for months, then carry them down the river in rowboats and put them in the tupelo trees, which bloom for only a few weeks a year. It's a dicey business. The swamp, the gators, rowing those hives down in the boats, the short growing season. That's why the honey is so expensive. It is the result of many things that could have gone wrong but that have somehow managed to collectively go right.

He hands me a jar. A small jar, but the tag says eighteen dollars, and I start to tell him my mama bought a jar of honey at this very stand—or at least one like it—for less than two dollars, but that was such a long ago that it hardly matters. At his insistence, I raise the jar up to the sunlight and study the color. It's a light amber gold, with just the slightest touch of green.

"Its rarity is what makes it so expensive," he says. "Its rarity and its purity."

There's a billboard just past this little roadside stand. I didn't see it when I pulled in, but I see it now as I raise the jar to the setting sun. Another one of David Beth, and he's stretching out a hand in invitation. It's a normal-looking hand, not like his or mine. The index finger is the right length and he's staring in a way that makes it seem like he's looking just at you. Come to the Father, the billboard says, and I look down at the Band-Aid in the crook of my elbow.

I laugh, which the guy working the roadside stand seems to take as a laugh of disbelief as to the value of tupelo honey. One honeybee only produces one-tenth of a teaspoon of nectar in its lifetime, he hastens to explain, and it takes two million tupelo tree flowers to produce one pound of honey. He goes on and on like this for some time. He's a born salesman, wasting his talent at this little produce stand by Highway 45, or maybe it's my sustained silence that upsets him, because I can't seem to think of anything to say.

Of course you must pay for rarity. And purity. And the sacrifice of many, even if the many is only flowers and bees and swamp farmers. So even though this small jar is eighteen dollars, I give him twenty and tell him to keep the change. I open the jar on the spot and stick my finger in. The honey is buttery and smooth and something else. Something I have no word for. I stand here, flat-footed by Highway 45 with my finger in my mouth, and try to think of the word for what I'm feeling.

"They say it is impossible to describe," says the man working the stand.

"They're right."

"And so you see what I'm saying? You aren't disappointed?"

I tell him no, that I'm not disappointed. I take my small, expensive jar and climb back into the Blackhawk, and begin to drive north. Toward Memphis, my last stop. Toward Memphis, where it seems like I've been heading my whole life.

HONEY

It takes us the better part of an hour to find the cemetery. Marilee drives us over half of Tupelo, and at some point we even stop at a roadside stand and buy some fruit to eat on the way. Marilee pays for everything—out of what I don't know, since I still have the money—but when she gets back to the car she hands me a jar and says, "Here. Tupelo honey. To remember the day by."

Remember the day? Is she kidding? I'm not likely to forget any day that started with screaming and ambulance sirens. Any day that started with me throwing drugs off a dock into the Mississippi River, me leaving the man I love passed out in a Rest-A-While, me wondering what the hell I'm going to do with every mile we put behind us. But I thank her and put the jar of honey down by my feet and we talk a little then. Speculate on the other girls, the other backup singers. Where they will go, what they'll do next, if in all the hysteria of the day anyone will notice that the Blackhawk has gone missing. Gone missing along with Marilee and Nunchucks and Honey.

"We haven't done anything wrong," Marilee says, taking a bite from one of the apples she bought at the stand.

"Nothing except destroying evidence and stealing a car."

"Evidence is only evidence if there's been a crime," she says. "And there's no crime here, just an accident. And nobody stole this car. Elvis gave it to you free and clear."

"They've only got our word on that." I look over at her. "Were you close enough to hear when he said it? That I should take the car and go?"

"Not exactly. But you say that's what he said, so I say that's what he said."

"Great." I sit back in the seat and look at the scenery, or at least what there is of it. "Do you even know where this graveyard is? Do you have a map?"

"I've been there before. I'll know the turn when I see it."

But just as I'm thinking we need to give up and get going for sure, Marilee begins to mutter and pulls the car down a road. A nothing road, going from nowhere to nowhere without a single sign to mark it, but she seems to think she's onto something, because she turns, and turns again, and soon enough we roll up to a little graveyard.

"Here we go," she says, pushing open the door.

I'm not sure why we've come, except that she needs to pay her respects somehow, just like she seemed to feel she needed to buy that jar of tupelo honey. The road to redemption is long and thorny. That's what my daddy always says, and today, for the first time in my life, I'm starting to see what he means. Because this makes no sense, the way Marilee and I are picking our way among the tombstones, half of them tilted and cracked, the names and dates worn away through the years. There are no monuments, no flowers or concrete angels or quotes from the Bible. The bodies of poor people lie beneath us and it's hard to understand why Elvis, who was so sentimental about family and so superstitious about signs, would leave his dead baby brother to rot here, in this wrecked place.

"Did you ever hear him talk to Jesse?" Marilee asks.

"Sure." I'd wager we all did at one time or another, whenever he was high or in an especially bad way. It was creepy. In fact, I remember the first time I ever saw Elvis standing backstage before a show, his head bent forward, whispering to a blank wall. I'd thought he was just rehearsing the lyrics and I took it as a good sign. But Fred had shaken his head and said, "Oh Lord, he's talking to Jesse tonight, and that ain't never good."

We find the grave. Or at least what Marilee claims is the right one. It has a little marker that says 1935–1935, but there's no name. We stand with her on one side and me on the other, both looking down, and she says, "It explains a lot, doesn't it?"

I nod automatically, like a preacher's daughter has been trained to do, but personally I don't think it explains shit. It makes no sense that the Presleys would leave their little lost boy here, in this dump of a graveyard at the end of a nothing road. Why didn't they exhume him and bring him to Graceland and lay him beside his mama—and now his brother—in the fancy meditation garden with its marble and fountains and roses?

"I wanted you to see this," Marilee says. "I'd seen it, but I wanted you to see it too."

"And so you keep saying, but now that we're standing here at the end of this dirt road, Marilee, I've got to ask you why." Maybe it sounds like a mean question, but I'm not trying to be mean. I'm a little bit scared, the two of us out here all alone under the hanging moss, looking down at this tiny marker, with an unembalmed baby beneath it, faded down to his soft, curving bones. I shudder and Marilee looks up.

"I'm just trying to explain things. You came to Graceland so recent. You don't really understand him. Don't understand what all this means."

"Maybe I don't want to." I shake my head and start to walk toward the car, hoping Marilee will follow me. Because we've got to get the hell out of here. Put miles behind us. When something has gone as wrong as all this has, driving away is pretty much all you can do. Put miles behind you and direct your faith toward the territory ahead.

But Marilee doesn't follow me. She stands stock-still, looking down at the pitiful little grave, and I turn back toward her, exasperated.

"You brought me here to learn something and I guess I'm too stupid to learn it. So spell it out."

"I hoped that you seeing the grave might make it easier for you to forgive."

"Forgive who?" I snap the words.

"To forgive Elvis for dying on us, leaving us like this." She shrugs. "And anybody else who wasn't what you wanted them to be. Maybe your daddy, I don't know. Nunchucks, that's for sure, and I'm guessing Fantasy Phil back in Macon. Or it could have even been your boyfriend back home in Beaufort. There must have been some reason you took to the road. We all got some-body we need to forgive."

"And you think looking at an unmarked grave is going to do that? Gonna give us the peace that passeth all understanding?"

"It's where it starts."

"Fuck you, Marilee."

"Don't you talk to me like that. Not in this holy place. Not when we've come to pay tribute to Elvis."

"Elvis is in Memphis. Shit, Marilee, don't you get it? The ambulances have come and gone by now. The news is out. Peo-ple are lining up around Graceland, waiting hours for a moment at the foot of his casket. Reporters are camped on the lawn. Ce-lebrities are flying in from all over the world to attend the ser-vice. They're gonna give him a big send-off. Gospel and twenty-one gun salutes and eternal flames. He was the King."

"Maybe so," Marilee says, turning away at last from the grave. "But part of him never made it out of Tupelo."

PART FIVE

Memphis, Tennessee

HONEY

August 14, 1977

Every day at Graceland is strange, but this might be the strangest yet.

Gladys Presley had been forty-two years old when her heart stopped beating. Elvis is forty-two now. And since he's superstitious about everything—especially numbers and family—he's gotten it in his head that he's going to die today, on the exact anniversary of his mama's death.

I guess if you use Elvis logic it makes a kind of sense. Last night at midnight he went upstairs and locked himself in his room and no one has seen him in the eighteen hours since. The whole house has stood silent all day. Nobody's gone to the pool or is watching TV or playing tennis and even the lights in the kitchen are out.

"This ain't right," Marilee says to me. "Him being alone in the dark all that time,"

"Alone?" I say, and when I glance up the back staircase I feel a little tickle of fear. Elvis is never alone, and especially not in his bedroom. It's not because of the sex. I've heard rumors—even me, and I'm the last one to hear anything—that he's no longer interested in women "that way." He's got a new girlfriend, a local beauty queen named Ginger, because if you're Elvis you always have a girlfriend, each one younger and prettier than the last. But Elvis is waning either way. David told me one time that it's like the man's soul is already in the process of leaving his body. He's letting go of this world, inch by inch, but yet—

He still wants someone sleeping next to him in the darkness. It gives him a sense of security, I guess, to know there's another beating heart in the bed.

"Come on," says Marilee. "I know he loved his mama and I mean no disrespect, but we can't walk around quiet as a funeral for twenty-four straight hours. This is getting foolish and I'm getting hungry."

So she and I turn on every light in the kitchen and fix ourselves bowls of cereal and then we carry them down to the jungle room along with our guitars. We're playing softly, just working on something new like we sometimes do, and despite the fact it's nearly ten at night—usually about the time Graceland's getting into full swing—there doesn't seem to be anyone else downstairs.

The jungle room is my favorite place in Graceland. The walls and even the ceiling are carpeted in green, so it's like hiding away in a cave. It reminds me of home. Not that my daddy's house had tiki gods and waterfalls, a thought that makes me laugh, but because the mossy green is like the woods where I used to roam as a kid. There are animal statues everywhere and those big, woven, high-backed chairs that look like thrones—all as a tribute to Hawaii.

It was the scene of his greatest triumph. When the *Aloha from Hawaii* special aired four years ago it was the highest rated television show of all time. More people saw Elvis singing that night than saw Neil Armstrong walk on the moon, and I remember just where I'd been, at home in the den, staying up late with Daddy and Mama. Ordinarily they weren't much for what Daddy called "that pop pop music." He took his reputation within the congregation too seriously for that. But Elvis was an exception. He openly declared his faith in Jesus and was southern, with old-fashioned manners. Maybe he wasn't the perfect role model because everybody remembered him swiveling his hips in that jail-cell movie, but I guess Daddy figured that if I had to listen to some sort of pop pop, Elvis was our best bet. So when *Aloha from Hawaii* came on, I was allowed to stay up and watch the whole thing. I'd sat there on the couch in my pajamas with a big bowl of ice cream in my lap and I'd been transfixed. It was the most glamorous thing I'd ever seen.

"You're not paying attention," Marilee is saying to me now, resting her cheek against the neck of her guitar. "Where's that mind gone?"

"Wandering," I admit. There's never any point in lying to Marilee.

She's been humming some little scrap of melody over and over. It sounds good. Because of the carpet on the walls, the jungle room has great acoustics, and we've recorded here more than once. Some people say it gives better sound than our actual high-dollar studio out back. I move to pick up my guitar and join her, and just in that second, I look up and see Elvis standing in the doorway.

We're caught. He's come down the back staircase and caught us.

I don't know why I'd say it like that. All of us girls have free run of the mansion, or at least the part downstairs, but still when we look up and see him just standing there in his light blue bathrobe, not saying a word, me and Marilee both freeze like we're doing something forbidden.

Maybe we were. We were making music at Graceland without Elvis.

But all he says is, "Play that last part again."

So we play it for him, as much as we have, and after a couple of times through, he starts to sing along. He's in a strange mood tonight, gentle and shy, as if those hours in the dark have sucked the swagger right out of him. At some point he goes to get his own guitar and tells Marilee to set up a microphone.

And then we record, just a little bit. First of him singing with me and her on backup, and then trying out different combinations of melody and harmony.

"The words need to say he's looking into the water," Elvis says. "Nothing's any sadder than a man looking into the water."

"We gotta be careful how we phrase it," I say. "Nothing rhymes with water."

"Daughter," says Marilee.

I'm shaking my head but Elvis is nodding his. "There you go," he says. "Daughter can be a sad word too."

So we've got *water* and *daughter* in the first two lines, despite my reservations about both of them, and if you had told me four years ago, on that night I sat on my daddy's couch with a bowl of ice cream, that I'd be jamming in the jungle room with Elvis Presley, I think the top of my head would have flown off.

At some point the clock chimes. Twelve low bells. Midnight. It's August 15. The day of death has come and gone and the heart of Elvis Presley still beats. I look at Marilee and she looks back, her eyes wide and solemn. Only Elvis seems unaware of the time. He is hunched over his guitar, his face as sweet as a child's.

Remember this, I think, moving my head side to side as if I were a camera trying to take in the scene from every angle. Elvis on the stool with his guitar. Marilee fiddling with the recorder. Me with my legs crossed Indian style, scribbling lyrics onto a yellow legal pad. *Remember everything about this night,* I think. *Because you will never be this happy again.*

CORY

June 3, 2015

I bought one of those disposable phones back in Tupelo, specifically so I could leave the number with Express Paternity. Even so, I'm startled when it buzzes and it takes me a second to dig it out of the passenger seat, where it's slipped below Lucy's shredded chew toy and the jar of honey. I've just come into the outskirts of Memphis, and I'm in what Bradley would call "not the good part of town." But the sign on the interstate swore up and down that this was the Graceland exit, and based on the street numbers I think I'm almost to the airport La Quinta where Lucy and I will be spending the night. I fumble for the phone.

"Miss Ainsworth?"

"Yeah. Yeah, that's me. Are the tests done already?"

"You said you wanted them today, didn't you? That was . . . that was our agreement?"

"Right." I feel suddenly flushed and dizzy, and ever since the phone first buzzed, I've been looking for a place to pull off the road. It normally costs $179 to have DNA tests run at Express Paternity, but as the young male nurse had been drawing my blood I'd asked him if they could put the double rush on it for $250. He'd hesitated, turned away for just a split second, and I had panicked like I always do and said, "Or how about $300?" I suck at negotiating. I think he'd only been looking out the door to make sure his boss didn't hear our conversation, and then I'd gone and flown off the handle and offered up damn near every dime David Beth had just given me.

But maybe that's fitting, who can say. Maybe it's nothing more than Express Paternity karma. And either way, this kid was as good as his word, because here it is barely two hours after he drew my blood, and he's already calling me. I find a strip center and whip the car in. It's the kind of place that has a check-cashing service and a tattoo parlor and a Ho Ho Chinese take-out and three empty storefronts. I make sure all the doors are locked before I cut off the engine.

"The DNA was collected from the toothbrush and the razor match," the nurse begins. "We couldn't do anything with the earwax from the Q-tip. But the saliva and the hair are clearly from the same person."

No big surprise there. "And?"

"We can say to a degree of ninety-nine percent certainty that these samples come from your biological father."

"Ninety-nine percent?"

"They won't let us say a hundred."

"So ninety-nine means a hundred?"

"I guess it does."

I look down at my hands on the steering wheel. *I'm half Jewish,* I think out of nowhere, and even though I was expecting exactly this, the world still swims before my eyes.

"And the blood on the tissue paper," the young man's voice continues, "is a match as well."

"What do you mean 'the tissue paper'?"

"The Kleenex."

"What?" The world snaps back into focus. "That's not possible. Those samples came from completely different places. They were collected years apart."

"I don't mean the blood on the tissue matched the saliva and hair samples," the voice hastens to explain, although I'm having trouble hearing him, for I truly must be near the airport. A jet roars overhead as he speaks, coming in low for a landing, and the Blackhawk shudders in response. "I mean that they match your own blood."

"I'm not following you," I practically shout into the phone. "Say it again?"

"The hair and the saliva are a match to you," he says. "And the blood on the Kleenex is a match to you as well."

"How can two different people be my father?"

"They can't," he says with a little giggle. "Two different people can't be your father, but two different people can be your parents. That's why you're a DNA match for both samples."

I still can't seem to understand what he's saying. How can Graceland be near here? This whole part of Memphis is so ugly and loud. It's like the whole world is roaring. From the backseat Lucy begins to whine, as if even he knows that sitting still in this particular parking lot is a bad idea. "So what you're telling me . . ."

"What I'm telling you is that the saliva and the hair came from your father," says the voice on the phone. "And the blood on the tissue came from your mother."

HONEY

August 15, 1977

The next day, all the magic of our night in the jungle room is gone. The house comes rumbling slowly back to life, but everyone inside of it is edgy and out of sorts. Elvis had slept again after our recording session, and he must have slept long and hard, because it's late afternoon before he comes down the steps and heads straight into the media room. A bunch of us are clumped in the kitchen, but he doesn't say anything when he passes. He can be like that. He can plain ignore people, even when they're standing right in front of him. Sometimes it's like Elvis sees through your skin and into your soul, and at other times it's like he sees through your skin and straight through to whatever's on the other side.

"Take him a sandwich," Wanda snaps at me. "I don't think the boy ate a bite all of yesterday." She's short of temper, just like the cook before her and probably the one before that. I don't blame any of them. They're just a bunch of good Baptist women who are used to people eating breakfast in the morning and dinner at night. They likely had no idea what they were signing up for when they came through the gates of Graceland.

So Wanda fries up a peanut butter and bacon sandwich, one of his favorite breakfasts, and sends me to take it to him. I call out that I'm coming as I head down to the media room, stomping as hard down the hall as 108 pounds of girl can stomp. Anything to make sure I don't startle Elvis. Whatever else you do, you don't want to startle Elvis.

I find him sitting in his white leather swivel chair with the TVs fanned out in front of him. The media room has three televisions going at all times, so that Elvis can see what's happening on every network at once. He heard that Lyndon Johnson watched TV like that when he was in the White House, and I guess he figured that if three televisions were good enough for the president, it was good enough for him. The evening news is on, so two of the screens have men dressed in tan suits with wide striped ties, and on the third there's the woman from ABC, Barbara Walters. Her face is strained, her brows pulled together in a slight frown, like she's giving the world bad news. "The Tower of Babel," that's what my daddy would call the media room, but having the whole world talking to him simultaneously doesn't seem to disturb Elvis. In fact, I think it soothes him.

"Well, hey there, Honey Bear," he says.

He isn't facing toward me, but that doesn't matter. Not only is the ceiling mirrored, but there's a whole wall of mirrors behind the TVs too. It's a good room for a paranoid man, because you can see everything, as it's coming toward you and leaving you both. Years ago someone had seen fit to decorate the place like a disco, in bright blue and yellow, with a painted lightning bolt streaking across one wall, and shiny silver surfaces everywhere. So as I walk toward Elvis holding out the sandwich, I'm not only bombarded with three talking heads but I'm seeing all this times four, with Barbara Walters ricocheting at me off every wall.

"They're gonna let me ride in the car tonight," he says with his eyes darting back and forth among the screens.

Let him? Elvis doesn't require permission from anyone to do anything. But then I realize that this must be one of those nights when the Memphis cops have invited Elvis to do a ride along, probably on a drug bust. Elvis loves drug busts. I think on some level he realizes he's being humored by the local boys, that the uniform they give him is nothing better than another stage costume, that there's a reason they make him stay in the car when something real is going down. But he is still smiling when he tells me this, so I just put down the sandwich and say, "That's great."

In a way it is great. Today is bringing us a bunch of good signs. That he's hungry and that he's excited about riding with the cops. His eyes flick away from the TVs and focus on the sandwich. If I thought for one minute that our recording session last night bought me any new status in his eyes, that idea is dying fast. He's lost interest in our conversation. I've been dismissed.

But just as I turn to go out of the room one sentence jumps out from the hubbub of voices swirling around me. One of the male TV anchors is saying something about "eighty-two seconds of extraterrestrial communication."

"Did you hear that?" I ask Elvis.

He mumbles something, his mouth full of the sandwich, but for some reason I'm bold in the moment. I reach down and grab the remote control, even though I'm not entirely sure how to work it. It must have twenty buttons. It looks like the dashboard of an airplane. But I start punching one of the arrows and the volume begins to go up on one of the TVs. The wrong one. ABC with Barbara Walters. I punch her back down again and keep trying until the story about the alien finally rises above the rest of the Babel.

It's almost the end of the report. Just a few lines left. Apparently an observatory at Ohio State has picked up some sort of space signal. The transmission lasted just over a minute, and appeared to be coming from the direction of the constellation Sagittarius. I look down to see if Elvis is listening. Normally this would be just his kind of news story. But he's still preoccupied with his sandwich.

"Aliens are trying to communicate with Earth," I tell him.

"Shit," says Elvis.

"No," I say. "This is a real news channel reporting this and it was a real school that got the signal. A state university, a respectable place."

But he sticks a finger in his mouth and starts digging around, pulling out wads of half-chewed bread. "Shit," he says again. "What's in this fucking sandwich?"

"Bacon. What do you think they want from us?"

"I've lost a goddam filling," Elvis mutters, spitting into his napkin. "You're going to have to call somebody."

I nod, still staring at the TV screen. The news of the world has moved on. Now the reporter is talking about the Panama Canal. It makes me wonder if I dreamed the whole thing. I back out of the room, the plate in my hand. The anniversary of Gladys's death has come and gone, but it would seem we're still in danger. The Memphis police have invited Elvis on a ride along. Aliens from Sagittarius are trying to contact Earth.

And my period is nine days late.

For whatever reason, they decide that I should be the one to take him to the dentist. I guess because I was the one who was there when he busted the filling out. Otherwise it makes no sense. I'm not used to driving the cars, which are low and powerful, and anybody can look at me and tell I'm not suited to handle a man the size of Elvis if the dental work makes him woozy. So I ask Marilee to come too.

I expect her to grumble. Nobody wants to go to the dentist in the middle of the night. But she not only says yes, she says, "Of course."

The dentist said he'd meet us at midnight so Marilee and I are waiting in the foyer at eleven fifty when Elvis comes down the stairs wearing a black silk shirt and pants. He's in a surprisingly good mood considering his ride-along got canceled, and we're even almost on time.

As he descends, I call up, "Can Marilee come with us?"

He smiles and says, "Now you know she can. How you doin' tonight, Miss Marilee?" He doesn't appear to be in any pain from the lost filling. I guess he self-medicated before he left his room.

The three of us head out to the garage, where someone has already pulled his newest Stutz Blackhawk out of the pack. It's sitting diagonally in the driveway, with both doors open, like it's on display. Even after a year at Graceland, I've never quite understood how the coming and going works—if Elvis called down tonight and asked for a certain car, or if Rusty, the mechanic, made the decision about what he would drive. Maybe they have some sort of rotation system to make sure all the cars get driven on a regular basis, the same way you have to exercise a horse. But the Blackhawk is waiting and Elvis waves Marilee over to the driver's-side door.

I scramble into the backseat first, getting in on the driver's side. There's a tuft of blue fur on the leather and I brush it off my pants. It looks like it came from a child's stuffed bear, most likely one of the carnival toys Elvis won for Lisa Marie and her friend a few days ago. His little girl was flying back to her mother in California soon and he was spoiling her big-time in these final days, in the only way Elvis knew how to spoil someone: with his large, silly, and over-the-top gestures, like having a whole amusement park opened up in the middle of the night, just for her and a friend. I wonder what that must have felt like for the child, if it was fun to run from ride to ride without ever having to stand in line and wait, fun to know you'd win every prize in the arcade, no matter how bad you threw or shot. Or if maybe it was sad and creepy to be the only two kids in a deserted park, the only two screams on the roller coaster, with both the cotton candy and the caramel apple coming right toward you the minute you glanced in their direction.

Too much, that's what I sometimes think. *Too much sugar, too much salt. Too much noise and too many toys.*

But I pick a few strands of the blue fur off my white pants and make up my mind right here and now that when I have a child—whether it is eight months from now or eight years—it'll be raised much differently than Lisa Marie. Because it seems to me that having everything must be sort of like having nothing. Elvis's daughter will never know the pleasure of choosing the one from among the many, the pleasure of waiting, of dreaming and planning. There's a deep joy in yearning. Maybe it's the deepest joy in life, and I feel sorry for the child, even though I know it's a silly thought. Most likely Lisa Marie doesn't resent the difference between her life and that of other little girls because she doesn't know there is a difference. She's been rich and famous since the day she was born.

Marilee is driving slowly down the driveway and through the gates, which swing open as we approach. The movement excites the clump of people waiting outside it. I look out the backseat's small triangular window to see the photographers jostling and the tourists with their cameras too. Elvis lifts a hand in greeting, gives a smile and a wink to a couple of the women. I'm not sure how much they actually see. It is pitch-black here at the end of the driveway and the windows of the Blackhawk are tinted dark too. But he makes the gesture and maybe they do feel it, felt the vibrations of the King's power reaching through the hard metal walls of the car. Because they surge toward us as Marilee hesitates, as we pause just that one little second before she pulls the Blackhawk onto the main road.

Marilee says something to Elvis and he answers. They're

talking softly and the engine of the Blackhawk is loud enough that, sitting in the back, it's hard to hear. But once she pushes in an eight-track and the music starts, it isn't hard to hear at all.

Smart girl, I think. *No wonder you wanted to come. And aren't you slick as butter, using this rare time alone to remind him of our song? When did you get it converted to an eight-track? You must have been out in the recording studio the whole time I was sleeping.*

I lean forward and strain to listen as we drive through the dark and deserted streets of Memphis to the dentist's office, with Elvis slapping the back of his hand against the side of the car door. When we get to the dentist office, a building Elvis does not appear to recognize, even though we'd all been there before, Marilee cruises the Blackhawk around the block a couple of times just to make sure he has plenty of time to hear out the whole tape, all our versions, to the very end. The music stops just as she's finally rolling the car into the parking lot and Elvis says, clear as day, "Now I'm gonna tell you something, girls. The three of us need to get this pretty little song on the radio."

Three people are waiting inside the office. They're lined up like a military troop and probably have been standing just that way for twenty minutes or better. Because, as usual, we're late. The dentist escorts Elvis down the hall, and both the hygienists are all set to follow when Elvis abruptly stops and jerks his thumb toward me and Marilee.

"Do somethin' for them too," he says. "Clean them up or somethin'."

So the hygienist who is last in line whips around and directs me toward a second office. I don't want to have my teeth cleaned and I doubt she wants to clean them. But I climb into the chair anyway, and she starts setting up. She doesn't make small talk. She drops the metal instruments to the tray with a clatter. She's pissed and I can't say I blame her. She was probably home for the night when she got the call to come back in. Making dinner, watching TV, or sleeping beside her husband. Who knows, maybe she has kids who need to get up and start getting ready for school in just a few hours. But then the word goes out across Memphis that Elvis Presley has lost a filling.

So this girl gets up and gets dressed and drives back to work just before midnight, only now she finds out she's not going to be attending Elvis at all. The other hygienist gets the important gig and she's been cheated out of a good night's sleep to clean the teeth of two nobody backup singers who just happened to come in with him.

She takes her disappointment out on my gums, gouging at them with that little curved pick thing and talking hateful about plaque and flossing and how it was clear I'd been rushing things when it came to good oral hygiene. Rushing things, or maybe even skipping steps entirely. "Sloppy," she mutters, scraping away in the back of my mouth, hurting me so bad that at one point I pull my feet up to my butt and close my eyes. "Yes, I'm going to say that somebody's been very sloppy indeed."

By the time she finally releases me, my white cotton bib is splattered with blood. I walk back into the lobby with a balled-up Kleenex in my hand, bleeding into that too. Enough so that Marilee raises her eyebrows when she'd looks up from her *Cosmopolitan* magazine and sees me coming toward her.

"Good luck," I whisper as she stands.

But just as Marilee is going in, the door to the other office jerks open. The dentist looks down the hall and calls out, "Can one of you girls run down to the pharmacy?"

He explains that since this medical office complex is so close to the hospital, an all-night pharmacy is just below us on the first floor of the building. God knows what he's doing to Elvis in there, but whatever it is, he seems to think Elvis might need painkillers later.

What he doesn't realize is that Graceland is practically an all-night pharmacy in itself. We have little brown vials with white tops sitting on every table, and stuck in every kitchen and bathroom cabinet throughout the house. We have pills to ease you up and some to ease you down. Pills to make you big and some to make you small. I don't understand half the names or what particular brown plastic vial is meant to do what, but I do know this: if we flushed every brown bottle at Graceland down the toilet and into the water supply, the whole city of Memphis would go to sleep for a week. Maybe the whole state of Tennessee.

And so I hesitate for a second, standing there in front of the dentist with the Kleenex pressed to my mouth. I'd started to crumple it in my hand and hide the blood from him—hiding things is my natural tendency—but then I think no, he needs to know how rough his hygienist is on the normal patients.

So I very pointedly press the Kleenex to my lips and he very pointedly ignores it. He holds a piece of white paper out, pinched between his thumb and index finger, and says "Just in case there's pain later."

Just in case there's pain later. If life with Elvis has taught me anything, it's that there's always pain later.

"All right," I say. "I'll go."

The idea doesn't hit me until I'm out the door and in the hall. That this prescription in my hand is a gift, because it gives me an excuse to go to a pharmacy alone, and in the middle of the night.

In other words, it gives me the chance to get an at-home pregnancy test without anyone finding out.

So I ride the elevator down to the ground floor and follow the signs to the twenty-four-hour pharmacy. It's predictably deserted at this hour, except for a man sitting alone in a wheelchair, staring into space, as if he has no idea who brought him here or who, if anyone, is ever coming to fetch him. And then there's the woman behind the counter, who seems bored to death. She looks down at the prescription that I hand her, and then at me, and I blurt out, before I can lose my nerve, "I also need an EPT."

They're brand-new, but I've seen them advertised in magazines. *Cosmopolitan* and *Mademoiselle* and *Glamour*. The ads show a woman who's the dead opposite of me, a young housewife with her husband beside her, and they're both smiling like they want nothing more in life than a positive test and a baby on the way, and then a hundred more behind it.

Peace of mind, the ads say. *Our family found it with EPT.*

This lady pharmacist knows that the girl standing before her is nothing like that beaming young wife in the ad. I'm nineteen, but I look more like fifteen, and it's the middle of the night in a twenty-four-hour pharmacy near the only hospital in

Memphis, Tennessee. I'm bleeding from my mouth, which is unfortunate, but I'm not bleeding from anywhere else, which is even more unfortunate, and this pharmacist looks at me like she can see my whole life in just one glance.

And then, as if the situation isn't sordid enough, it occurs to me that I don't have any money. No money for the painkillers and no money for the test.

"And just put it on the Graceland account," I say, taking a chance. Graceland has credit all over Memphis, and the minute I say the magic word *Graceland*, the attitude of the woman behind the counter changes. She's all smiles as she plops the square white box that holds the EPT test kit onto the counter and goes into the back for the Parafon Forte.

Ten minutes later I'm back in the elevator. I read the side of the square white box and it tells me that with four easy steps I will have my results. Four easy steps and twenty minutes and then a circle will either form at the bottom of the test tube or it will not.

My whole life hangs on that circle.

CORY

I wake up early, so early that I'm the first person in line for the breakfast buffet, which is really saying something when you're staying at an airport hotel. A whole flight crew comes in right behind me, looking so spiffy in their uniforms that I feel guilty about being in the lobby in my pajama bottoms and a T-shirt. I eat fast, then pack up a couple of waffles and a bowl of grits for Lucy. After I feed and walk him, I'm going to have to leave him alone for an hour or two and just pray he doesn't eat the room.

Because I've decided I'm going to Graceland. I'm going to make a first trip by myself and try to get the lay of the land before Dirk gives me the all-clear to come back with the Blackhawk. I called Dirk last night to give him the number for my disposable phone, and he said he'd call me today when he got his daddy "used to the idea."

For some reason I failed to ask him exactly what idea he's trying to get his daddy used to. Dirk has been working on some kind of plan ever since I drove the Blackhawk into his line of vision, and it seems like this car is proving to be the redemption of all sorts of people, not just Mama and me. *It's streaked its way across the South like a vengeful chariot,* I think, even though I know I'm only talking like a preacher's granddaughter again. I do that whenever I get nervous, or drunk.

I'm not drunk now, but I'm definitely nervous. I decide to take the shuttle to Graceland, leaving the Blackhawk just where it is. The fact you have to park your car behind a gate with a security code and a barbed-wire fence is just further proof that we are not on the good side of town.

But even if this location is kind of sketchy, there are still plenty of little old ladies lined up for the first shuttle to Graceland. They all look like good small-town church ladies, wearing their matching pantsuits in those Easter egg colors. I don't even know where you go to buy lilac or mint-green polyester pants anymore, but the ladies relax me a little bit, the way they chatter and chirp as they wait for the bus. They're excited. Happy. Most of them have probably been to Graceland before. Some of them probably come here every year. But it's still a treat, a special day, and when the bus rumbles up, I climb the steps and file back to the very last seat.

We don't drive far. The hotel billboard told the truth about that part, at least. The bus puts us out in a parking lot and we make our slow way across a white bridge, then follow a winding sidewalk until we find ourselves not in Graceland, but in a series of small connected museums located across the street from Graceland. Each section is dedicated to a different period of Elvis's life, from his hardscrabble childhood in Tupelo to his stint in the army to his movie era to Vegas.

The Sirius radio station that plays only Elvis is sitting out in the courtyard blasting "Love Me Tender." I've listened to this station before. Of course I have. Poor as I am, I always manage to scrape together enough money to keep Sirius in my car. The annual bill comes through in January, which is lucky, since I always get a lot of gigs around the holiday season.

Last year I thought . . . I don't know what I thought. It was our first Christmas without Mama and I knew things would be different, and I wondered if Bradley would even pull it together enough to get me a gift. We met at a Waffle House early Christmas morning, which breaks my heart just to say it because I know that a better woman, a better daughter, would have found a way to make him a holiday breakfast. But I'd had a gig the night before and another one coming up that afternoon. It stinks to work like that on the days when nobody else is ever working, but I knew I needed to milk the holiday cash cow as long as it was mooing. Three lean months lay ahead, starting precisely on January 2, when my only choice was to either chase the snowbirds down to Florida or hole up and spend the winter eating ramen noodles.

So I think Bradley knew I had to take any work I could get through New Year's and he didn't make the slightest peep of protest when I said I'd just meet him Christmas morning for breakfast at the Waffle House out by the interstate, even though the only people there with us were hookers and truckers and a waitress who had brought her kids and their Santa toys to work with her. I gave him his gifts, a fishing cap from Cape May and a book about the Civil War, and he gave me an envelope, apologizing the whole time because it wasn't a store-bought gift.

But I was relieved. I peeked in while he was paying our bill at the register. Cash, more than ever before. Either he was feeling guilty that his wife had up and died on us, taking her casserole-baking, muffin-making Christmas brunch skills with her, or because he'd never been entirely certain how much money Mama had given me every year.

Either way, this envelope held enough to get me Sirius and electricity and ramen noodles through spring. I hugged him good-bye and we went our separate ways—him to church for a holiday service, me to the bar to set up. I watched his car pull out of the lot just ahead of mine and sat there for a minute, my mouth feeling like it was full of onions and ashes.

Welcome, I'd thought, *to the new normal.*

And it had fucking sucked.

But that's what I'm remembering as I stop now, in front of this radio station that's plunked here right in the middle of the Graceland museum complex. The sign on the front promises ALL ELVIS, ALL THE TIME, and behind it is a diner serving the foods Elvis liked to eat, including the famously gross stuff. All those banana and bacon and peanut butter concoctions that pitched in together to kill him. It's a funny thing. Having this diner sitting here is like having a guillotine in the middle of a Louis XVI exhibit or a shooting range at the Abraham Lincoln birthplace, but even so, the diner appears to be a moneymaker. It's hardly past time for breakfast but the Elvis faithful are already lined up for lunch.

I turn slowly in the square, taking in the view from all directions. A four-lane highway separates this shiny new museum complex from the actual grounds of Graceland. I can barely see the famous gates, big and brassy, festooned with musical notes. The airplane called the *Lisa Marie* is parked in its own separate lot, part of the package tour I've paid for, and I consider climbing aboard. Mama flew on it several times. It took her, I guess, to that broken-down runway that runs beside the Juicy Lucy. But Macon seems far from me now, and I look down at the phone in my hand. Dirk hasn't called.

I amble through the sections of the museum. They're cleverly done, with the music and clothes from each era greeting you as you enter, taking Elvis from the 1930s through the '70s. But it's not just Elvis. This place is like a museum of America—all our hopes and dreams and failures, laid bare for anybody to see. Perhaps I think this because so many of the visitors seem to be foreign. I hear a variety of languages around me: German, French, Japanese. They are systematic and studious, stopping at every bejeweled outfit, every black-and-white picture.

The whole thing culminates in a section about Elvis and his cars.

The theme is cute. They've set it up like a drive-in movie: clips of Elvis films play on a big screen reminding us—as if anyone who comes here is likely to forget—that the young Elvis was a god. I pause for a second, watch the segment of *Viva Las Vegas* where he first meets Ann-Margret. *She's just as hot as he is*, I think. Or perhaps it's more accurate to say that Ann-Margret was freakishly beautiful in the exact same way that Elvis was. She had the same finely chiseled features, the same powerful hips, ready to uncoil and snap at any moment, the same curling, slightly contemptuous lip. In fact, if you had dyed her hair black, she would have looked just like him. She would have looked like Priscilla.

So he had a type, I thought. *Big deal. Lots of guys do. So his type was . . . himself.* Okay, that's weird, but I guess this one fluke of Freudian psychology is why I'm standing here now, the keys to the Blackhawk in one pocket of my jean jacket, the eight-track in the other. Because I know that just as Ann and Elvis and Priscilla shared this certain resemblance, so do my mama and me. We're all peas from the same pod, and if Honey hadn't happened to remind Elvis of himself, none of the rest of this would have ever occurred.

It's funny to think of it like that, but true. If I didn't look like Elvis, I wouldn't exist.

I lean against a trash can, watch the clip play out. Ann-Margret was the love of his life, that's what my mama always said. Well, in truth there's no "always" about it. In truth, she only said it once. She told me that Ann-Margret had been as talented as Elvis, and so when they met on the set of *Viva Las Vegas* it had been electric. Electric because she was his equal. And, I guess, it had also been impossible because she was his equal. They surfed and sang and danced and raced motorcycles and made what I can only imagine was the most combustible love on the planet, and yet eventually he gave her up and went back to the teenage Priscilla. All this happened long before Mama was at Graceland, but I guess she heard the gossip. She said Ann-Margret was the one who broke his heart, or maybe it would be more accurate to say she's the woman he used to break his own heart. He crashed on her like waves on rocks and then receded because he couldn't face the possibility of a wife just as famous as he was.

It was the closest Mama ever came to saying Elvis had a weakness, that time she told me about how he let Ann-Margret go. But she said Ann kept loving him on some level, just like he kept loving her, for all those years they lived apart. When somebody called to tell Ann he was dead, she screamed. Screamed before she heard the words. She'd known it the minute the phone rang.

I watch the clip play out to the very end. Ann and Elvis really do sizzle on screen, especially in their first scene, where she walks into his garage and he rolls out from under a car and looks up at her. Pretty boy, pretty girl, but together? *Jesus Christ*, I think. *It almost hurts to look at them.* But then the clip ends and Elvis swivels on to someone else—Mary Tyler Moore in *Change of Heart* or Dolores Hart in *King Creole*. It hardly matters. The films are pretty much interchangeable. The girls are all young and pretty and hopelessly smitten, for who wouldn't have been, with Elvis in his prime?

I push myself away from the trash can and move on. Walk through the exhibits of sports cars and jeeps, motorcycles, and even the golf carts they used to race around Graceland. The Blackhawk will end up here eventually, I guess, and it seems fitting. It stings a little less to let go of it, walking through this museum and seeing how it will be valued. Maybe it will even be one of the cars that sits up high on a pedestal, with the doors flung open and mirrors strategically placed so that the tourists, forbidden to approach, can see inside. Dream of what it would be like to sit in those soft red leather seats, to feel that kind of energy vibrating beneath their fingertips.

I head out through the gift shops, which are large and strategically placed. Elvis is singing in all of them and you can buy approximately a million things with his picture on it. I see a waffle iron that presses out his image on your breakfast and a Christmas ornament, a dangling replica of Graceland. The tag says twenty-six dollars. I look at it again. Surely I read it wrong. Surely most of these people passing through the shops—for they are crowded already, even though it's nine forty-five on a weekday—look to be working class, and I'd imagine they have plenty of other things they could do with twenty-six dollars. But no, that's right. That's the price and they're willing to pay it.

The people will do anything for even the slightest sliver of Elvis, I think. That fact makes me sad, and yet that fact is also the one that's going to save me.

A bus is waiting outside. I pull a set of headsets off the huge rack holding dozens of them and climb aboard. We are one of the first batches of people of the day and the bus pulls out of the museum complex, crosses the road to where Graceland awaits. The fence with the musical notes swings open as we approach and the woman beside me squeals. We drive slowly through the grounds, past tall oak trees and a bright green rolling lawn.

I'm prepared for the fact that the house itself is not really that big. That it looks like lots of other houses, with a redbrick facade and a flat, understated entrance. Elvis bought it in 1957 for a hundred thousand dollars, which I guess was a fortune at the time. It was already named Graceland, after one of the previous owners, a woman named Grace, but he liked the name and kept it. As we file out of the bus, all clutching our headsets, most of the people trot right up to the door, but I linger a bit in the yard in front of the house, looking up. Despite the fact there's a busy highway just past the musical notes and even an airport nearby, the house strikes me as a spot of calm. I can imagine Elvis, barely in his twenties, proudly handing the keys to Gladys and Vernon, certain beyond measure that he had done what everybody wants to do in the end: he had made his parents proud. What a paradise this must have seemed after the shotgun house down in Tupelo, like the three of them had vaulted as far and as fast as a family could travel. Now he and that father and mother are buried out back in the meditation garden, along with one of his grandmothers, and Dirk said there is a marker for his dead twin brother as well.

The meditation garden is the last stop on the tour. I can see people coming up the sidewalk that leads from the back of the house. Some of them are weeping. While the tourists who rode over with me on the bus were squealing and chattering, singing snippets of songs, the people now getting back on the bus at the end of their tour are sobered. They whisper. They point their cameras or phones toward the front of the house for pictures, but they take them quickly and then step back, as if they are ashamed of their own curiosity. They hang their headsets back on the pegs with reverence, and I pull my own up and over my ears as I head toward the front door. For some reason, I'm already wiping away my own tears, and I haven't even begun.

HONEY

August 16, 1977

My hand is shaking as I lift the dropper to the mouth of the test tube. One, two, three . . . four. The last drop is reluctant to fall. It dangles at the tip until I give it a gentle flick, and finally it releases and plops into the tube with the others.

I use the funnel that came with the kit to add in the second mixture. It's so clear that it looks like nothing more than regular water and it turns the contents of the test tube from gold to pale yellow. I read the rest of the instructions quickly. Something about sheep's blood and hormones and dark floating circles and reflections in mirrors. The whole thing sounds like voodoo.

They say to agitate the test tube steadily, in a swirling motion, and then after that to let it rest completely still. And so I agitate, first one direction and then the other, and I wedge the tube into the little cardboard slot just like it shows in the picture. Finally, I stand up straight, exhaling for the first time since I began.

Twenty minutes to wait.

It's cruel.

I've set up this whole chemistry set on a plastic table where people are supposed to change their children's diapers. It pulls out of the bathroom wall like a Murphy bed, and I've never seen one quite like it. I guess the fact it's even hanging here is further proof that we're in the most modern office building in all of Memphis, one that offers its clients the latest bells and whistles. There's a picture of a fat, gurgling baby on the part that drops down, and he's looking right at me. In fact, his eyes seem to follow me side to side, like one of those creepy portraits in a haunted house, and I back carefully away from the whole contraption, trying not to consider the irony that I'm setting up an EPT pregnancy test across a baby changing table. The instructions said that something has to settle. I forget what. But something has to settle over the course of the next twenty minutes, and after that a dark brown circle will either form in the bottom of that test tube or it will not.

I don't even know if the four golden drops I measured into the test tube qualify as early morning urine. It's now 1:36 a.m., which by one way of reckoning is early morning, although you could just as easily argue that it's nothing more than late night. But I have to do the test here and now, no matter what time it is. There's no privacy at Graceland.

I slip out of the bathroom stall and go to the ladies' room door. Open it slowly and look across the lobby. No one is there. The doors to both of the examination rooms are still closed.

I could wait in the lobby. Get a magazine and try and distract myself with a *Cosmopolitan* quiz. "What Song Describes

Your Sex Life?" "Are You in Love or Just Faking It?" "Is It Time to Cut Your Hair?"

But instead I turn back and check the test tube, even though I know there's nothing yet there to see. I slide down the wall and sit on the floor, looking up. I am seventeen minutes away from news that will either save me or end me and I suddenly feel nauseous, even though I can't remember the last time I ate. Normally this is where I would try to make up a haiku, just to pass the time, but for some reason I can't seem to think of any words. All I can think is five, four, three, two, one, my mind counting down, just like a rocket launch.

CORY

The phone rings while I'm still in Graceland. While I'm standing on the puke-green shag carpet and looking down into the jungle room, as a matter of fact. Dirk says that Fred is prepared to see me now. He says it like I've been granted an audience with the pope or the queen of England.

I'm to take the car to the back, he says. Not even to try to get it through the front gates, which is liable to cause a riot on the spot. Instead he tells me this complicated series of turns that'll lead me back through the service entrance and to a hidden parking lot. I don't tell him that I'm in Graceland right now. I don't tell him I've got nothing to write these complicated instructions down on. I don't tell him that it's a miracle I even felt the phone vibrate, down deep like it is in my pocket and with the headphones on my head, saying something about tiki gods and what they symbolize. I just tell him to give me thirty minutes.

He doesn't like the fact it's going to take me so long to get there and he makes no bones about it, but I know even thirty minutes is cutting it close. I have to get out of Graceland, catch the shuttle back to the main museum part, and then transfer to the hotel shuttle back, throw my shit in my backpack, get the dog, check out of the La Quinta, get the Blackhawk out of the armored parking lot, and return to Graceland. It's a lot to do, but it's a good thing I have a lot to do, because otherwise I might panic. I've come all this way for just this particular moment, but now that it's finally upon me, I feel numb and blank. I make Dirk give me the instructions to the parking lot round back once again and then I repeat them back to him.

I must sound scared because he tells me to pull myself together. It won't do to show up nervous and uncertain in front of Fred, who Dirk says "jumps on any sign of weakness just like a June bug."

"Isn't this what your mama and daddy left you?" he says. "Isn't this your chance to get what's coming to you after all these years?"

I nod, even though I know he can't see me. I've stepped away from the crowd to take this phone call. I think it's against the rules to take a phone call in the middle of a Graceland tour, but I don't see a security guard in this particular section and most of the people are on their headsets. I lean against a pine-paneled wall out from the kitchen and my eye falls on a group of photographs. One of Elvis with the whole traveling band behind him, and I guess one of these tiny blobs might even be my mama. Of course, there were lots of traveling bands and backup singers through the years, so it's not likely. Even if this picture did happen to be taken during her singular year at

Graceland, the girls are so small and squeezed together that it's nearly impossible to tell them apart, everybody with the same hair and clothes and eyes. But there's no denying that the picture hanging right beside that one is my daddy. David Beth in his full karate gear, the jacket loosely belted, the hair on his chest peeking out of the top. He is in a pose, his fists balled up, his feet bare, one sole pointed straight at the camera. I guess his expression is meant to be intimidating, but it only looks silly. I bring my face closer to his and stare at him.

"Isn't this what your parents wanted for you?" Dirk repeats when the silence between us has stretched.

"My parents?" I say vaguely.

"What your mama and your daddy planned all along for you," Dirk says with exasperation. He's beginning to think he's gone out on a limb for a crazy woman. "Wouldn't they tell you to get your full inheritance at last?"

"Better make it more like forty minutes," I say, and I end the call before he has time to yell.

HONEY

Marilee is rapping on the bathroom door. I open it.

"What the hell are you doing?" she whispers. "We're waiting. Elvis is ready to go."

I'm surprised by the *hell*. Marilee never cusses. But of course Elvis never has to wait for anything either, and if he's finished in the dentist chair and ready to go, then by all means the time for going has commenced.

"Just a second," I whisper back, looking down at my watch. I still have almost ten minutes on the EPT test, but of course that's shot now. "Just give me one second."

"You got the Vicodin? He asked about the Vicodin."

"Yeah. Of course I have it."

She nods, and I shut the door. Go back into the stall and look at my little chemistry kit. Should I throw the pieces away, try to stuff them down into the narrow trash can or just walk out and leave everything as it is for some cleaning crew to find in a couple of hours? I begin to pick the whole thing apart and for some reason, even though the instructions very specifically said not to rattle the test tube, I decide to take it with me. I wrap the Kleenex around it, blood and all, pull my purse over my other shoulder and head out the door.

Elvis is already at the elevator. He's leaning against the wall, staring up at a perfectly ordinary office building light fixture like it's the second coming of Jesus. His mouth is sagging open. He seems woozy.

"You drive, Honey Bear," he says. "Miss Marilee's sick."

I glance at Marilee. She doesn't look sick exactly, but she does look strange. There's something in her that seems washed away and she mumbles something about a cavity, so I guess they drilled on her. She hands me the keys to the Blackhawk, which I take in my left hand because the test tube and the Kleenex are still in my right.

"Get him down and wait under the awning," I say to Marilee. "I'll fetch the car."

She nods and presses for the elevator. I start down the staircase beside it, still trying to not jostle the tube even though anybody can see that's a lost cause at this point.

Once down the stairs, I push open the lobby doors and step out into the hot, wet night. There's no one in sight, only a single streetlight out in front of the pharmacy, making the parking lot look like the opening shot in a slasher movie. I used to be scared of the dark, before I came to Graceland and night started to feel more normal than day. My feet against the pavement sound light and fast, like a heartbeat, and I fumble with the key, then slide into the driver's side of the Blackhawk. I put the test tube into the cup holder, even though I know that no ring will form at the bottom of this test tube filled with urine, not after this much motion. So the EPT will read negative, but not the kind of negative that will give me any peace of mind. My heart sinks with the thought I'm going to have to figure out a way to do this all over again in a couple of days or maybe even take the crosstown bus to Planned Parenthood.

Marliee's legs are a mile long, so I have to adjust the seat, and the rearview mirror too, but then I crank the car and swing around to the front of the building. Elvis comes out leaning on Marilee's arm. She takes him straight to the passenger side and I hop out and flip up the seat to let her crawl in behind me. Elvis settles back, not bothering to fasten his seat belt, putting his head against the red leather and mumbling, "You got the perscription, didn't you?"

He does that sometimes. Mixes up words, like *perscription* for *prescription*, and I've never known him to call a single drug by name. They're all just perscriptions. Maybe it's another one of his superstitions. If you don't name something, you don't give it any power.

I nod and we pull out of the parking lot in silence. I glance at the eight-track player. Our demo tape is still inside of it, and I could offer to play it again, freshen up the memory in everybody's minds. But then again, none of us are at our best. More than an hour in the dental chair has exhausted Elvis, and the hygienist must have done something wicked to Marilee, who has laid her head back in an absolute imitation of Elvis's position. I can see her in the rearview mirror.

I doubt any cop in Memphis would stop the Blackhawk, which is known across the city as Elvis's favorite car, and besides, there's hardly anybody on the road to hit. But I'm careful anyway as I drive through town, and when I turn back into the gates of Graceland, there are a few photographers waiting on us, even now. I guess they figured that if the Blackhawk drove out just before midnight, it would have to return eventually, so they stuck around. I feel sorry for them sometimes, although I wouldn't dare say that to anyone else. We're supposed to call them vultures and leeches, to sneer at them for not having anything better to do than stare at us through long lenses. But I wonder about their lives, standing outside Graceland in all kinds of weather, just standing and waiting without the slightest evidence any of it will ever pay off. I take the turn slow and deliberate, both because it would never do to smash up the famous musical fence and the Blackhawk in one fell swoop and—I'm sorry to say—also to give the photographer on the right-hand side of the car a good shot at Elvis.

For he has lifted his head from the seat now. He even manages a halfhearted smile and a floppy little wave at the photographer as we roll by. I stay slow all the way down the driveway and stop short of the garage door, not trusting my ability to actually park the car.

"Damn," says Elvis. He's drooling from his numbed-up lip and he starts groping for a Kleenex, coming up only with mine. As he pulls it out of the cup holder, the test tube comes with it. He fumbles, almost drops them, and then stops, studying both of the items in his palm with a frown.

The funny thing is, he knows at once what he's looking at. Elvis, who can seem a bit slow sometimes, like self-centered people often do, lifts the test tube to his line of vision and then turns his gaze quizzically to me.

I'm caught and I know it. Lying or pretending will only make it worse. I flick up my gaze again to the rearview mirror, but Marilee appears to have gone to sleep.

"So you're in trouble, Honey Bear?" he says.

My eyes flood with tears. I shake my head, unable to answer.

Elvis opens the door so that the interior light will come on and holds the test tube up again, higher than his head, looking at the contents from the bottom. Later I will think of what a strange moment in time this was, Elvis squinting up at the test tube, his chin cocked to the side, studying it just like the scientist on the cover of my old high school chemistry book.

"It won't tell you anything," I say. "You're not supposed to shake the tube and here I've carried it down the stairs and across the parking lot and then driven it all over town rattling away in a cup holder. If the test is positive, a ring forms, but I haven't given the ring a fair chance to form. I've messed it up, so tomorrow—"

I stop. It's the longest speech I've ever made in front of Elvis. Maybe the longest speech I've made since I got to Graceland. But I have to stop, not just because I know I'm running on like a madwoman, but because I don't know what I'm going to do tomorrow. I don't know what I'm going to do tomorrow or the day after that or the day after that.

Elvis looks at me with sorrowful eyes. Like he knows what's ahead and he hates it, both for himself and for everybody else.

"You went home a few weeks ago, didn't you?" he says gently, crumpling the Kleenex and throwing it back into the cup holder. "Went home to see your mama and your daddy?"

I nod, even though I don't have the slightest idea where he's going with this or how he even remembers the event. My daddy had turned forty and they'd had a party for him at the church and I'd asked Fred, at the last minute, if I could have some time off to go. We'd been touring anyway, were somewhere on the southern swipe between Charlotte and Atlanta, and Fred said yeah, he'd get one of the roadies to drive me to Beaufort just as long as I was back for that night's show.

We made it just in time for the end of the Sunday service. I walked up the steps of the church I'd grown up in—prodigal daughter, returning star. My hair was fixed and my makeup was set and I had on one of the short lace dresses Elvis favored. Just as I got there they were getting ready to bring in the cake and one of the women said, "Oh, let Laura carry it in."

So the church doors had opened and there I was, carrying a sheet cake with forty candles, walking slow and steady up the aisle like a bride. I'd seen certain people out of my peripheral vision as I'd passed. Mama, of course, and two of my high school friends, already married and done for, and Bradley, even Bradley, although I couldn't quite bring myself to turn my head and look at him.

But it didn't matter. When my daddy had seen me coming toward him he'd said, "Praise Jesus," and rushed down the aisle toward me and everyone had clapped. I was back in the car an hour later, barreling toward that evening's venue in Atlanta and never having said a word to Bradley Ainsworth at all. I can't think why Elvis would remember such a trifling event. But he's like that—sometimes aware of nothing and then, in the next breath, aware of everything.

"I went for my daddy's fortieth birthday," I say. "To his church. He's a preacher." I don't know why I feel compelled to remind Elvis that I'm a preacher's daughter, but I do.

"That's right," says Elvis. "And you saw your high school sweetheart while you were home, isn't that right?"

Oh. Okay. So that's what he thinks. I'm still the virgin of Graceland in his eyes. Always have been, always will be, even if I got liquored up and started swinging from the chandeliers. The only way he can reconcile the possibility I might be pregnant with his image of me is to tell himself that when I was home I must have been with my high school sweetheart. It's the sort of truth he can live with—in other words, a truth that isn't true—and he likes it better than he'd like the reality of the situation. The reality that I was already nobody's virgin when I went walking down the aisle of my daddy's Presbyterian church wearing an eggshell-colored lace dress and carrying a cake with forty candles. I'd already lain with Philip Cory, such as that was, and was plotting to lie with my real target, David Beth, the moment we got back to Graceland. My high school sweetheart was nothing more than a face in the crowd, someone I didn't even bother to exchange words with, but I can't tell Elvis all that. In fact, I find myself nodding before he's even finished talking.

"That's right," I say. "I went back to see my mama and my daddy and my high school sweetheart. Bradley Ainsworth."

Elvis sighs and looks toward the house. "I won't sleep tonight," he says.

It's like him. Two minutes of thinking about somebody else

has worn him out and now he's back to thinking about himself. I feel like snapping at him, asking why can't he see what I'm going through, but of course I don't. Instead, I wipe my eyes with the back of my hand and say, "I got something from the doctor."

"That picayune little shit won't help," he says, even though there's enough Parafon to drop a horse zipped up in my pocketbook. "I told ya, I'm not gonna sleep tonight."

Perfect. Just great. We all know what a night at Graceland is like when Elvis doesn't sleep.

We're both still waiting in our car seats, Marilee dozing in the back, the two of us staring toward the house. Elvis's face, when I glance over, is a mask of fear. As much as I know that if he doesn't sleep we're all facing a night of misery, as exasperated as I am with him for switching from my problem to his in half a second, I still feel a trickle of sympathy. He fears going to sleep and he fears being left behind when everyone else goes to asleep, and the result is the situation now before us. A house where nobody is allowed to shut their eyes, where we're all nervous and wakeful, like a bunch of people waiting for bad news that hasn't yet come.

They say that Elvis has a recurring dream, in which he always wakes up alone. The girls who have spent the night tell stories of it, of him sitting up with a gasp, clammy and terrified, his hands reaching for them before his eyes are fully open. Marilee said once it's because his baby brother died when they were both in their mama's belly, that the first thing Elvis ever knew was what it felt like for somebody to go on ahead without him, to leave him behind to face the morning all alone. That he's carried this sense he was getting ready to be abandoned again, any minute, with him throughout his whole life.

"Is he a good boy, this one you left behind in South Carolina?" Elvis asks me, still looking toward the darkened shell of Graceland.

This conversation is enough to give you whiplash, but I nod. "Yeah. Maybe too good." I don't add that I'm no longer a good girl and that I suspect Bradley and I could make each other's lives a living hell if fate gave us half a chance to do just that. But it turns out I don't have to say anything else, because Elvis laughs.

"Then you take this car, Honey Bear, and you drive back east as fast and as hard as you can." He holds out the key. "Make him marry you. From what you say, it won't take much."

My mind does what it always does when it's surprised. It goes straight to something trivial.

"I can't drive this car to South Carolina," I say. "How am I supposed to get it back to you?"

He laughs again, a gesture that evidently gives him pain, because he immediately winces and rubs his jaw. "If I give you a car," he says, "I ain't gonna be calling for it back."

"But this one's your favorite. Nobody drives the Blackhawk but you."

"Now that's hardly the truth, is it? Miss Marilee drove it earlier tonight and now here you sit behind the wheel. And looking mighty fine there, if I say so myself."

I'm stunned. I'm not a lucky person. I've never even won movie tickets or a piece of Tupperware in a church bingo game, and now this man is giving me this car. This car that I know without thinking costs more than my daddy's whole house.

Elvis reaches over and grabs my hand. Presses it into the steering wheel with his own. "Drive, Honey Bear," he says. "Get your pretty little ass out of here and keep driving. Go as far as you can go until the water stops you."

I blink back tears. "Why are you doing this?"

He holds out the test tube. It must have been in his hand all along.

"Because you're pregnant," he says.

CORY

Lucy doesn't like Fred. That seems like a bad sign, because Lucy is the most indiscriminate creature I've ever met. Even that time he lunged at the Montgomery La Quinta desk clerk, it was just a matter of being overenthusiastic about a treat and he was wagging his tail again two seconds later.

But Lucy has had a low growl rolling around in his throat since the moment we pulled up in this back parking lot and got out. The hair is standing up on the back of his neck as I drag him toward the side yard, where Dirk and a scrawny little man are leaning against a white split fence. I probably shouldn't have brought the dog here. He kept getting progressively agitated as I drove through the mazelike back roads that lead away from the front gates, the tour buses, and the crowds. And now we are walking slowly toward Dirk and what must be Fred. His gray hair is thin and longish for a man, curling up on the ends. He's wearing a string necktie that makes him look like he's getting ready to sell me some fried chicken.

On top of all that, the first thing he says to me is a criticism.

"I cannot believe," he says, "that you let a coonhound ride in Elvis Presley's very own Stutz Blackhawk."

He has his palm outstretched and for the briefest of moments I think he wants to shake my hand. But then I see that no, he's held his hand out palm up. He wants the key.

"You're expecting me to hand over my car just like that," I say. "You think you'll take it from me the second you see me. Candy from a baby. "

"You can't lose something that wasn't yours to begin with," he says.

"Elvis gave my mother this car," I say, but even I can hear the fear in my voice.

"Oh, I'm not suggesting Honey stole it," Fred says. We're both talking louder than two people normally talk. Shouting across an unnatural distance, because Lucy's still straining on the leash and I'm afraid to take him any closer. At least he's stopped growling.

"Honey was a good girl," Fred goes on. "All I'm saying is that she borrowed it. Borrowed it for an extended period of time."

"Thirty-eight years."

"Thirty-eight years. Fair enough. And now her daughter has brought it back."

I look down at the keys in my hand, suddenly aware of how hard it will be to hand them over. I've been in that car for four days, more or less, and I know I've driven it thoughtlessly, despite all of Leary's warnings about how the whole thing could blow at any minute. But the tires haven't shredded and the engine hasn't overheated and I know I've been lucky. The Blackhawk was a gift from fate that I damn near squandered.

Stalling for time as much as anything else, I walk back to the car and start pulling my possessions from the back. It occurred to me on the shuttle that once I release this car to Fred, I won't have any way to get back to the Memphis airport La Quinta, or to Beaufort for that matter. I haven't thought out this part of my adventure at all. In fact, this part is pure Cory Beth Ainsworth, to be so focused on how you're going to get to a place that you never stop and think twice about how you're going to get yourself back.

Fred's expression sours even more as he watches me yank out my backpack and toss it in the dirt, then lean back and get the guitar, which I set against the backpack, and finally Bradley's waders. I line them up too and there you have it, the sum total of my worldly possessions.

"What the hell are those?" says Fred.

"Waders. For fly-fishing."

"I know what they are. Why the hell did you bring them here?" he asks, and just then, before I can say something else stupid, Dirk steps forward. He has a gift for inserting himself into a situation at the perfect moment, and the minute he comes toward us, Lucy calms down. He extends a hand toward the dog and suddenly Lucy's all licks and wags and sniffles.

"Here's what's going to happen," says Dirk.

His tone is calm and perfectly pleasant, but I'll wager the man has never said those five words all together in his life, at least not in the presence of his father.

"Cory here is going to hand over the keys to the car," Dirk

says. "And you're going to sit down and listen real carefully to a tape she has. It's the last recording anybody on earth has of Elvis Presley singing, and he is furthermore singing with this girl's own mama.

"That's right," Dirk goes on when Fred frowns and tries to break in. "It's Elvis and Honey Berry on that tape, collaborating on an original piece of music. And since both of them are unfortunately deceased at this point in time, the girl standing here in front of you, Miss Cory Beth Ainsworth, is now going to sing that song in their place. She finished it and she's going to record it, and Graceland is going to release it."

There is a moment of dead silence and then Fred's eyes slide back toward the guitar. "Can she even sing?" he asks.

"She can sing real good," says Dirk, and he smiles at me. "I heard her yesterday when we were walking around the church, letting the dog take his crap. She's a lead singer by nature, that's my opinion. Not meant to stand in the back with a bunch of other girls, meaning no disrespect to her mama."

Fred starts to say something, probably to ask his son what the hell he's talking about with the dog and a church and me singing lead when all he was supposed to do was go straight to Tupelo and fetch my troublesome ass to Memphis. He gets as far as opening his mouth to drown Dirk in a flood of questions, but then he stops himself. He wants the car. He wants it real bad. Bad enough to take a bit of guff off two people he sees as no better than kids.

"Show him what I'm talking about," says Dirk, and he hands me the guitar.

I give Fred a few quick lines of "Love Me Tender" standing

right here in the gravel. Dirk likes it. He closes his eyes, rocking back and forth between one big foot and the other. Lucy's pleased too. He gives me a little backup, in fact, pulling his mouth into an O and crooning along. Only Fred is unmoved by my rendition. His expression never changes and he folds his arms across his chest.

When I finish he says, "You sound like your mother."

"Only when I sing."

"Only when you sing? Fool answer. What you should be saying is thank you. 'Cause I hired her, didn't I? There must have been a hundred girls at that open call and your mama was the only one I took."

"Then thank you. You're right. That's what I should have said the first time."

But Fred is still frowning. "You grew up singing Elvis? Your mama taught you?"

"Actually, no. I just started singing Elvis . . . the day before yesterday."

I can tell he doesn't believe me. He thinks I've spent a lifetime moving up and down the East Coast, stopping at every little bar I can find and ripping off my slight connection to the King. He thinks I'm nothing more than another pretender, a poser and a wannabe, but he stops himself before he pushes too far. There's still a negotiation in the works, after all.

"So you claim you got a tape of Elvis," he begins, "and you claim he's singing some song nobody's ever heard of . . ."

"It's my mother and Elvis together," I say. "And I think the tape was made just a day or two before he died. My guess would be they were in the jungle room." I don't tell him that I hatched this theory today, staring down into the room, thinking that the way it was covered in cloth from the floor to the ceiling and sunk down three steps, it would be a perfect place to sing. And if I thought that, I bet Mama once thought it too. I'm finally starting to face the fact that despite thirty-eight years of protest, I'm exactly fucking like her, both the good and the bad.

Fred is nodding, almost despite himself. I bet he hardly ever nods. I bet his head is used to going side to side but not up and down. It's probably getting ready to snap off right here in the parking lot.

"They sang sometimes there in the jungle room," he admits. "Recorded some too."

"So I think she started out alone, late at night," I say, "and he heard her and came in and he took the lead and she came in on the harmony and I've got it all on tape. Right here." I pull the tape from my jacket pocket and hold it out. Fred looks down at it.

"And why am I supposed to think this recording is authentic?" Fred asks. "The world is slap full of people who think they sound like Elvis."

"Oh, it's authentic all right," says Dirk. "You can have them run whatever tests people run on this kind of thing and I swear to you, Pop, they'll every one come back telling you that this little eight-track tape sat undisturbed in that car for all those years. Honey started the song and Cory finished it and now we're going to take her over to Sun Records and—"

"Sun Records?" Fred looks down and spits. "Hell, Sun Records ain't no more than a hole-in-the-wall these days. A tourist trap."

I'm thinking it takes a lot of balls for a man standing in a

Graceland parking lot to spit on the ground and call anything a tourist trap, but Dirk is ready for that one too.

"No, sir," he says. "I'm asking you to reconsider. Elvis did his first record at Sun, back in the day, and it's only fitting that his last one comes out of there too. It gives the whole thing . . . what's the word, Cory Beth? The word that means something's exactly equal going back and forward?"

"Symmetry," I say, because for once I know where Dirk is heading. "So yes, it's only fitting that Sun Records releases Elvis's first record and his last one, sixty-two years apart. May lightning strike me if I don't have a little bit of him singing on this tape. You'll hear it clear enough when you listen."

"We can start with that little clip of Elvis and then fade into Cory's voice," says Dirk, like it's all been decided. When the hell did he get so smart? "So she's going to give you the keys to this car and you'll gonna call up Sun Records and tell them that we're delighted—"

"Delighted?" Fred says skeptically, then he spits on the ground again. "Nobody here is delighted about goddamn anything."

"Well, I guarantee they're going to be delighted about this," says Dirk. "Because they're gonna be hearing the sound of cash registers clinking all the way to California." He's been my champion without fail for the last two days, and I'm going to have to find a way to thank him when this is all over. But then again, judging by the way he's smiling, maybe Dirk is going to have to find a way to thank me. Something about this situation is making him stand up to his daddy for the first time in his life, and he likes it.

"We're going to call Sun Records and tell them this is their lucky day," Dirk goes on. "Tell them that we are delighted . . . extremely delighted . . . what's the word, Cory Beth?"

"Ecstatic," I say.

"Ecstatic to have found, after all these years, the last recorded words of Elvis Presley. We're going to tell them that this treasure was brought to us by the daughter of one of Elvis's long-lost backup singers, Honey Berry, and that now, after all these years, the song will be released. Tell them that Cory could have taken this . . . this . . ."

"Artifact," I say. "This precious piece of American history."

"She could have taken it to any record label in America," says Dirk. He's rocking so hard back and forth on his feet now that I'm afraid he's going to topple over. "Any record company in America would have rolled out the red carpet just to have a chance for the last recording from the King, but Miss Ainsworth wanted there to be . . ."

"Symmetry," Fred and I say in unison. Lucy thumps his tail.

"And furthermore . . ." says Dirk.

"Good God," says Fred. "There's a *furthermore*?"

"There is," says Dirk. "And furthermore, we're gonna see to it that this song debuts on the Sirius Elvis station across the street and it'll be for sale in every gift shop at Graceland. The fans will gobble this story right up like butter on a biscuit."

"But Graceland and the estate of Elvis Presley—" Fred starts.

"Dad," Dirk says gently. "You got no business standing here speaking for Graceland or the estate of Elvis Presley. You know as well as me there's a whole lot of people who've gotta be asked. But I believe they'd think all the better of you for bringing this to their attention. You being the one who helped find this . . . this . . ."

"Artifact," I say.

"This guaranteed number one hit," says Dirk.

Fred looks at me. He looks at the car. One of us he wants bad and the other one he doesn't particularly want, but a lifetime in the music industry has taught Fred how to smile while he swallows a bitter pill, and he smiles now.

Lucy is waiting right by my side, whining a little low in his throat. I'm shaking, and I guess the dog can feel it. But this time I'm not shaking because I'm nervous, I'm shaking because I know Dirk is right. His plan, in fact, is nothing short of brilliant. A new release with Elvis, even just a line or two from Elvis, will be big news. If I play my cards right—spiff up the lyrics and sing it as good as I can—this eight-track can be the start of my whole new life.

Of course the person getting screwed in all this happy-happy is Marilee. It's not quite right to say that Mama wrote the song free and clear when she probably only wrote the lyrics. I think about calling her down in Fairhope. Telling her what's unfolding and asking her what she thinks, but then I remember her holding out her strong, dark hand to me and saying, "Take this tape, it's yours," and I know that all this is nothing more than what she expected would happen. She knew I'd end up turning the car over the moment I drove it onto the property of Graceland, and she also knew that the tape was my true legacy, with the power to lift me to a higher plane. *She still feels bad about Mama*, I think. *Still feels bad about sending her out onto the highway pregnant. This whole thing has been her way of evening the scales. Doing for the daughter what she wasn't able to do for the mother.*

"If this is really Elvis—" Fred says, but I cut him off.

"If you've got the slightest doubt," I say, "we can get into this car right now and listen to the tape. You'll know if it's legitimate. A thousand impersonators couldn't fool his old tour manager now, could they?"

He's tempted, tempted by the chance to hear, even for a few mangled seconds, the sounds of Elvis crooning in the jungle room. I hold out the keys to him.

"All right," Fred says. "You and me. You and me only." He jerks his head toward Dirk. "You hold that damn dog out here. He's not getting into Elvis's car."

It's sort of a ridiculous order in light of the fact this damn dog has been in Elvis's car for the last thousand miles, but I see he's just trying to reestablish in everybody's eyes that he's the one calling the shots here. That he's not going to let some half-wit bar singer from South Carolina and her coonhound and even his own son join forces to sass him. I can tell from the way Dirk's finessing him that Fred hasn't had any real power here at Graceland for a long time. That he's pretty much rattling around like a relic of the old days, with a title like "authenticator" that doesn't mean squat, and that's okay. Let this little man be a big man. Let him sputter and spit and make declarations. Because after he's had time to think about it, he'll see the genius of Dirk's plan. How it will behoove Graceland as well as me.

I hold out the keys. "You want to crank it?"

As he reaches for them, a bolt of static electricity passes

from his fingers to mine, enough so that that both of us jump. I step back and run my hand over the chassis a final time, letting my palm drag the length of the flank of the car. *You've been wrapped away all this time,* I think, *waiting for something. The chance to go home, maybe, or some kind of release. And I hope I gave it to you. 'Cause God knows you gave it to me.*

Even Lucy has caught the sentimental mood. He sniffs the back left tire of the Blackhawk, then lifts his leg and pees good-bye all over it.

And with that, we're done.

HONEY

I'm standing in the kitchen, debating whether or not to go upstairs and at least try and sleep when I hear Elvis pick up the phone. From the way he's talking, I can tell he's asking for David. I don't know why he'd be wanting to practice karate now, at three in the morning, when he's all sore from dental work, or why he'd be asking David to come up to the house instead of meeting him in the studio.

But it's clear soon enough. Elvis isn't in the mood to kick. He's in the mood to talk. Talk and eat. Because in the next instant he calls the cook and pretty soon David's burst in the door, clearly awakened from a deep sleep, and the three of them are huddled in the kitchen. Pans are rattling and water is running. David has come with an armful of his philosophy and religion books and has spread them across the counter.

As for me, I'm lurking in the hall outside the kitchen, waiting for the moment when Elvis and Wanda are distracted and I can wave at David. He and Elvis are sitting at bar stools, with their books and papers spread out all around them like two teenage boys doing homework. Wanda's moved to the stove and started frying something. She has two pans going—one for each man—because none of the rest of us can quite stomach the volume of grease and sugar that Elvis casually consumes on a daily basis. I don't know what she's cooking for David; an egg, or a hamburger patty most likely, or something equally simple. Elvis is having his standard fried banana and peanut butter sandwich. No bacon this time, or at least I can't smell any. I guess all that dental work must have put him off anything hard.

It takes awhile, but I finally get my moment. Elvis stands up and goes over to Wanda, mumbling something to her, poking at the contents of the fry pan. I hiss, just like a character in a cartoon, and David looks up from his books.

He smiles. He thinks I'm was calling him out into the hall to set a time for a tryst later—or at least for a kiss. He has no idea he's about to be confronted by a madwoman with a test tube of urine in her hand.

But when I pull it out, his face changes in a second. It would seem that, just like Elvis, he can recognize an EPT test kit at twenty paces.

"How could this have happened?" he whispers before I can even get the words out. "I thought you said you took care of it."

I try to sputter out my story but he cuts me off.

"Never mind," he says. "I guess that is my fault as well as yours. But you're going to take care of it now, right?"

And in that one sentence he tells me everything I need to know. I said *baby* and he said *it,* and even though I'm not surprised by his attitude, I still weave a little on my feet.

"Wait downstairs," David says, and he is concerned enough to reach out and grab my arm, to give me a brotherly peck on the cheek. "We can talk later. Right now, I've got to be here for Elvis. We're talking about the true face of God."

I shake his hand off my arm. "So duty calls."

He nods. "Exactly." Sarcasm is totally lost on the boy. Always had been, always will be.

I wrap the EPT in toilet paper and dump it into the trash can of the downstairs bathroom and then go down to the jungle room to wait. I curl up on one of the couches and cover myself with a leopard-skin blanket, even though I don't think I'll sleep. With my mind racing like this, I don't think I have a prayer of sleeping, but I guess I do, because I suddenly feel myself jerk. That feeling you have, like you're falling from a tree.

Somebody is screaming.

You hear a lot of sounds at Graceland. Gunshots and gospel. The roaring engines of go-carts and the girlish giggles of Lisa Marie and her friends. But I've never heard anybody scream, at least not like this. It's high-pitched and shrill and desperate. I struggle to sit up, tangled in the leopard-skin blanket and hoping that I'm dreaming.

I'm not. The scream has come from right above me, and I move toward it without thinking. It's a preacher's daughter impulse, bred in me from birth, to automatically move toward trouble when any sensible person would move away from it. But I'm on my feet and running now, past the empty kitchen and up the wood-paneled staircase. It's so dark that I stumble more than once, banging my knee and finally emerging into the upstairs hall that leads to Elvis's bedroom. I look both ways, feeling lost. It sounds crazy, to say you're lost in a house you've lived in for over a year, but I had only been past these double doors once or twice. I must have been on some sort of errand, taking something to or from Elvis, and for a moment I'm turned around, still in that stumbly dream state.

Another scream sets me right. It lets me know which way to run, through another set of double doors, these already thrown open, and toward Elvis's bedroom.

I burst in and see that it is already full of people. Whatever is happening is happening fast. Ginger is the one screaming. She's shrieking with every breath in her body and somebody, one of the audio boys I've seen but whose name I can't remember, catches my eye and whispers, "She's the one who found him."

Found him?

As crowded as the room is, the action is focused somewhere else, at the door of the bathroom. Four or five people are clustered there, but then somebody moves and I can see halfway inside, enough to see a man's feet stretched out on the floor.

Marilee is here. She claps her hand on my shoulder and spins me around to face her. Her mouth is trembling. Marilee is the calmest person I've ever met. She moves through the world acting like God himself has already told her what's going to happen next. Like she's living her life in a circle or maybe even backward and she's immune to fear, or even surprise. But now her lips and her eyes are wide and her fingers claw at the air as she's struggling to get the words out.

"Fred wants us to get him out of here," she finally manages to say.

Wants us to get him out of here? It's another phrase that doesn't seem to make any sense. Elvis is sick, that much is clear. Somebody has called for an ambulance. I know that because everyone keeps saying to one another, over and over, "the ambulance is coming." Elvis's father is wailing. His daughter is moving through the room like a sleepwalker.

They shouldn't be here, I think. *Somebody needs to get hold of the situation and get Vernon and Lisa Marie out of here.*

"Come on," Marilee says. "If we work together, we can carry him." Her voice is barely a whisper. With all the hollering and running and the pounding sounds coming from the bathroom, I have to lean toward her to hear what she's saying. Even then it doesn't make any sense. Fred wants me and Marilee to carry Elvis downstairs to wait for the ambulance? Won't the rescue guys come up the stairs to Elvis, with their stretchers and IVs and cardiac machines? I think of him earlier that night, bobbing his head in time to the eight-track, smiling. Holding the test tube out to me, his face serious this time, and kind and wise and tired. Bending down over the frying pan to sniff whatever it was that Wanda was making.

"Did Elvis faint?" I ask Marilee. It is all I can think of to say. He must have fainted. Maybe hit his head when he fell. There are so many things a person can hit their head on in a bathroom.

"Elvis is dead, Honey," she says. She almost shouts it and, loud as the room is, several people turn toward her, all shaking their heads and frowning. She is the first to speak the D-word. No one must speak the D-word. To speak it aloud is to call the possibility into being, to practically invite the roof of Graceland to collapse down upon our heads.

And then Marilee steps aside and for the first time I understand what she means, who she has been whispering and yelling about all along. Behind her, crumpled in a light blue velvet
chair, is David.

David. What was he doing here, at the end of this long hall,
in the bedroom Elvis shares with Ginger? And how can he be
dead when just an hour earlier he was telling me I needed to
take care of something? Perhaps I should be the one screaming
and crying now. From the bathroom I hear Elvis's daddy wailing,
"Don't leave me, son . . . Don't leave me," and the entire room
flinches at the sound. One of the other backup singers, a girl
from Detroit we call Lou Lou, finally has the sense to latch onto
Lisa Marie's hand and pull her out of the room. A man says to
me and Marilee, "Where's that fucking ambulance?" and we
both shake our heads.

David is dead?

How can he be dead?

I turn toward him and study his body, folded in on itself,
like he's assumed the crash position in an airplane. His
hands dangle down by his feet, and his head is utterly limp. I
start to drop to my knees, to try to reason with him. Because
it seems that he's being so utterly unreasonable, just sitting
here like this, staying so still and silent while the world is
falling apart around our ears. But then Fred is by my side,
and, numb as I am, I find myself nodding as he spits out or-
ders into my ear, willing to agree to anything he asks of me.
I'm just relieved that someone, somewhere, seems to have a
plan.

"You've got to get him out of here," Fred says, patting David's shoulders with both of his hands. "One can be explained as an accident, but two . . ."

And he's right. Trust Fred to be the only one who is thinking ahead, already trying to guard the reputation of the man who is either dead or dying in the bathroom, the reputation of the entire house of Graceland. If the body is found in a bathroom, there can be any number of plausible explanations. It can be an accident. A medical emergency. Elvis had a heart attack. Yes, it's his heart. He went just like his mother went, and weren't we all more or less expecting it? It's the most likely and easily accepted cause of death.

But if you have another dead body, curled up and waiting not twenty feet from the first? There's no way of calling that an accident. Now you're heading down the slippery slope of "foul play." You're inviting the doctors and policemen—who must surely be here any minute, because it feels like we've been in this room for a lifetime—to start looking for an explanation of what could have possibly killed two men at once.

Fred hands Marilee a white plastic bag. She takes it, without saying anything or looking inside. Then Fred turns back to David. "Steady, Nunchucks," he says, and for the first time my heart lurches. I've been watching all this like it was a show on TV, happening to somebody else, half expecting that any moment Elvis will pick up his gun and blow the screen out, save us all from having to watch this stupid, unbelievable story. But when Fred said "Nunchucks," calling David by that awful nickname, my heart twisted in my chest.

Fred reaches under David's armpits. He's hopped up on adrenaline, but it's still not going to work. Fred's too frail for the task at hand. A middle-aged tour manager who goes a buck thirty dripping wet is not going to be able to move the body of a young karate instructor. If anything he's only going to knock him over and make him harder to lift. Marilee seems to be having the same thought, because in an instant she's moving to help Fred, pushing the white plastic bag into my hands. I glance down into it. Vials of pills. Maybe twenty bottles, maybe five hundred pills.

I guess we're supposed to get these out of here along with the body of David.

And as for David, he has just rolled to the floor. He is splayed out on his back, arms flung wide, staring at the ceiling, and Marilee and Fred are arguing with each other about who's to blame. As they are yelling about who should have grabbed him where, I see a foamy little river of slime begin to ooze out of David's lips.

"He's alive," I say.

Marilee and Fred both look at me. Then they both look at the bathroom door as if hoping against hope that I'm talking about Elvis. As if the King has somehow gotten to his feet and is coming out of the bathroom saying, "Well, I'll tell y'all that was a close one."

But no, of course the person who is alive is David. The fall to the floor, the thud to his back, seems to have shocked him back into life. It must have forced some of the poison up his throat and onto his mouth and cheeks.

"Shit," says Fred. "Goddamn it and shit." I guess Nunchucks half alive requires as many explanations to the authorities as Nunchucks dead.

"We should move him down the back stairs," I say. "The ambulance people will come up the front."

"Should we let them take him to the hospital?" Marilee asks. "Pump his stomach maybe?"

"Hell no," says Fred. "At least not a hospital in Memphis. What we need is a car."

"I have a car," I say. Marilee and Fred look at me like I'm speaking Greek. "The Blackhawk. We can take him in that."

And so I tie the loop of the white plastic bag to my belt buckle and the three of us working together manage to get David off the floor. Fred takes his head and Marilee and I each take a leg and we start toward the hall and no one makes any particular note of us or even asks us what we're doing. The center of the world is still the motionless body of Elvis, except for a few people who are going around opening drawers and checking out counters, trying to find any pills Fred might have missed in his earlier sweep. The truth is now slowly dawning on the faces of at least half the people in the room. Their focus is changing from saving Elvis the man to saving Elvis the idea. So no one says anything as Marilee and Fred and I bump our way through the door and down the hall to the back staircase. We're trying to hurry and we're rough. David's head gets whacked more than once. We lose one of his shoes. He throws up again halfway down the stairs, starts to choke on it, and we just twist him over like a dishrag, taking care not to step in the vomit as we continue.

The stairs let out near the kitchen and Marilee and I both freeze. Lisa Marie is in there, with Lou Lou and Wanda, but Lou Lou is turned toward the staircase and sees us coming around with David's limp body. Not a sight the little girl needs to witness with so much else going on, but evidently they're making a milkshake, so Lou Lou thinks real smoothly and cuts the blender on. The noise covers up our thuds and groans as we get David out of the stairwell and down the hall leading to the garage.

The Blackhawk is waiting in the driveway, exactly where I left it. We pile David into the back. I turn toward Marilee but she's still shaking.

"I'll drive," I say, and Marilee nods. For once, Fred doesn't have anything to add. He doesn't say good-bye or good luck or give us any last-minute instructions or scold us for something that happened yesterday, or the day before that. As I seesaw the Blackhawk around and head toward the gate, I see him lean against the wall of the garage, looking like a man who's had the fight knocked clean out of him.

The sky is barely starting to lighten as we move down the driveway. A crowd is already gathered on the far side of the gate. Three times the number of reporters you'd normally find on a random weekday in August.

They know something's up, I think. *How? The ambulance isn't even here yet but the vultures are already descending.*

"They listen to police scanners," Marilee says tonelessly, as if she'd heard my unspoken question. "Always tuning in hoping to hear trouble. And they got it today, didn't they? Got it in spades."

I pull onto the main road without slowing, almost enjoying the sight of the reporters scattering, diving this way and that to avoid the strong curved bumpers of the Blackhawk, cursing at us and pounding the sides of the car as I roll out. And almost immediately after I'm through the gates I see them coming, a whole string of ambulances roaring down the highway, with police cars and a fire truck to boot. A dozen sirens screaming, all bearing down on Graceland.

Marilee and I talk briefly as I drive. She gets a map from the glove compartment, spreads it across her lap, and manages to direct me through town and to the river. Early as it is, traffic is picking up with people starting to work, so we pull down to one of the landings where they let the boats in. I position the car beside the bank and stomp on the emergency brake. We seem to be having a real run of bad luck, we three people in this Blackhawk. It wouldn't do to top it off by having us all roll into the Mississippi.

"I'm sorry," Marilee says. "My legs are gone to rubber. You're gonna have to do it."

"Do you think we can get in trouble for this?"

She barks out a little laugh. An angry laugh. "Can we get in trouble for this? Well, I ask you, Honey Berry, what do you think?"

I yank the bag from my belt, tearing the top in the gesture, and glance into the backseat as I get out of the car. David's head is resting against a child's blue plush toy, the one that got the blue hairs on my white pants last night on our drive to the dentist. I didn't see it in the darkness, not then, and it's a pathetic droopy little thing here in the growing light of morning.

For some reason I reach back and pull it out too. David's head bumps against the side of the car and he moans. I don't know why I'd do such a thing, if I'm so mad that I want to deny

David even the comfort of his little bear pillow or if doesn't seem right for him to be drooling on a carnival prize Elvis had won for Lisa Marie, or if my rattled mind is just viewing everything in sight as evidence. Evidence for some crime that doesn't yet have a name.

But I grab the toy and stand up out of the car, looking down at my white pants as I do. Not a great traveling outfit, but we peeled out of Graceland without any clothes or money or even our purses. I don't have my driver's license or my gas credit card or a change of underwear. All I have is this car and a sack full of incriminating drugs and Marilee and David, neither of whom seems remotely inclined to help me sort this all out. I've picked a hell of a time to become the person in charge.

I walk over to one of the little docks. Stretch to look up and all around me, but I don't see anyone. The cars are driving steadily by on the bridge overhead, not a one of them slowing down to take notice of the Blackhawk or the people riding in it. The water before me is dark and deep. It's as good a place as anywhere to hide your sins, I guess, and I open the white plastic bag. Shake out the bottles one by one, and watch them plop in the water below.

All that's left is the furry blue animal lying at my feet on the dock. At first I thought it was a bear, but as I stoop to pick it up, I see that it's a hound dog. It looks up at me, all mournful eyes and floppy ears, and I guess that's why Elvis asked the carnie for this toy in particular, because hound dogs had always been good luck for him. "Hound Dog" was his first number one hit. The start of what made him Elvis.

Marilee honks the horn. She's wondering what's taking me

so long. I look up at the sky, at this day that's coming straight at me, no matter how hard I try and stop it. Coming at all of us, splitting time in half, so that no matter what happens after this, we'll only see our lives in terms of before Elvis died and after, dividing our world just as neatly as the Mississippi divides this town. Just as neatly as the Mississippi divides this country, this world.

Marilee has rolled down the window. "Hurry up," she yells. "We gotta get going."

"I know," I say. "I'm coming." Then I throw the dog into the water too.

CORY

I'm standing looking down into the rolling water of the Mississippi when the phone rings. I jump, startled. Funny how fast you can get used to the silence, to life without a phone or computer. It takes me a few minutes of digging around my backpack to even find the damn thing. I'd been working on the lyrics of the song, and the steady roar of the river had me nearly hypnotized. It reminds me of the sound of the bay back in Fairhope.

It's Dirk, of course. He dropped me and Lucy off here by the docks maybe an hour earlier, because I told him I wanted to explore the city and think about Fred's offer. It's a good offer, I know. As good as a girl like me is ever going to get in this world, and yet I'm hesitant. Maybe it's because the song isn't finished. It doesn't feel right signing the paperwork before the lyrics are done.

It's hard to hear Dirk over the hum of the river. He has to say it three times before I grasp what he's called to tell me. Some man claiming to be my father has tracked me down, he says. He called Graceland no more than five minutes after I left. Told them he'd driven all the way to Memphis to fetch me home.

"What'd you tell him?" I yell.

"I didn't say shit," says Dirk, who's rapidly moving into the category of Best Damn Friend I Ever Had. "Why would I? I figured it was up to you to tell him what, if anything, you thought he needed to know. But he said to tell you he'd be waiting at the Smokin' Pig for lunch at one. It's at the end of Beale Street. Do you feel like going?"

"Yeah. I'll go."

"Want me to come get you?"

"No, it isn't far. I'll walk."

"Girl, you got them waders with you, and that guitar and that dog. Let me come for you in the car and take you there proper. So you step out like a lady. Like a lady who has the world by the ass."

"I can walk," I say. The Graceland Security squad car always caused too much of a fuss for my taste, and besides, I wasn't more than a handful of blocks from Beale and I'd intended to walk it anyway. It's the music street of Memphis and I've never been there. I tell Dirk good-bye and look down at the phone. It's not quite noon, so I have plenty of time, and I'd like to stand here a minute longer, looking down into this dark water, watching it flow, and waiting for the words to come.

I think of Mama, think of why she put the word *daughter* in the lyrics when she always said she thought I was a boy right up to the moment I popped out into the world, looked her right in the eye, and proved her wrong. Besides, there's a lot more words that rhyme with *son* than with *daughter*, which pretty much tops out at *slaughter*, unless you slur the word as Marilee suggests and make it sound like *water*. I keep murmuring options to myself and my mind drifts back to one night we were out at the lake house and Mama and I had been sitting out under the stars, looking up. She knew a little something about astronomy. She could always find the Dippers and the North Star, and that night she pointed to Venus. I never could see it, but I told her I could and then I asked her for a ghost story.

Mama wasn't much for ghosts. She didn't like Halloween or scary movies, and she wouldn't let me read Stephen King, even though all my friends did. But on that particular night she reached over and stroked my hair and told me that somewhere on Earth—she didn't know where, but somewhere—there was another little girl who looked just like me. Who walked like me and talked like me, even though she was living somewhere else. Somewhere far away, with a whole other life. She was my double, Mama said, and everybody's got one. When I wake up in the morning, that other little girl was lying down to go to sleep at night and when she woke up . . . well, you get the idea. It made me sad to think of having a double somewhere out there. The Cory Beth I couldn't see, living with some other mama and daddy.

I said, "What happens if I find her one day? What happens if I walk past her on the street?"

And Mama said, quick and flat as a river, "Well, then one of you will just have to die."

She could be like that sometimes. Weird and weirdly mean, thinking the kind of thoughts no one else ever thinks, and I burst out crying because I knew I was going to have to spend my whole life scared that someday I'd accidentally meet the other Cory Beth. That I'd pass myself in some airport and then I'd just clutch my chest and drop dead on the spot.

I guess now that I've taken this long drive I understand her a little bit better. Or at least I know a little more of what she meant. She was trying to tell me that we all have a lost twin out there in the world, some part of ourselves that's broken off and gone in another direction. And we're haunted by it. We feel an absence and it pains us, like a Civil War soldier who's lost a leg. It's everyone's personal ghost story, this sense that we're only half here, but we also know that if we ever find and reclaim that lost part, that the cost will be the death of everything we are now. It's harsh and it's dark, but I guess it's also sort of true. I try not to think too hard about the Cory who's going to have to die to let this new Cory be born into the world.

I pick up the pieces of my present life, including the leash of my dog, and turn away from the river. Start back in the direction of Beale Street and whatever waits for me when I finally reach the end.

The day is up and bright and by some counts even half over, but Beale Street is still lying like a whore in the mess of last night. I pick my way through the orange rinds and cherry stems, the crushed beer cups and the pork ribs sucked bare of their meat and scattered around like evidence in a crime scene. Lucy is interested in all of it and I let him have a bone, even though everybody says they splinter. But that dog just isn't going to walk until he has a bone in his mouth, and even then he picks it up wrong, idiotic creature that he is. He carries it back to front instead of side to side, with the end of the bone sticking out of his mouth like a big broken tooth.

It's early, but there's music. People are set up and singing in almost every bar. I can hear them as I pass, and most of them are good. Damn good. The bar doors are open. Sunlight is spilling into the buildings, and the blues are spilling out, and every now and then I pass an alley with picnic tables and an open bar and a little stage. I can't believe this many people are playing this early, before the world's even had the chance to get drunk, but they're here. All with their dreams and most of them knowing that those dreams are going to get dashed. Nobody understands the odds better than me, and yet I'm humming as I go, picking up a piece of a song on one corner and then a piece of another on the next, walking through zones of music, the debaucheries of the night before squishing beneath my shoes, forming part of the beat, and the hot southern sun on my face.

And then I see him. He's sitting outside at one of the picnic tables, waiting for me, just like he always has been. At the edge of every softball field and stage and high school parking lot, there that man has been, sitting and biding his time. He smiles and waves. Waves hard, as if there's a chance I might get confused and walk on by him, and then he frowns a little bit, seeing that I've got his waders and this crazy-ass coonhound, who's now dropped the bone and picked up a corn dog and is eating it, stick and all.

I pull up beside him, drop the backpack on the picnic table, and put down his waders and my guitar.

"Hey, Daddy," I say.

Bradley says he's driven straight through from Florida in his pickup truck. It seems he called Gerry on Saturday, and Gerry told him I'd come in for my check then disappeared, which was all Gerry knew. But then he called Leary and Leary had broken like an eggshell. Spit out the whole story of how I'd taken off heading west on four bald tires with no money.

"I didn't plan this too well," Bradley says, reaching down to scratch Lucy behind the ears. I've looped his leash around the leg of the picnic table.

"You planned it? It's hard to believe anybody planned anything about this at all."

"It's not a bad trip, you know. Straight north from Sarasota, till you get around Charlotte, then hang a left. Interstate the whole way, north and west. It's boring, but it's fast."

I try to do the math in my head. He left two days after me and still just about beat me to Memphis. He looks exhausted. His eyes are red and he's got stubble on his chin.

"I thought you'd end up here," he says. "On Beale Street. It seems like your kind of place."

The waitress comes up. There's no menu—in fact, I'm not even sure which of the four or five restaurants crammed on this corner lay claim to this picnic table. But it doesn't matter, because the only real question is pulled or sliced, so Bradley and I order our barbecue and sit back. The break, brief as it was, seems to have pushed him back down into himself a little bit and given him confidence, because he finally looks at me straight on and comes to the point.

"I made a mistake thirty-seven years ago, Cory Beth."

"Claiming me, you mean."

"That's what you think? You think I drove a thousand miles to tell you that?" He takes off his ball cap and fans his face. "No, claiming you was one of my best moves. But when your mama came back from Memphis she . . . she tried to tell me what happened to her at Graceland. All the ways she'd been changed, and I shushed her. I couldn't stand to hear it. Here she'd been out into the big world and I was afraid she'd think of me as small. See me as a small man."

There's silence. He waits, like he's expecting me to say something. Maybe make some stupid joke about Honey being five feet and him being six, and just a few days ago I might have said just that. I might have rushed in with something silly just to give us a way to break the tension. But the road has taught me that sometimes the smartest thing you can do is just shut up and listen. People want to tell you their truth and they'll do it, if you give them half a chance.

Bradley sighs, begins again. "I told Laura that none of that stuff had ever happened. I erased it, don't you see? I erased a part of her life. We hid the car. Wrapped it up and both acted like we'd forgotten it existed. I think I was a bad husband . . ."

Now that's too much. I hear myself speak. "Come on, Bradley, you were a good husband. The best. You loved Mama."

"Cory Beth, there's more to being a good husband than loving a woman. Loving a woman is the easy part. The hard part is seeing her as she really is and letting her be all those things, even the ones that are not particularly convenient. So I pretended there wasn't anything more to Laura than the girl who'd climbed on the bus to Memphis after graduation, and I think we were all the worse for the deception." He looks at me evenly. "I think we hurt you."

"You think that's why I grew up rootless and feckless. A loser."

"You're not a loser. Don't you ever say such a thing again. You're not too old for a whipping."

I'm already shaking my head. "Don't think Mama didn't play along with all your secrets. It wasn't like she was in love with the truth. Not any more than you were. Maybe less."

"The truth?" Bradley says quietly. "Now I'm not sure about that. The truth's a hard ball to throw and a hard ball to catch."

The waitress is back. She plops two iced teas in front of us and puts a bowl of water down on the ground for Lucy. He's been awful still and quiet.

"Laura and I only really fought about one thing during our whole marriage," Bradley says. "And that was about how much to tell you."

"Whether or not to tell me you weren't my blood daddy."

"Oh, you knew I wasn't. You figured it out for yourself soon enough, didn't you? When you had to draw that family tree in fifth grade or whatever it was? I remember it plain as day, you sitting at the kitchen table, getting all the dates lined up. Doing the math and frowning. You were looking up at me and then Laura and both of us holding our breath, waiting for you to say something. But you never did."

"I was a kid. I wasn't totally sure what it meant."

"But you figured it out eventually and you still didn't come asking. No, when I say the truth, I don't mean that I'm not your biological father, but that I wasn't sure who it was. Neither was Laura. That's as far as I let her get with her story. She said there were two men and I put my hand over her mouth and we never discussed it again. I felt bad about it. Just 'cause I couldn't stand to know didn't mean you couldn't."

"Then why'd you set the cops on me?"

He takes a sip of sweet tea. "I didn't set the cops on you, or at least I didn't see it that way. I reported you as missing, which is exactly what you were. When Leary told me you took off with the car in that condition, I just about lost my mind with worry. He convinced me to give you two days to get to Memphis, but when two days came and went and you still hadn't shown up . . ."

"I took a circular route."

He looks at me cautiously, like he's afraid to ask the next question, even though he knows he has to. "And did you," he finally says, "find what you were looking for?"

"No," I say. "I found something else entirely. I thought I'd been looking for my daddy, but it turns out what I found was my mama. Parts of her, at least. I think she was a complicated woman."

He snorts. "You got that part right. There were rooms inside that woman that nobody ever saw."

But I'm still trying to sort it all out. "So you're the one who called everybody, told them I'd be coming."

"I called everybody in your mama's book. She'd looked up a

few people up near the end, you know. I guess she wanted to make her farewells."

"And you told them to help me?"

"I told them to do whatever they thought was best. Although by the nature of the question, I'm thinking some of them must've helped you, and I'm glad of it."

"Did you call Fred?"

"Who's Fred?"

"He works at Graceland."

Bradley takes another slow sip of tea. "No, whatever you found at Graceland you found on your own."

"Mama wrote a song," I say. "And Elvis sang some of it. She had a tape of her voice and his. Did she ever tell you that?"

He shakes his head.

"The tape was in the car. I've just about finished the lyrics and the melody is already there. They want me to record it, let Sun Records release it and Graceland sell it. I don't know, because you never know, not really, but it could be the start of something big. It could change my life."

"Well that sounds good."

"It is good."

He swallows. "So you're staying in Memphis?"

"For a while."

The waitress is back with a plate of biscuits. She sets them down in the middle of the table, fat and brown and warm, I can tell from the steam, then she plunks a bowl of whipped butter and a squeeze bottle of honey beside the plate.

"We didn't ask for biscuits and honey," Bradley says.

She shrugs. "They come whether you ask for them or not."

I pick up a biscuit and pull it apart, then reach for the squeeze bottle. *In the end, people are whatever they choose to be.* Who said that? I've been talking to so many people about so many strange things during the last five days that I have to stop to remember. But it was David Beth who let fly with that particular nugget. He said it to me as he was sending me off with his guilty paternity check and a bag of his stolen DNA. It's a surprising little piece of philosophy coming from such a fool but, then again, I guess through the ages fools have always been a source of wisdom.

People are what they choose to be, and over and over again, Bradley Ainsworth has chosen to be my daddy.

"If you're staying in Memphis to be a big recording artist," Bradley says cautiously, his mouth full of biscuit, "who's going to look after that dog?"

"I was hoping you'd take him," I say, even though the idea had not occurred to me until just that very second. And it makes me ache to think of Lucy and Bradley driving home to Beaufort, happiness and sadness all squished together in the same breath. "Maybe you could watch him until I get back."

He's still being careful. "You're coming back?"

"Of course I'm coming back. It's home, isn't it? Just promise me you won't let him ride in the flatbed. He's not the smartest dog in the world."

"What you call him?"

"Lucy. It's a long story."

"Lucy," Bradley repeats, looking under the table at the dog, tossing him the last of a biscuit. "Good boy."

"He's not that good either. He tried to bite a clerk at the La Quinta in Montgomery, Alabama."

"Now, I have trouble believing that," says Bradley, starting that crooning tone he gets with dogs and children. "Listen here, Lucy Boy. Are you and me going fishing out on the bay? We gonna catch us some crabs and fry them up in the pan?"

"These biscuits are good," I say.

"Nothing beats honey on a warm biscuit."

"Tupelo honey's not from Tupelo, did you know that?"

"It seems like it would be."

"I know. But things are never exactly what they seem, are they?"

"Nope," says Bradley, wiping the gold from his mouth. "They never are."

AUTHOR'S NOTE

I got the idea for *Last Ride to Graceland* one Sunday morning, when I was lying in bed reading the newspaper. It seemed that after thirty-eight years, the estate of Elvis Presley had decided to restore the Stutz Blackhawk Elvis had driven on the last day of his life and add it to the fleet of cars on display at Graceland.

One detail from the article jumped out at me. The writer described how the car had been wrapped in plastic since Elvis died, and that finally opening it was like unearthing a time capsule. There was still trash on the floor and the faint smell of a man's cologne. That was just enough to get the writer part of my brain all shook up. Before the end of that rainy Sunday, I'd written out a full outline for the novel.

Last Ride to Graceland is a work of fiction. For example, the famous Stutz Blackhawk wasn't found in a fishing shed in South Carolina, but rather has been stored at Graceland the entire time. Honey and Cory are entirely of my own imagination, as are the people they meet along the way in their separate fictional journeys to and from Memphis. The snippet of song featuring Elvis's voice and the eight-track in the car is another of my own inventions.

The last hours of Elvis's life have been exhaustively studied and documented and I did research them before writing, along with firsthand accounts of what life at Graceland was like during the waning days of the King's reign. Unfortunately, the sadder the detail, the more likely it is to be true: Elvis did have a twin brother who died at birth and many biographers speculate that he suffered a kind of "survivor's guilt" his whole life. He had a fascination with religion and spirituality of all kinds and was a deeply superstitious man who did in fact die shortly after the anniversary of his mother's death, with both of them passing at the age of forty-two. His last words were spoken to his girlfriend, Ginger Alden, who found his body in the bathroom hours later. Most painful of all, his father, Vernon, and daughter, Lisa Marie, were at Graceland that night and witnessed the panic and confusion.

But with the exception of Elvis, Priscilla, Lisa Marie, Vernon, and Ginger—who are real but I've used here fictitiously—the characters are entirely of my own imagination.

I drove the route from Beaufort, South Carolina, to Memphis, Tennessee—in the summer, no less, and accompanied not by a coonhound named Lucy but rather by a terrier named Thad. We stopped in Macon, Fairhope, and Tupelo before arriving in Memphis and touring Graceland. When I told a security guard I was a writer, he let me step behind the ropes and approach the Stutz Blackhawk they have on display there. (Not the one Elvis drove the day he died, but an earlier model which was very similar in design, if not quite as storied.) I must confess it took my breath away. When I asked if I might maybe dare sit in it—purely for the sake of research, of course—the young man regretfully shook his head.

"Ma'am," he said, "nobody touches this car but the spirit of Elvis."

So there you have it.

ACKNOWLEDGMENTS

Books are rarely born in a vacuum. I got the idea for *Last Ride to Graceland* on a rainy Sunday morning when I was looking at my local paper, *The Charlotte Observer*, and saw an article about how they were hauling the Stutz Blackhawk Elvis Presley drove on the last day of his life from Memphis to the NASCAR museum in Charlotte. Once it was spiffed up, it would be added to the collection of Elvis cars at Graceland. One line in the article leapt out at me. The car had been sealed so tightly for so many years that one of the restoration experts described it as "like opening a time capsule"

For a Southern girl obsessed with the past, that line was like waving a red flag at a bull.

The idea for this book completely came to me that day. Honey and Cory Beth started talking immediately, as I lay in bed scribbling on a yellow legal pad, with the newspaper open beside me. While I have relied on real facts about Elvis and his family for the background of the book, all the other characters are utterly fictional. And the Blackhawk wasn't found in a fishing shed on Polawana Island in Beaufort (where I own a spit of land), but had rather been in Graceland since 1977, holding its secrets there.

In order to give the road trip a breath of authenticity, I

drove the route from Beaufort to Memphis in the dead middle of summer, making stops in Macon, Fairhope, and Tupelo along the way. I wasn't in a big black muscle car with a half-witted coonhound. I was in a Prius with a half-witted terrier. But I did stay in many pet-friendly La Quintas and I did have an Elvis Presley milkshake. I cannot recommend either highly enough.

And books are also never published in a vacuum so I'd like to thank the wonderful people at Gallery Books: my unflappably calm editor, Karen Kosztolnyik, and her infallible assistant, Becky Prager; Jennifer Bergstrom, VP and Publisher; Louise Burke, President; Jennifer Long, Associate Publisher; Lisa Litwack, Art Director; Liz Psaltis, Director of Marketing; and Wendy Sheanin, VP of Marketing at Simon and Schuster. An extra-big hug to Senior Publicist Meagan Harris and VP and Publicity Director Jennifer Robinson, who've offered so much support to all three of the novels I've published with Gallery Books.

I rely totally on the council and guidance of the stellar staff at the Gernert Company, especially my agent, Stephanie Cabot, who always has my back. Thanks to her assistant, Ellen Goodson, and Director of Marketing Anna Worrall, and to the tireless Rebecca Gardner, the VP and Rights Director, who has given more of a boost to my career than she will ever know.

Finally, I'd like to thank the staff at Graceland for giving me such a kind welcome, even as the author of a unfinished book about the King. A special shout-out to the security guard who took me behind the velvet rope for a closer look at a Stutz Blackhawk. "Don't tell anybody I let you touch it," he said, and I promised that I wouldn't.

Never trust a writer.

LAST RIDE TO GRACELAND

Kim Wright

INTRODUCTION

When Cory Beth Ainsworth discovers a 1973 Stutz Blackhawk in her parents' shed, all of her suspicions are confirmed. She was not a nine-pound nine-ounce preemie. She was a product of her mother Honey's single wild year in Graceland, and it's time that she learned the truth about her real father, Elvis Presley.

But truth is a tricky thing, as Cory soon learns. Retracing Honey's journey from Memphis to South Carolina, she stops in Georgia, Alabama, and Mississippi, finding that the road is taking her further from her destiny at every turn. Her desperate search for a father yields instead a complex portrait of her mother, whose beautiful voice and rebellious spirit inspired the King even as his own song was fading.

In this latest novel, Kim Wright stuns with a wrenching portrayal of a mother and daughter whose powerful love for music binds them in a way they never could have expected.

TOPICS AND QUESTIONS
FOR DISCUSSION

1. The epigraph quotes Bruce Springsteen on Elvis, "It was like he came along and whispered some dream in everybody's ear, and somehow we all dreamed it." What do you think Springsteen meant by this, and how does it resonate throughout the novel?

2. Cory Beth begins her story with an introduction to the South, where half-truths necessarily infiltrate a culture built on propriety and kindness. But when do half-truths become more harmful than helpful? Name a few moments in the text when they morph into full-blown lies, and discuss the consequences of that.

3. Memory plays a powerful part in this story. Cory is overwhelmed by her sensory reaction to the 1973 Stutz Blackhawk, calling it a time capsule. When else do memories arise unexpectedly from a sound or a smell, and how does that influence her decisions?

4. Before she sets off on her quest, Leary tells Cory, "That road out there can't tell you a single thing that you don't already know." Do you think he ends up being right? Why or why not?

5. In our first glimpse of Honey, we learn that she desperately wants to avoid the life her mother prescribed for her. How does this generational divide trickle down to Cory? How much can we really resist our inheritances?

6. As she drives through the imposing gates of Graceland, Honey experiences a sense of foreboding and wonders whether the place is as much a prison as it is a dream. What does she mean here? Can the two be one and the same?

7. Philip tells Honey that his life "was written for me before I was born. I'm just turning the pages and living it, year by year." Discuss how destiny can inhibit certain freedoms.

8. Honey initially records her thoughts in brief diary passages, eventually winnowing them down to haikus. Why does she find it easier to "edit reality," reducing and simplifying her experiences into something more digestible?

9. Cory has a hard time reconciling the contradictory accounts of her mother from Fantasy Phil and Marilee. Are they both correct? How can our personality be fractured, based on how we present ourselves differently to different kinds of people? Does Cory do the same? How so?

10. Marilee, wistfully taking stock of the run-down Doozy's Barbecue, claims that "things that get that wet are never quite dry again." Is she just talking about the restaurant? What else could she mean here?

11. Discuss the significance of place of origin as it pertains to the novel. David Beth, for instance, is from both nowhere and everywhere. He claims that "people are whatever they choose to be." How does this mantra bleed into his life's work? What do we lose when we lose our home?

12. Why do you think Cory is finally able to perform Elvis's "Love Me Tender" in Fairhope? What parallels do you see between her life and his?

13. Elvis suffers the loss of his unborn twin acutely. Honey tells Cory that we all have a kind of twin out there in the world who cannot live if we survive. What does this particular brand of "symmetry" say about the larger message of the novel?

14. Why does Honey throw the blue hound dog toy into the water?

15. Discuss the last scene with Cory and Bradley. What has he become to her, and how has forgiveness played a part in this new relationship? Where do you think Cory will go from here?

ENHANCE YOUR BOOK CLUB

1. Write your own haikus that express your daily joys and anxieties. Share them with one another and discuss what it was like to condense your personal experiences down to syllables.

2. Marilee says "there are lots of ways to sing." She, for example, enjoys expressing herself through cooking. How do you "sing"? Tell one another a little bit more about your passions and how they inform your everyday life.

3. Give "The King" his proper due! Make your own peanut butter and bacon sandwiches and host an Elvis listening party, or have a movie night to watch films like *Jailhouse Rock* and *Blue Hawaii*. And feel free to try out your best impressions.